WHERE YOU ARE

Michael Burns

WHERE YOU ARE

ISBN 13: 978-0-9840984-0-8
ISBN: 0-9840984-0-2
Library of Congress Control Number: 2009905558

This is a work of fiction; any resemblance to actual persons, living or dead, is purely coincidental.

Cover design by All Things That Matter Press
Published in 2009 by All Things That Matter Press

To My Wife

Acknowledgement
to my dear friend Sandy Smoller,
with my deepest appreciation
for all his help and support.

I speak of the hopes we had in youth,
The diminishing powers we had as time went by,
Of sufferings old and new, and always doubt.
And of death the less said the better.

Richard Eberhart, from "Plain Song Talk"

PROLOGUE

My wife deserves all the credit for curing my nostalgia, a cure that seems to have endured for the past thirty-five years. Perhaps only my wife could comprehend what it was that drew me back to Garrison, New Hampshire, after all that time. I can say with assurance, however, that if she had been able to accompany me east for my mother's funeral, she would have been displeased at my detour to Garrison.

I had heard from my mother, among others, that Garrison had not escaped the "scourge" of gentrification that had afflicted so many other similar old cities and towns in New Hampshire. So I was somewhat surprised to discover that Mrs. Pappas's sagging old apartment house was still standing on Washington Street. The sight of it filled me with excitement and sorrow. Caplan's Auto Supply had endured as well, but not Spiro's Sweet Shoppe across the street, or Archie's Grocery on the corner of Green and Washington.

Sitting in my rental car in front of what was once Mrs. Pappas's apartment house on this cold April morning in 1998, I experienced an urgent need to discover who and what I was during that watershed period in my life:

ONE

Early August 1963:

I had gotten used to finding Laura working the *New York Times* crossword at the kitchen table when I came home from work. She didn't like to cook. We would heat up a TV dinner or make sandwiches. There was no Laura at the kitchen table today, no *New York Times*. Instead, I found a note written on the electric bill envelope propped against the salt-and-peppershakers:

> *Dearest Paul,*
> *I can't take it anymore.*
> *Love,*
> *L*

I studied the note for a long time. I carried it into the bedroom and lay down on the bed next to Honcho, our foundling black cat. I showed him the electric bill.

"What's this all about?" Honcho yawned fish breath in my face and jumped down from the bed. I fell asleep and woke up two hours later, sweating like a horse. We lived in three square low-ceilinged rooms. There were two windows in the living room, two in the bedroom; the kitchen was windowless. Laura had not come home while I was asleep.

"Can't take what anymore?" I asked myself out loud in the kitchen. There was some cold meat and mayonnaise in the refrigerator, a few slices of day-old bread left in the loaf on the counter. I made a sandwich and washed it down with a glass of milk that was on the verge of going bad.

"What's with your mother?" I asked Honcho, who was winding his body around my legs trying to get me to feed him. "What is it she can't take anymore?"

It wasn't until I got to the living room and was in the act of putting a record on the turntable when it hit me that maybe my wife had left me. For a moment I felt light-headed. I dropped the needle hard in the middle of the record. It careened across the vinyl and caught in the label. It was not like Laura to pull a thing like that, to leave me without warning, without telling me what was on her mind. She was not the kind of person to keep things to herself. That would better describe me. If there had been something on her mind, something bothering her, you can bet I would have heard about it. We hadn't fought in a couple of weeks.

As far as I was concerned, everything was fine between us. It made no sense. What was it that she couldn't take anymore? I asked myself again.

I went into the kitchen with the intention of phoning her parents. I made it through the first three numbers and hung up. Devlin's screen door squeaked open and slammed shut. We shared the back landing with Devlin and his common law wife Maggie. Our apartments were mirror images. We also shared a thin wall between our bathrooms. The first couple of weeks we lived in the apartment, Laura was bothered by Devlin's morning gagging and hawking. To be honest, I'm still not that comfortable going to the bathroom knowing that they can hear as much on their side of the wall as we can on ours.

Devlin sat down on the steps and ran a hand through his thin hair. He placed a shot glass of rye beside him.

"Dave, mind if I join you?" I asked Devlin. "Apartment's like a freaking oven."

"Sit down, my boy." Devlin moved his shot glass to make room for me. "Can I offer you a drink?"

"No thanks, Dave." I sat down on the step beside him. The sun was setting, a ball of blood red on the horizon.

"Now that's what I'd call a beautiful sunset." Devlin drank off the top of his shot as he admired the sunset.

"Yes." The back of Mrs. Pappas's apartment house faced almost due west. There were fifty feet or so of sloping lawn that led down to the bank of the polluted Cocheco River. A rusted railroad trestle spanned the river. It wasn't used much anymore now that commuter train service to Boston from Garrison had fallen off. Occasionally we would see a freight hauling goods to Boston and points south. Devlin predicted that it was only a matter of time before the trestle collapsed, and there would be hell to pay for Boston and Maine Railroad's negligent management, thanks to McGinnis. Devlin had been a railroad man for over thirty years. Now he sold kitchen appliances at Montgomery Ward. Maggie worked there, too, in the office.

Before he died, Mrs. Pappas's husband had planted shrubs and some hemlocks around the perimeter of the backyard. There was a grape arbor, and a rose trellis, and a glider that Laura and I liked to swing in on pleasant evenings. Out back, one got the impression of a nice, middle-class neighborhood; out front it was a different story.

"Sure you won't have a drink? Maggie," Devlin yelled through the screen door, "let's have the bottle out here."

"No, Dave, really."

"You want the bottle, come get it yourself," Maggie said from the kitchen table where she worked on her jigsaw puzzle. Like Devlin, Maggie liked her whiskey neat. She drank hers from a coffee cup.

"Say, have you guys seen Laura? She wasn't here when I got home from work ..."

"Can't say that I have, my boy. Maggie, you seen Laura today? Looks like Paul's misplaced her." Devlin laughed and took down the rest of his shot.

"Probably at her mother's," I said.

"She didn't leave you a message? Just like a woman," Devlin snorted in amusement.

"No." I didn't quite know how to explain to Devlin what Laura had said in her note.

"She'll be along," Devlin said, not sounding concerned, not even interested. Maggie hadn't seen her either.

Devlin and Maggie got home from work around five-thirty. They would start drinking immediately. Sometimes they ate a supper, but more often they would skip eating and just drink. From where I sat, I could see Maggie at the kitchen table. Her hair was up in curlers. It was what she did every evening as soon as she got home from work, before she got too drunk to bring off the task. I couldn't be sure of their ages, but if I had to guess I'd put them in their late fifties, or early sixties. They were both very thin. Devlin's face, especially his shapeless nose, was a dendritic network of tiny broken blood vessels. He was a chain-smoker; his long, bony nicotine-stained fingers were wrapped around his now empty shot glass. He stared into it as if he were contemplating its metaphysical properties. I could tell he was annoyed at Maggie for not bringing the bottle out to him. Soon they'd be into their evening quarrel. It was practically a ritual with them. They'd have at each other for forty-five minutes or an hour, and then, as if by mutual consent, the fighting would stop. Or, for all I knew, they just passed out simultaneously. I liked them both. So did Laura. It was hard not to like these poor besotted souls. They had us over for supper a few times. Maggie was a decent cook, which was more than I could say for Laura.

Laura had no skills as a cook or a homemaker. She made no apologies. On the contrary, she was proud of the fact that she would never be a "house slave," as she put it. House drudgery was not what she was put on the planet to endure. She expected me to share in the household chores, chores that could not be avoided unless we wanted to live in total squalor. I didn't work ten hours a day and come home in the mood to perform housework. We had more than one disagreement over the issue. She would remind me that she worked eight hours a day in the bank herself, and it was only fair that I do my share of the house chores. She had a point. I'd never use my true feelings as a counter argument, namely, that I believed that housework ought to be done by the woman of the house. That would not be a concept Laura would be receptive to.

If the guys at Archie's or at Caplan's Auto Supply knew my wife made me wash dishes and scrub floors, they'd eat me alive. We hadn't had a division-of-labor spat in a long while. She wouldn't leave me over so trivial a matter. Of that I was sure.

I excused myself and went back inside my stifling apartment. I was aimless, confused; I didn't know what to do next. It was the time of night when television watching was out of the question in our building. Devlin's theory was that some son-of-a-bitch in the neighborhood was probably running a high-speed electrical tool, which could account for the interference with reception for about a half-hour to an hour most nights of the week in summer.

I flipped through our record albums, not really seeing the covers. I selected a record at random. Nina Simone's heroine exhorted her husband not to smoke in bed, while I brooded over my current circumstances. Then Charlie, Mrs. Pappas's fourteen-year-old mongoloid son, started up. At night, sometimes, Charlie would have what I could only describe as fits. Mrs. Pappas said it was because he saw monsters in the dark. Whatever it was Charlie saw in the darkness, it would get him howling like a wolf. His howling, now, I could hear over Nina Simone. I got up and turned the volume up a notch. Then Prufrock, our cockatiel, began to act up. For no reason that I could figure, he dropped off his perch and began thrashing and jumping around on the bottom of his cage.

"J. Alfred. You want some chow?" I pulled a handful of sunflower seeds from the bag beside his cage, put one between my lips and pressed my face to the bars. Prufrock cocked his head and gently plucked the seed from my lips, husked it and ate it with great skill; the way nature had designed his beak to do. Laura had taught the bird to take seeds from her lips. I was leery about letting him do it to me, but then discovered it was really quite pleasurable to feed the thing like that. My contribution to its education was to give him a taste for beer. He liked to perch on my shoulder when I sat on our ersatz Dutch Modern sofa to watch TV. One night he wandered down my arm and dipped his beak into the glass of beer I was nursing. He liked what he got out of the glass enough that it became a habit with him. J. Alfred had no interest in a glass of water or soft drink. Beer was what he liked. Laura actually accused me of turning our cockatiel into an alcoholic. It got to the point where he'd scream like a banshee whenever I'd bring anything in a glass into the room. Laura swore the bird had woken up with a hangover one morning. I found it amusing. She did not.

"Your mother didn't happen to tell you where she was going, did she, J. Alfred? Did she tell you what it was she couldn't take anymore?"

Ten o'clock came. I began to panic. Then panic gave in to worry. It would be too late now to call the Sargents. Laura's father would be asleep already, and her mother made it plain that she did not like to be disturbed when she was watching her shows. This I learned when I was courting Laura. On impulse I dialed Noelle's number. Noelle's husband, William, answered the phone.

"No," William said, "she hasn't been around tonight. What, did she finally ditch you?" William laughed. I had always found his laugh unpleasant. That was only one of the reasons I could name for my dislike of the man.

"I got home late and she wasn't here. I thought she might be at your place. Sorry to bother you."

"No sweat."

I poured myself a glass of cream soda. In the freezer, both ice cube trays were empty. Laura was derelict when it came to refilling ice cube trays. I drank my cream soda without ice. Devlin and Maggie were in full throat. I closed my kitchen door quietly against their fight. I could still hear most of what they hurled at each other anyway. Pretty soon, I heard the sound of breaking glass, Maggie's sobbing, and Devlin's incoherent muttering. Then, silence. I suddenly felt profoundly sad, and all alone, like a child whose parents have gone out for the evening leaving him alone and wondering if they will ever return. I'd had that feeling many times growing up.

I did now what I hadn't dared to do earlier when I found Laura's note. I went into the bedroom and opened the closet door. Laura's things were gone from her side of the closet; her travel bag was not on the shelf. I checked her bureau drawers and found only a dish of potpourri with its cloying fragrance.

I sat down on the bed and stroked Honcho's silky pelt. This got him purring.

"Is this really happening?" I asked my cat, "or am I in some kind of bad dream? Where could she have gone? You know as well as I do that she'd never go running back to her mother. Her sister wouldn't have her, either. Where can she be?" Honcho continued to purr.

The room was so hot that I had difficulty breathing. Laura had asked me a couple of times, when the heat wave started, to pick up a fan for the bedroom. I never got around to it. I wondered if that was her reason for splitting: if you can't take the heat, get out of the bedroom. I undressed and lay down on top of the sheets, sweating and sweating and sweating. I wallowed in sweaty misery for maybe half an hour, and then got up to draw a bath. In the kitchen I was met with the smell of gas. The pilot light on the range had gone out again. Sometimes I wondered how I would go: in the night from asphyxiation, or in a ball of flame trying to light the front burner?

The bathroom was one step up from the level of the kitchen. The walls had been salmon pink when we moved in last January. Laura's first act had been to paint them white. She was about as handy with a paintbrush as I was, and in a couple of weeks the pink bled through, leaving the walls a hideous mottled faded pink. She couldn't be bothered to apply another coat, so we lived with what we had, the way we learned to live with Devlin's morning noises.

I turned on the faucet, half expecting to see brown water spewing out. It was not so unusual to get brown water from our faucets. The faulty pilot light, the brown water, the fact that the temperature in the apartment seldom fell below eighty degrees in the summer, or rose above sixty in the winter, made me wonder why I forked over seventy bucks a month to Mrs. Pappas without putting up a stink, no matter how sweet she was as a person. Devlin's apartment, identical to our own, didn't seem to be equal in its deficiencies. At least Devlin never complained about any. He tolerated, even seemed to enjoy, the suffocating heat of summer, and not to mind the winter cold, as skinny as he was. The fact that he and Maggie consumed prodigious quantities of rye whiskey in all seasons could explain their apparent indifference to temperature extremes.

I managed to get half a tub of clear, tepid water. I crawled in with it hoping it might cool my fevered brain and sweating body at the same time. I seemed to be able to think more clearly soaking in a bath, or as clearly as I was capable of thinking. I slid down until the water rose to my chin, and tried to fathom what was happening to me. But Devlin had regained consciousness and was hawking his phlegm, bumping around on his side of the wall. He ran water, prepared for bed. Then I heard his bowels move. I slid down underwater, and held my breath for as long as I could. The toilet flushed. Devlin's hacking receded into his apartment. I held my breath again, this time in anticipation of Maggie's turn in the bathroom, but she never made it.

Then, out of nowhere, Perry Potter was in my head when I hadn't given him a thought in a couple of months. Potter was a bank officer at Garrison Savings and Loan, Laura's supervisor. I had come home early one day in May with stomach cramps (brought on by bad seafood, Tommy Laroche had said) to find Perry Potter and my wife finishing up lunch at the kitchen table. Potter got to his feet in a hurry, manicured hand extended in greeting, his face in a smile full of perfect teeth. He had on a black three-piece pinstriped suit with a pointed hankie in the breast pocket. His hair was perfectly barbered, his face so clean-shaved you couldn't have found a whisker with a magnifying glass.

I suppose he could be considered handsome—in a dandyish way. I'm sure even Laura would concede that he was better looking, and certainly better dressed, than I was, even if she would deny vehemently any interest in mere appearances. Laura went a little overboard in a show of concern about my stomach condition. She made me take Pepto Bismol before she pampered me into bed. I told her that I never wanted to see that twerp in my house again. She never said a word, but she had a look, a look that frankly scared me. Her eyes narrowed and conveyed contempt and amusement at once. Her mouth twitched slightly; she grabbed a handful of her long hair and tossed it over her shoulder, turned and left the room, closing the door behind her. In a little while, I heard them leave; Laura said something that made Perry Potter laugh. I was tempted to jump out of bed and go after him. Instead, I waited until I heard them go out the front door. Then I went to the window and waited until they appeared on the street, get into Potter's black late-model Oldsmobile, and drive off. Feeling guilty and perverse, I actually smelled the bed sheets.

I didn't bring the incident up that evening when Laura got home from work. She had nothing to say on the subject either. In a week or so, I put Perry Potter out of my mind; the expression on Laura's face was harder to shake. Now here he was, back in my head. I couldn't help but consider the possibility that she had run off with her supervisor. That could be verified easily enough with one phone call to the bank. If she had run out on me, she must have given her notice at least a week ago. Laura would not be the kind to leave her employer in the lurch. Her husband she had no compunction about leaving high and dry, apparently, but her employer? Never.

I suddenly had a powerful urge to talk to someone, to confide, to be comforted. It was late. Even Archie would have gone home by now. I should have said something to Devlin and Maggie earlier. All the friends I once had in Garrison had either fled or got married, which amounted to the same thing. The turds I worked with at Caplan's would be about as understanding as a parking meter. The only couple Laura and I saw regularly was Noelle and William. As I said, I had no use for William, and it had nothing to do with the fact that he had once dated Laura. I chose to believe I disliked him because he had bad character. In any case, he was not a person I could trust.

Archie and the boys would show me no mercy when they found out that my wife had left me. They'd needle me about not being able to satisfy my wife's needs, and by that they'd mean I wasn't able to satisfy her needs in bed. Sexual dominance, and independence from the wife; these were the two chief virtues of true manhood, in their opinion. Part of me agreed, even if I knew better in my head.

I was already sweating again before I could finish toweling dry. I really wanted to get out of the apartment, but I didn't want to be gone if Laura took it in her head to come home. I put on a pair of shorts and went out on the back landing to sit on the steps. Honcho went out on his nocturnal errands. I could hear Devlin and Maggie snoring from inside the apartment through their screen door. A knot formed in my throat. The night was starless and alive with the sound of insects and automobile traffic. Sweat poured into my eyes, trickled freely down my sides. I had no idea what I was going to do. Mosquitoes drove me back inside. I could have listened to some more Nina Simone, whose melancholy songs suited my mood, but I liked to listen to music with the volume turned to at least forty-five degrees. I was afraid it would disturb Mrs. Pappas, or worse, send Charlie into one of his fits. I returned to my bedroom, lay down on the bed, and fell asleep in spite of myself.

TWO

I spotted Archie in front of his store clad in a loose, unbuttoned Hawaiian shirt, his barrel chest and hairy bay window hanging out for the whole world to see.

"Hot enough for you, Paulie?" Archie scratched a kitchen match on the utility pole and fired up his dead cigar butt. "I'll kill them little bastards, see if I don't." The urchins taunted him from the corner of Washington and Green; they opened their dirty mouths to show off the penny candy they had just robbed him of. One of them turned around, dropped his pants, and waggled his white little ass at Archie. Archie made a move toward them and they bolted, shrieking with laughter.

"The boys are down back. Come on in and have a beer."

"I was going around Primo's for a pizza."

"Primo's open till midnight. Drink a couple of beers. It'll cool you off."

"You're not going to believe what happened to me, Arch." I hadn't intended to tell Archie or anyone else about Laura. Not right away. The words were out of my mouth as if they had a will of their own.

"These days I'd believe anything."

"My old lady left me, Arch."

"Sorry to hear that, Paulie. All the more reason you should drink a beer. Women."

I followed Archie into his decrepit store. His brother Duane was on duty behind the counter tonight. I worked for Archie a couple of nights a week and Sundays from eleven in the morning until eleven at night at a buck an hour.

"Paul's old lady left him. Ain't that a bitch?" Archie said to Duane.

"That's too bad," Duane said, his nose in a Boston tabloid.

"Yeah. I never saw it coming."

Duane shook his head, his attention on the sports page.

Archie's Corner Grocery was a menace to the public health. If Archie hadn't been Doc Robinson's drinking and whoring buddy, his place would have been shut down a long time ago. As soon as you crossed the threshold you found yourself on an uneven, creaky floor covered by filthy green linoleum with bare spots worn down to the plywood. Archie kept token canned goods on the dusty shelves. He sold a lot of ice cream, candy, and soda to the neighborhood kids, but his business was mainly beer, beer he sold mainly to minors.

The glass of the meat showcase was opaque from grease and condensation. It was probably just as well that customers didn't get too good a look at the beef steeped in coagulated blood, the desiccated pork chops, the slimy link sausages, discolored chicken legs, and mold-grown frankfurters.

How people could actually want to purchase meat out of that showcase never failed to amaze me. Archie quoted the prices of regular ground beef and chuck. Regular you could get for forty-nine cents a pound, chuck for sixty-nine. The ground beef was all from the same source. Archie justified this deception on moral grounds, arguing that anyone who could afford sixty-nine cents a pound for hamburger could afford to be hosed every now and then. He'd weigh out the meat with the fat part of his hand on the edge of the scale, and customers went away none the wiser.

Most of his customers kept a tab because they were as likely as not to be out of work, and had run out of unemployment compensation. Archie carried a lot of bad paper. He had a heart as big as his hairy belly; he couldn't bear to see people suffer, even if the majority of them spent most of what they had on beer instead of food.

Doc Robinson was in the back room stretched out on Archie's Naugahyde recliner, a glass of vodka and milk in his big paw. He'd been off beer for a couple of months, since his ulcer started acting up. He had on a blue serge suit and Panama hat. His wide florid face was bathed in sweat; the tiny room Archie used for an office was windowless and airless. Doc's black-framed glasses were steamed up. I had never seen Doc remove his jacket, no matter how hot it got. Oblivious of the heat, Doc counseled Norm White on the virtues of early retirement. Doc was a general surgeon specializing in "viscera," as he put it. In Doc's opinion, surgery was no more exalted than any other mechanical activity; it was no different from the work Ray Duffy did under the hood of the Oldsmobiles and Cadillacs he serviced at Cavanaugh's. Doc had operated half drunk enough times to have little respect for the skill. The fact that he had stitched up a patient with a hemostat in his abdomen last week only proved that nobody was perfect.

Whitey listened to Doc's counsel, though I doubt he heard much, and understood less, of what Doc had to say. He was drunk, practically out on his feet; he used the doorjamb to support himself. He had on his work denims, even though he hadn't worked in a couple of weeks since getting laid off from the Portsmouth Navy Yard. He wore his Red Sox ball cap askew on his balding head. Whitey's eyelids were growing heavy. He didn't look long for the conscious world.

"How do, Paul?" Ray Duffy greeted me as Archie fetched two bottles of beer from the cooler. Ray turned toward Whitey and smiled. I shook my head. "You better sit down, Whitey, before you fall down." Whitey regarded Ray with a blank look. Then, as if Ray's words had taken a little time to register, he grinned.

"Paulie ain't feelin' too hot tonight," Archie said, chuckling. He handed me a beer. "Mama hit the road on him. Right, Paulie?"

"Yeah. Never saw it coming." I tried on a laugh, but it sounded tinny, even to my own ear. Ray shook his head and smiled. He was no stranger to abandonment himself. His wife had left him twenty years ago. He had a grown son living in town who would have nothing to do with him. Ray had his name stitched over the Cavanaugh's Cadillac/Oldsmobile logo above his shirt pocket.

"You don't have to worry about nooky, Paulie, you know. I can get you all you want," Archie said in all earnestness. Ever since I had started working part time in the store, Archie and the boys had tried to fix me up with something "strange." I couldn't let on that I would have no interest in what they might offer up. Besides, I was married less than a year, hardly a respectable waiting period before a man went out on the prowl. They would never understand that way of thinking. To get along, I had even taken to using expressions I frankly considered vulgar and demeaning, like referring to my wife as my "old lady."

"Thanks, Arch," I said, "but I can take care of myself."

"I'll bet he can." Ray said. "You been sampling that college poon tang since you started night school, Paul?"

I smiled half-heartedly.

"Hey," Archie whispered from outside the door. "She's here."

"Who?" Doc asked.

"The Black Dahlia." Archie grabbed a handful of his crotch and made an obscene gesture toward the front of the store. Whether or not the Black Dahlia saw this I couldn't say because I had only a view of Archie.

"What are you waiting for, big-balls? Get her down here," Doc said with his odd lisp. Odd because he was such a big man, a man who exuded masculinity.

Doc had tagged her the "Black Dahlia" the first time she showed up in Archie's store wearing a skintight mini-skirt and halter-top. She had perfected a slutty, ass-swinging walk designed to get the attention of men. In that effort she hadn't failed.

"All she's got on is a fucking bikini and spiked heels," Archie said, grinning lecherously around his cigar butt.

"Well, get her down here, for Christ's sake," Doc said, rearranging his bulk in the recliner so that he presented himself splay-legged. One huge testicle bulged at the threadbare fabric of his trousers.

She'd come on to everyone in the store since she'd materialized in the neighborhood, sometime in late May, early June. She had even come on to old Whitey who, Doc said, had a prostate the size of a Maine potato. She was maybe nineteen or twenty. Archie claimed that she'd taken on four of them one night after he closed, right in the Naugahyde recliner. I had always been skeptical of Archie's claims of her sexual advances, but early on she'd had a go at me, mincing up to the counter and placing her purchases down in such a way as to deliberately treat me to her breasts. I made it a point not to flirt with her, so after she'd given me her come-screw-me smile a few times and I didn't respond, she probably wrote me off as a fruit. That didn't stop her from coming on every chance she got.

Archie wandered toward the front of the store.

"Sorry to hear about your pretty wife, Paul. I wondered why I hadn't seen her at her window the last couple of times I was in the bank," Doc said to me. Ray followed Archie; Whitey swayed on his feet, beer bottle clutched to his chest.

"Yeah, she really blind-sided me. What can I say?"

"I thought she was different."

"Me too."

Doc made no secret of the fact that his own marriage was a sham, more an arrangement of convenience, one insisted upon by his wife, whom he described as a "social climbing bitch." She despised Doc for keeping company with the likes of Archie and the people who frequented Archie's back room. I had occasion to talk to her once when she called the store looking for her husband. She had sounded imperious enough, as if she were calling her husband at the Harvard Club instead of Archie's smelly store.

"The place is ripe tonight," I said to Doc, trying to steer the conversation away from my wife. There were no toilet facilities in the store, so the boys, and about a dozen stray cats, used the dirt-floor cellar as a latrine.

"Yeah. I told big-balls to spray, especially in this weather. He has no sense of smell. Don't expect him to make it better."

"I'd be happy to spray myself. It'll take more than a few cans of Lysol to deal with the miasma coming up out of that cellar."

"Miasma. They're teaching you some pretty fancy words at the night school." Doc laughed. "Besides, Archie's customers like the smell. To them it's ambiance. They'd be disappointed if he prettied the place up."

Doc was right. Even the college kids, who represented Archie's greatest source of income from beer sales, liked the fact that the store was a pig sty as much as they liked Archie's prices, not to mention his liberal policy on I.D. cards. In their condescending way, the college kids thought of Archie as a "character" with his down east Maine accent, and his "colorful" expressions.

"She run off with someone?" Doc asked.

I shrugged my shoulders. "I don't know for sure. She left a note but it didn't have much to say."

Doc shook his big silver-haired head. "I never would have guessed she'd do something like this to you. Not Laura."

"Me either." I took it as my cue to leave. I left my half consumed beer on Archie's desk and bid Doc goodbye. Whitey was passed out on his feet. "Shouldn't we put him in a chair?"

"Don't worry about Whitey. He's used to napping on his feet."

Archie and Ray flirted with the Black Dahlia while Duane ogled the girl who was, just as Archie had said, clad in only bikini and spiked heels. Her hair was dyed jet-black, but the dirty blonde roots were starting to move north. Tonight she had on a ton of black eye liner and mascara. She batted her gooey eyelashes at me and winked.

"I'm going for that pizza now, Arch. Catch you later."

"Keep it in your sneaker, Paulie."

THREE

There was a time when going to work at Caplan's wasn't an altogether unpleasant experience. That was before Chessy turned on me. Louis Chessman was Caplan's purchasing and inventory manager. Everyone called him Chessy, not Louie. When I started working at Caplan's as inventory clerk, Chessy was friendly with me in a chatty sort of way. It was the way I imagined women were with each other. To tell the truth, the first day I met him I suspected that he might be a closet homosexual. He was in his early thirties, married, with two young daughters. The better I got to know him the more convinced I was that he was definitely a homosexual, if not in practice, at least in temperament. His taste in musical artists, for example, was my first tip off. He "adored" Judy Garland, and the new Broadway sensation Barbra Streisand. The way he held his cigarette, the way he used his hands, the way he walked and talked—his entire frame of reference pointed to the fact that he was that way. For example, one day he made a big deal out of the fact that Jackie Kennedy would be the first First Lady since Grover Cleveland's wife to give birth. What man do you know would want to share that kind of information with another man, even if he was really interested in such a fact?

One day in early April he went mum on me. He didn't blab on about what he and his wife watched on TV the previous evening; he didn't share his endless anecdotes about what his wife said, what his wife thought, what his wife did; I heard no reports of new restaurants in the area that he and his wife had discovered; nothing about movies, about Judy's or Barbra's songs, nothing. Silence, pointed silence, is what I got. After about a week, being the perceptive guy that I am, I began to sense that something was wrong. I didn't—and don't—have the knack for confronting someone head-on about something they might have done that bothers me. Instead, I tried the oblique approach with Chessy. I'd ask him questions about the job, steering deliberately away from matters that did not concern the job, questions that were emotionally neutral, or I believed them to be. His answers were always perfunctory, and he never looked me in the eye. It was clear that I had done something wrong, or something to offend him. For the life of me I couldn't figure out what it was. I was left baffled and hurt, the way I was baffled and hurt by my wife's sudden disappearance.

One theory I had was that it was in April when Chessy clammed up on me and started giving me the cold shoulder, and April was when I started the second semester of French I at the university extension night school. On days when business was slow in the office, when I'd caught up on posting sales slips and receipt invoices to the inventory cards, I'd tear off a few sheets of paper from Chessy's memo pad, sheets with Caplan's letterhead, and practice conjugating French verbs. Chessy never said a word to me, but I sensed his disapproval. It could have been pure coincidence, but in retrospect it seemed more than coincidence. The truth is, I was never any good at "looking busy" on a job to cover up the fact that there was no real work to do. Therefore, it didn't seem to me that spending a few minutes on my French homework when there was a lull in the workflow really constituted slacking off, or cheating the company. When business was slow out front, the countermen didn't have to pretend to be busy. They'd chew the rag with Sid, who would install himself on a stool at the end of the counter, lip his unlighted Chesterfields and oversee his in-store business. Besides, as my supervisor, Chessy should have let me know if he thought I should be doing something else when I'd finished posting, like checking physical inventory out in the storage areas or whatever. Could it have been as simple as that? At the time, I didn't think so. So, Chessy's abrupt change in attitude toward me remained a mystery.

Now there was a new guy on the job, a young guy with yellow hair that looked dyed, to me. Chessy mumbled an introduction and told me he'd be working in the office from now on. His name was Justin. He wore a green Banlon shirt, polished chinos, and penny loafers that actually had shiny pennies inserted in the slots. Justin offered his limp hand in such a way that I didn't know whether he expected me to shake it or kiss it. It was a lot like grasping a handful of overcooked pasta.

"Nice to meet you, Justin."

Chessy guided him to the machine facing the big double-paned window that looked out on Washington Street. There were two such machines in the office, machines that bore metal trays of inventory cards, and operated like a Ferris wheel with the push of a button. Chessy explained the inventory system to Justin. I wondered if it meant no more overtime. Ordinarily this would have been good news, but now that I was apparently reduced to a single income, the loss of overtime could be a financial hardship for me.

"Check a number for me, will you, Paul?" Tommy Laroche yelled from the next office, separated from my office by a waist-high partition. Tommy was Caplan's head bookkeeper. His assistant was a young crippled boy named Phil. Phil had long greasy black hair, thick glasses, and fingernails like talons.

Justin, maybe trying to show Chessy what a quick study he was, got busy looking up the part number, and had it before I had a chance to sit down at the machine.

"That's Tommy Laroche," Chessy said to Justin. "He'll bore you to death with his fish stories and bowling exploits. Say hello to Justin, Tommy. He'll be working in the office starting tomorrow."

"Hey there, Justin," Tommy Laroche said, attacking his ten-key calculator with the stubby fingers of his broad hand. He had on a short-sleeved shirt that revealed large, hairy, "Popeye" forearms.

I left the office to take my coffee break, feeling like an extra teat.

* * *

I came home from work to find a note from Noelle taped to my door:
Paul,
We have to talk.
I'll come by around eight.

If anyone could throw light on my wife's disappearance it would be Noelle. Laura had been gone forty-eight hours now, more or less, and if the initial shock of discovering her note had passed, I was still anxious about her motives. There was a part of me that didn't want to hear what Noelle would have to say on the subject.

I'm not a drinking man, but I stopped by Archie's on the way home from work to pick up a couple of six-packs of beer. I opened one at the kitchen table and turned Laura's note over in my hand. Then it occurred to me that I hadn't seen Honcho since night before last. He had never stayed away more than twenty-four hours before. I went out on the back porch to call him, and found Devlin sitting on the steps with his shot of rye and a beer chaser.

"Find your wife yet, Paul?" Devlin asked me.

"What?"

"Night before last you asked me if I'd seen her. I'm just asking if you found her?"

"No. And now I can't find my cat either."

Devlin laughed. "It's one thing to lose your wife, but your cat? Well, that's serious."

"I'm serious, Dave. Laura's flown the coop." I told him about her note.

"I find that hard to believe." Devlin ran a nervous hand through his thin, slicked back hair, as was his habit. "There's got to be an explanation. She wouldn't pull a stunt like that."

"I wouldn't have thought so either. She's been gone two days, so I've got to believe it's no joke." I sat down, with my beer, next to Devlin. "Honcho," I called. "Where are you, you bad cat?"

19

Devlin had on a short-sleeved white shirt and tie. His arms were very thin with large veins, and splotches of dry red skin. I glanced at his screen door. Maggie was at the kitchen table sipping her whiskey out of a coffee cup, putting her hair up in curlers.

"Hi, Maggie. Did you hear what I said to Dave?"

"Yes, dear. I can't believe it either. Devlin's right. There has to be an explanation. She'll be back. You know how us women are."

The fact was, I didn't know how women were at all. If I did, maybe I would have seen this coming. "Honcho. Here kitty, kitty, kitty."

"He'll be back," Devlin said. "And so will Laura. Listen to Maggie. Women today, it's not really surprising when you think about it."

I didn't pursue this line of reasoning with Devlin. I felt relieved to have shared the news with Devlin and Maggie. As embarrassing as it was to have to admit that my wife had left me, it was better to have it out in the open than to let it fester in secret. People were bound to find out anyway. I would have to tell Mrs. Pappas sooner or later … and Charlie. Charlie would be devastated. Mrs. Pappas would be upset, too. The bond Laura had formed with the widow and her mongoloid son in so short a time was hard for me to understand.

Charlie had come to the door looking for her Monday night. He'd come again last night, and there was no doubt in my mind that he would show up tonight. Monday night I told him Laura was visiting her mommy, and I wasn't sure when she would return. Last night, I heard his heavy footsteps on the stairs, his clumsy knock on my door. I gave him the same story. He looked just as stricken as he had on Monday; his large black eyes (eyes that seemed to lack pupils), flickered, and saliva collected like cobwebs in the corner of his mouth. He turned without a word and descended the stairs, his pudgy chin on his chest.

"Maggie, better get Paul a shot."

"I can't handle whiskey. The beer will do me. Don't bother, Maggie."

"You sure, hon? It might make you feel better," Maggie said from the kitchen table.

"I'm sure. Thanks just the same." I think I must have been forever cured of whiskey drinking after one night of shot-swapping at the post enlisted men's club in Inchon my last night there. I was sitting in the middle of a semi-circular booth flanked by several of my buddies when I lost my insides on the third round. They had to carry my sorry carcass back to the barracks. I was sick for two days. Liquor hadn't passed my lips since that night. I was in no mood now to test the whiskey waters again.

"One shot won't hurt you," Devlin said, quaffing his own shot.

"For some reason, I can't tolerate the stuff. Makes me break out in a rash. Same thing happens if I drink more than two or three beers. Must be an allergic reaction, I don't know."

"That's too bad," Devlin said, as if I'd told him I had some kind of terminal condition. When I saw how alcohol ruled Devlin and Maggie's lives I considered myself lucky. Yet I would have been grateful for an escape from the way I felt.

I don't know why I should have been so taken by surprise by Laura's behavior, by the prospect of my marriage heading for the rocks, when broken marriages among my generation were becoming commonplace. Maybe it was comparable to the mindset one has about one's own mortality, or the dogged refusal to admit that you could ever become seriously ill, or even grow old. Surrounded on all sides by evidence to the contrary, I wondered why we still clung steadfastly to these fictions. I knew in my heart of hearts that Noelle would confirm all my worst fears when she showed up at my door tonight. This was the kind of thinking that could make me susceptible to Devlin's offer of a rye whiskey escape.

"Honcho. Here, kitty, kitty, kitty."

"He'll come back when he's ready," Devlin said.

"He's never stayed away this long." I felt guilty for not noticing sooner that he hadn't come home. For all I knew, he could have been crying at the back door all night. I was too absorbed in my own misery. The absence of my cat added to my desolation. I excused myself and went inside to feed the bird, clean its cage, give it fresh water… keep myself occupied.

Noelle arrived at a little after eight.

"Oh, Paul." She gripped my arm with both hands, her large eyes filled with concern for my welfare.

"You want a beer?" I extracted my arm from her grip.

"Sure."

"Let's go in the kitchen. If he spots us with beers he'll go ape."

"Hello, J. Alfred." Noelle put her face up to the bars of the cage. "Pretty bird." J. Alfred buried his hooked beak in his chest feathers. I closed my bedroom door on my way to the kitchen so Noelle wouldn't get a look at the disarray in there.

"Glass?"

"The bottle's fine."

I opened two beers, handed one to Noelle. She had those eyes fastened on me.

"What?"

"Oh, Paul, you must be …"

"Must be what? Maybe you can tell me what I must be. I sure as hell don't know. What's this all about, Noelle?"

21

Noelle took the chair nearest the door; there was barely room enough for two chairs at the kitchen table, which was cramped into the alcove with the sloping ceiling. I sat down across from her.

"She left you a note, didn't she? She said she was going to."

"I guess you could call it that. I'm not sure I understand what it means. What can you tell me?"

"You know how desperate she's been feeling lately."

I didn't know anything about my wife's "desperation," but I wasn't prepared to admit this to Noelle. "Yeah, well who doesn't?" Noelle's big eyelids flickered. "You sure you don't want a glass?"

"I'm fine. You must have known how she was feeling. Remember how she was last time you were over?"

"Yeah. I guess." We had been to their apartment for shrimp and steamers about three weeks ago. All I recall about that evening was what a tedious ass William had been with his need to dominate conversation, and direct it toward himself. In retrospect, maybe it meant something that Laura didn't seem to have any interest in busting his balls the way she liked to do whenever William got off on one of his egocentric journeys, or when he would get on Noelle's case out of spite or pure meanness. Laura had kept quiet. Thinking back, I realized that in my gut I sensed something was wrong. I didn't pursue this feeling when we got home, and Laura went to bed early complaining of a migraine. The migraine was as good an excuse as any for her behavior earlier in the evening.

"She had more serious things on her mind that night, Paul."

"She had a bad migraine that night."

"Paul, she hasn't had migraines in months."

"Well, she had one that night, but I suppose you're right. You'd know better than I would. I've come to expect dark moods from her. In my opinion, the way she was that night didn't seem so out of the ordinary."

Noelle finished off her beer. I had hardly touched mine. "You got anything harder?"

"You know me and hard stuff, Noelle."

"I thought Laura might have some Scotch on hand. She likes her Scotch, or does that come as a surprise to you, too?" I didn't answer. But I had a hard look, if not hard liquor, for Noelle. "I'm sorry, Paul. That wasn't a nice thing to say."

"There's no Scotch in the house, Noelle. I'll get you another beer if you want."

"No. I probably should be going before I make you really angry."

"I'm not angry. Confused, but not angry. Did she run off with, you know, someone?" I could hear the self-pity in my voice. Noelle got up and went to the refrigerator and helped herself to another beer.

"She left with someone, but it's not the way you think."

"What is it that you think I think?"

"She didn't run off with another man."

"Who, then?"

"She went to San Francisco with Andrea. Andrea's sister lives out there." Noelle took a long, unfeminine, swallow of beer. I half expected her to belch when she finished.

"Andrea Kincaid? I haven't laid eyes on her or her creepy friends for months, and I know Laura hasn't had any contact with her."

"Are you sure, Paul?"

I began to sense that my wife and Noelle had played me for the fool. "You know something? Maybe I lied about not being angry. And frankly, you seem to be going out of your way to see that I do." I averted my eyes, fixed my gaze on the door behind her.

"Do what? Lie or get angry?"

"Very funny."

"Listen to me. I'm sorry, Paul. I've got a big mouth."

I said nothing. I kept my eyes on the door. Peripherally, I could see Noelle looking down at her lap, her hand around the beer bottle on the kitchen table. She was terribly nearsighted, but had refused to be fitted for contact lenses, and was too vain to wear the kind of glasses that her poor eyesight demanded. Not even the fact that the state refused to issue her a driver's license unless she wore corrective glasses could budge her from her position. She would not compromise her appearance. William wouldn't let her behind the wheel of his new Corvair, in any case. She was pretty (some might even say she was beautiful); she had an ample front, and an eye-catching rear. Her eyes were green as malachite; her long straight hair as black as tar. Noelle, like my wife, had a bohemian temperament. They had been best friends since high school, and were alike in many ways, although different essentially. I believed Laura to be more moral and more intelligent than Noelle. Now, here was Noelle taunting me, cracking wise when I was trying to deal with a reality I didn't yet fully comprehend.

"Paul, I'm really very sorry. Please forgive me."

"We haven't been married a year. If you knew all along about Laura's intentions, I suppose that means William knows, too." I remembered what the supercilious jerk had said to me Monday night when I called asking about my wife.

"I know you won't believe me, but he didn't, and doesn't know about Laura."

"You're right, I don't believe you. What does it matter anyway?" What mattered was that if William did know, had known all along, I'd be very uncomfortable. Maybe there was a part of me that was jealous of William, even a little afraid of him. Laura had dated him briefly before he met Noelle. Whenever we were together with William and Noelle I felt conscious of the fact that he had knowledge of my wife that I was not privy to, and that they shared something between them that belonged to them and them alone.

"Paul, Paul." Her hand was on my arm. She had nearly finished her second beer. I looked into her myopic eyes, shiny now from the two beers. I think she truly believed she was conveying sympathy with her watery eyes. "This has been coming for such a long time."

"We haven't been married long enough for it to have been coming for a long time." I pulled my arm away from her hand. Noelle issued an exasperated sigh. We sat for a while in silence, not looking at one another. The heat in the room grew even more oppressive. I got up and opened the kitchen door. Devlin was on the back steps muttering drunkenly. I glanced at his screen door. Maggie was not at the kitchen table. Devlin didn't act as though he'd heard me open my door. I shut it quietly. "Maybe we should go in the other room."

"The bedroom?" I looked at Noelle, surprised at her words, and playful smile. "Come on, Paul, don't look so shocked. You must know how attracted I am to you. Don't tell me you haven't thought about the two of us. I've seen you looking. William finds it amusing."

"Aren't you supposed to be Laura's best friend?" Noelle laughed. "I said something funny?"

"It's just that your naiveté is so ... sweet."

I didn't enjoy being condescended to. I had no comeback, however.

"Why don't we get out of these old clothes and make sweaty love, Paul. You know you want to."

The truth was, I didn't know it before, caught up as I was in my own problems, but I had only to hear Noelle's offer out loud to know she was correct. I did want to. But not in my wife's bed. Not in this apartment. Noelle had me very much aroused ... aroused and maybe even a little frightened.

"You know something, Noelle? I think maybe you had better go now, before we do something I'll regret."

Charlie was at the door when I showed Noelle out. I wondered how long he had been there. I hadn't heard his knock. Noelle, apparently not inhibited by the presence of a mongoloid adolescent, put her hand on my crotch.

"Anytime you say, Paul. How's Charlie?" she said to Charlie, and patted him on the head before going down the stairs and out the front door.

"She's still visiting her mommy, Charlie. I'll let you know as soon as she comes home. That's a promise."

"Okay," Charlie said, turning to go back downstairs. But it wasn't okay with Charlie if I read his downcast eyes and quivering chin correctly.

I was still very much aroused by Noelle's parting gesture when my wife called. It seemed wrong to be talking to my estranged wife on the phone under the influence of Noelle's erotic spell.

"How are you, darling?"

"How do you think I am? Out of my mind is how I am."

"I'm sorry for that, Paul, but I couldn't see any other way."

"You're going to have to explain that one to me because I don't have any idea what you're talking about. By the way, your best friend just left, but not before she tried to put the make on me. With friends like her who needs ..."

"Watch out for her, Paul, she's a predator."

"I'm surprised it even matters to you."

"It matters, Paul. I love you. You have to believe that. Why do you think I did this?"

"You ran out on me because you love me. Forgive me if I don't make the connection between love and abandonment."

"I haven't abandoned you, Paul. I ..."

"You what?"

"I understand you're upset. You have every right. I don't think this is the time to talk about my motives, why I thought it was necessary ... to save our marriage. You're not emotionally prepared for this kind of discussion. Why don't I give you a few days, and call you back?"

"Wait. Aren't you even going to tell me where you are? How I can reach you?"

"Didn't Noelle tell you? Or was she too busy trying to seduce you?"

"She said you'd gone to San Francisco with Andrea. That's another thing I can't understand. Why that flake? Why all the damn way to California? Where'd the money come from?"

"I've got some money in my trust. Andrea paid her own way."

"You're staying with Andrea's sister?"

"Yes, Lydia and her boyfriend."

"Her boyfriend. You mean he lives with her?"

"Don't be naïve. This is San Francisco, not Garrison, which is just one of many reasons I had to do what I did. It was for us, Paul, not just for me."

25

I had no idea where she was going, and as she had already pointed out, I was not emotionally prepared to probe for her reasons. I wasn't in the mood to play games with my wife from a distance of three thousand miles.

"You got a number where I can reach you?"

"Lydia doesn't want me to give out her number. It's a private line."

"You think I'm going to broadcast her freaking number?"

"I'm sorry, darling. I can't."

"Or won't."

"Paul." She sounded imploring in that half bored, half exasperated voice I had come to know.

"So, when can I expect your call?"

"Let's say Friday at eight, your time."

"I used to think my time and your time were the same. Hey, that's my poker night."

"Friday at eight. I love you, Paul."

I didn't play poker on Friday or any other night. Laura knew this. In the nearly eleven months we had been married I had never once gone out in the evening without her. No night out with the boys for me. The guys at Caplan's, especially Tommy Laroche, needled me constantly about it. Archie once playfully observed that I was the most pussy-whipped guy my age he'd ever met. I took offense even if I knew it was the truth. There was many a night when I would have welcomed male companionship, would have enjoyed spending an evening shooting pool or playing poker with the "boys." I would never broach the subject with Laura. She would take it as a personal insult, say something like "You'd rather spend an evening with your friends than with your wife? Why did we bother to get married if that's how you feel?" On the institution of marriage, my wife was anything but bohemian. Which made it more difficult to explain why her absence made me ache so.

FOUR

"Mark my words, young man. The Yankees and Dodgers in October. And if the Yankees don't take them in five games, I'll wash and wax your car," Devlin said, raising his shot glass to his lips. My car, with its cracked block and dead battery, languished underneath Mrs. Pappas's back porch. For this piece of junk I had paid two hundred-fifty bucks. I had put maybe twelve hundred miles on it. The rocker panels started to show rust after I'd had it a month; the floor board on the driver's side caved in, and something had gone wrong with the linkage so that if I wanted to get into first gear or reverse I had to go under the hood to do it. I had bought this "sweet" '55 Chevy from the older brother of one of my high school buddies. I mistakenly believed that friendship counted for something in business. Now I was without wheels, without wife, and lately without cat. I hadn't told Laura about Honcho the other night, and I hoped he might make an appearance before she called tonight. This was not likely to happen. I would have to break the news to her; she would not be pleased with me.

"Thanks, Dave. Why don't you put a new engine in her after you finish the wash and wax job."

Devlin chuckled from deep in his whiskey-soaked throat. "I won't have to do either. You mark my words."

I had no interest in baseball, but that didn't stop Devlin from talking on the subject until I wanted to scream. He had no interest in basketball, so there really was no common sports ground between us. The fact that the Celtics had won their fifth straight NBA title last spring impressed Devlin not at all.

I was on edge in anticipation of Laura's call. Devlin's endless prattle about the World Series only stoked my agitation. "I've got to go in, Dave. Laura's supposed to call."

"You can hear your phone. Have another beer. Enjoy the evening air." The evening air was suffocating, as it had been for days. I was already sweat soaked and I'd been out of the bathtub maybe fifteen minutes.

"Beer only makes me sweat more."

"Sweat's good for you. Cools you off."

"Maybe Paul just wants some relief from your constant blabbing, Devlin," Maggie said from the kitchen table where she was putting together her jigsaw puzzle. Devlin made the yak-yak sign with his fingers, but said nothing back to Maggie.

"Anyway, I got some things to do. I'll see you later, Dave."

"All right. Give the wife our best."

"Thanks, Dave. I'll do that."

* * *

Laura called at precisely eight o'clock, as she'd said she would. We got off on the wrong foot at once. Probably out of spite, I told her that Honcho had gone missing.

"Since Monday! How hard have you looked for him?"

"I've called for him every night. I've walked up and down the street, looked in people's cellar windows. What more can I do?"

"Have you asked anyone if they've seen him? Have you posted a notice anywhere? At Archie's?"

"Who should I ask? I'm not acquainted with any of our neighbors; you know that. No, I haven't put up a notice. Nobody pays attention to notices for lost pets."

"Paul, you are so twisted."

"I might say that if you're so concerned about the cat's welfare why aren't you here to look after him?" And so it went. Finally, after we had sufficiently worn each other down, Laura sounded a conciliatory note.

"Paul, I miss you so. And I miss Honcho and J. Alfred, and Mrs. Pappas and Charlie."

"What about Devlin and Maggie? They miss you. And they send you their best, by the way."

"Of course. Please give them my love."

"When are you coming home, Laura? If everybody misses everybody else so much, what's the point in prolonging all this ... missing? All you need to do is get on a plane and come home. We can work this out."

"I've been trying to explain to you why that isn't an option. I said, plainly, I thought, in my note that I couldn't take it anymore, and I meant it. I still mean it. I know you feel the same way, too, Paul, even if you can't admit it to yourself yet. You're not a dullard."

"Yeah." But maybe I was more of a dullard than my wife gave me credit for because I didn't appear to share this "quiet desperation" she was going on about.

"Sometimes you just have to make a clean break without giving too much thought to what you're doing, even if the act looks impulsive or irrational on the surface."

"Don't you think we might have been able to bring this "act" off together if we'd maybe talked about it?"

"Do you know how you sound, Paul?"

Of course I knew how I sounded. It was the way I wanted to sound. It was to me reasonable to sound this way, to feel this way. I also knew that if I said these things out loud we'd be back to the same impasse. We would continue to move in circles.

"I'm sorry."

"Let me have a few days to get my bearings, honey, some time to deal with some issues. Believe me, Paul, my mind is in as much turmoil as yours. Think about us. Think about our future. Do you really see a future for us in Garrison, Paul?"

"Is that a rhetorical question?"

I could hear her audible sigh. "I'll call again in a few days. Look for Honcho. Ask people if they've seen him. Put up signs on the telephone poles, in Archie's grubby store. Do something. And make sure to give J. Alfred fresh water every day, and keep his cage clean."

"Anything else?"

"Goodbye, Paul."

FIVE

"Hello Mudda, hello Fadda. Here I am at camp Granada," Tommy Laroche sang, tunelessly. "You hear the new Alan Sherman song, Brother James?"

One of Brother James's jobs was to maintain parts catalogs. The catalogs were kept in the bookkeeper's office instead of the inventory control office. To my mind it seemed illogical to keep them there. Not that I was kept awake nights by the anomaly, but it was just one of many things that made Sid's operation seem quirky.

"Can't say that I have," Brother James replied. "Can't say that I care."

"You got no ear for comedy," Tommy said. He couldn't get his mind around the fact that Brother James found nothing amusing about Jackie Gleason's antics on TV. For his part, Tommy could quote verbatim lines from the show the morning after it was aired. What Tommy Laroche and Brother James really had in common was a passion for fishing, and for bowling.

The new guy's cologne was powerful enough to compete with the all-pervasive smell of gasoline from the machine shop across the corridor. It was this overpowering smell of gasoline that drove me to quit smoking cigarettes seven months ago.

Chessy and Justin were huddled by Chessy's desk, giggling like preadolescent girls. There was something calculated about their chumminess. I feared that my job at Caplan's was in jeopardy, yet it was Chessy's personal slights that wounded me. I had finished posting all the work that was in the "in basket," and it wasn't yet nine-thirty. I lingered over a sales slip I had posted ten minutes ago, trying again to give the impression of being busy. Chessy, of course, knew that I wasn't really busy.

"Hey, Brother James. Guess who's going to be the special guest at next Friday's game supper?" Tommy Laroche asked his fishing companion and bowling buddy.

"Haven't the foggiest," Brother James replied in his laconic way.

"C'mon, take a guess. You'll never guess, but try anyway."

"Ted Williams."

"Better than Ted Williams, though The Splendid Splinter would be a catch, if you get my drift."

"JFK."

"No. Lee Wulf."

"Don't try to shit me. You're not getting Lee Wulf."

"I swear on my poor mother's grave."

"Your poor mother's not dead."

"Trust me, we're getting Lee Wulf."

"Jesus Christ."

"Lee Wulf's better."

Phil, the crippled boy, had to work in the midst of this almost constant daily asinine exchange between Tommy Laroche and Brother James. He appeared to be oblivious as he punched his ten-key calculator, entered numbers in leather-bound accounting ledgers, so quiet and unobtrusive that half the time I wasn't aware of his presence. Only when he had to get out of his chair and clomp around with his aluminum canes coupled to his wrists would I remember he was in the room. Tommy and Brother James seemed to occupy all the available space, like a gas, with their banalities. And now Justin, with his fruity perfume, competed for my air.

I swiveled around for a look outside. I could see west as far as the post office, and east to Whitcomb's Stationery store. Directly across the street was Spiro's Sweet Shoppe where many of Caplan's employees took their coffee break and ate their lunch. Spiro catered to the Garrison High School crowd as well. It was a popular after school hangout, and had been for years. I had fond memories of the place from my own high school days, memories of English muffins washed down with vanilla cokes, as I pitched my line to the girls, always on the prowl for a date. Laura never frequented Spiro's. She was in the class behind me in school. In the years when our student days overlapped I was barely aware of her existence, which was saying something in a school of fewer than five hundred students. I got my license at sixteen, picked up a 1940 Mercury coupe convertible with money I earned working for my dad at the bakery, and was fairly social for a kid who was shy by nature. Laura I never saw at a school activity—a dance, or an athletic event. She was a straight A student, an intellectual, the class valedictorian. I earned my bourgeois Bs (this, I learned from her, was Laura's opinion of the grade of B, and of the students who received them) and if I was in the upper two thirds of my graduating class it was in the bottom range of that group, on the cusp as they say. After I got out of the Army and started dating her, Laura informed me that she eschewed all organized school activities with imperious disdain. This explained why no one, outside of her classmates, knew much about her. I doubt that even her classmates could claim to know anything really personal about her. Even though she was quite beautiful, no myth about her sprang up in Garrison. As far as we were concerned she might have been from another galaxy.

With no more work for me to do, and the unlikelihood that there would be any later, given Chessy's conspiratorial posture with Justin, I was left feeling desolate, cast out. The air in the office, saturated with gasoline and Justin's cologne, was beginning to nauseate me.

I announced to Chessy that I was going on break. He didn't give me so much as a look, let alone a reply. I got to the front door, then turned around and went back to the time card rack and punched out for the day. I'd have Sid to answer to on Monday.

* * *

Betty and Loretta, Archie's wife and bimbo respectively, were in the store at the same time. Loretta knew who Betty was; I doubt that Betty was aware of Loretta. I had seen them in the place together on only one other occasion. Archie had been amused then, and he seemed delighted now. Poor Betty was only twenty-nine years old; she looked fifty. Archie had knocked her up and married her when she was sixteen. He had been twenty. Thirteen years and eleven children had taken a toll on Betty. Now she hauled goods down from the dirty shelves, seemingly at random, an infant on one big hip, two squalling toddlers clutching at her heavy, varicose legs. The little boy's nostrils were clogged with snot as thick as candle wax; the little girl's face was smeared with something blue—like jam. Archie, elbow up on the meat counter, grinning around his cigar butt, caught Loretta around the neck with one arm and copped a feel, for my benefit, as soon as his wife and kids were out of sight around the corner, in the canned goods section. Loretta was around thirty; she was short, dumpy, and humorless, with dull brown hair and a permanent expression of insolence on her not-very-pretty face. She showed no change in expression as Archie pawed her in front of the filthy meat case with its festering contents. I shook my head at his antics, a gesture Archie no doubt interpreted as approval.

Betty piled groceries on the counter; Duane bagged them, hauled them outside, and stowed them in the trunk of Archie's '63 Ford Fairlane convertible. Then, without a word to Archie, or he to her, Betty left the store and sped off in the convertible. Loretta's purchases Duane entered on her tab, a tab which Archie would make a show of tearing up in front of the boys in the back room as if to remind them what Loretta's sexual favors added up to for him.

I had come in, after punching out early from work, to pick up something to eat. Somehow, nothing Archie had to offer appealed to me. I hadn't eaten properly since Laura had been gone (not that my wife's offerings could be considered "proper"), and it didn't look like I was going to start today.

After Betty was gone, Archie took Loretta to the back room and closed the door. I drank a soda and chatted with Duane for a while, then headed for my apartment, not knowing what I would do with myself the rest of the day.

*　*　*

Mrs. Pappas, a floral apron on over her black dress, swept the walk in front of her house. She had on a cameo brooch pinned at the neck, and she wore her black hair in a mesh net.

"You're home early, Paul." She pushed an imaginary wisp of hair from her face. Mrs. Pappas was a short woman, and quite heavy. Her extra weight exacerbated her diabetic condition.

"It's slow at the store. I punched out early."

"We haven't seen Laura all week. Is she feeling poorly?"

"She feels fine. A friend of hers from college called last weekend. She's suffering from multiple sclerosis and asked Laura to come out to be with her for a while. She's in San Francisco. I don't know yet how long she'll be out there."

"Oh my. All the way to California. Well, I'm not surprised, knowing the kind of girl she is. Charlie misses her so, poor dear."

"Yes, I know."

Mrs. Pappas stabbed her broom at nonexistent dirt on the clean-swept walkway. I amazed myself with this bit of extemporaneous lying. In a way, it was a medicinal lie. Mrs. Pappas had no need to share in our marital problems. She had troubles enough of her own with her diabetes, Charlie, and the fact that she was a widow on a fixed income. My problems were trivial by comparison.

"Is it comfortable in your apartment, Paul? This heat takes the life right out of you."

"I'm fine, Mrs. Pappas." The thermometer had not fallen below eighty-eight degrees for a week and a half. Mrs. Pappas kept her Venetian blinds shut against the heat, and from my apartment I could hear the roar of the fans she had running downstairs. It made me wonder why I hadn't sprung for a fan of my own.

"I might have an extra fan in the cellar if you could use it," said Mrs. Pappas, reading my mind.

"Are you sure you don't need it, Mrs. Pappas? That would be great. I'd appreciate it very much."

"I don't have any more outlets. Come inside. I'll see if I can find it."

Charlie sat in the middle of a large overstuffed sofa with his crayons and a coloring book. He wore a tank-top shirt and green shorts. His pudgy feet were bare. Mrs. Pappas disappeared into the kitchen leaving me uncomfortably alone with Charlie.

"What's that you're working on, Charlie?"

"Bozo," Charlie replied in his sepulchral voice. He didn't look at me, so intent was he with his coloring. I moved behind him for a surreptitious look at what he was doing, half expecting to see primary color chaos on the page. Instead, Charlie had been impeccable in keeping Bozo's colors inside the lines.

My aversion to the boy had not gone unnoticed by my wife. It had been the source of more than one contentious argument since we had been renting from Mrs. Pappas, and Laura had befriended the landlady and her afflicted son. If I suggested to Laura that Charlie spent too much time with us (meaning her) in our apartment, she would pounce on me, make it sound as though I were intolerant, a kind of bigot, down on the mentally "handicapped" (she would never use the word retarded). Charlie smelled bad. The odor he gave off was an unpleasant mixture of urine and baby powder. His looks gave me a chill; the saliva that perpetually collected in the corners of his down-turned mouth didn't improve them. He was fat and he had an eerie voice. I would cringe inside whenever Laura would unreservedly embrace him. I learned early on to keep my feelings about Charlie to myself. Mrs. Pappas adored Laura for showering her son with such unalloyed affection. Even I marveled at Laura's ability to teach the boy things I never dreamed a kid with an affliction as severe as Charlie's could learn. She taught him the Greek alphabet (she believed he should have some sense of his heritage), and to pick out the melody of "In a Little Spanish Town" on the portable electric organ his mother had bought him.

Because of all that Laura had done for her son, Mrs. Pappas went out of her way to do things for Laura, who was as enthusiastic about Mrs. Pappas's Albanian heritage as she was about her poor son. Given the fact that Laura had zero interest in cooking, it came as a surprise to me when she became a willing student of Mrs. Pappas in the art of Greek pastry making (which she must have learned from her husband's people). She once spent an entire Sunday afternoon in the woman's tiny overcrowded kitchen rolling out filo dough and hanging it to dry on a broom handle suspended between two chairs. They made their gooey pastries with crushed nuts and honey. Part of me resented Laura for not giving a fraction of that kind of effort to making the things I liked to eat.

Mrs. Pappas called from the kitchen for help with the fan. She had got it as far as the bottom of the cellar stairs. I went down the narrow stairs to the dank, dirt floor cellar whose cobwebbed ceiling was so low I had to stoop. The enormous fan was square, with a peeling enamel frame that housed a large rusty blade. It looked much too large to fit into any of my windows. I hauled the thing upstairs, thanked Mrs. Pappas, and wrestled it up another flight to my apartment. I was right about it not fitting in my window frame. I set it down on the floor, plugged it in and aimed it at my bed. It made a horrendous racket, like a jet revving its engine for takeoff. The important thing was that it moved air mightily in the little room. The noise I could put up with. I stripped off my clothes and lay naked on top of the sheets, letting the humid air wash over me. I fell asleep into an erotic dream and was startled when I woke up to discover Noelle performing *fellatio* on me.

"See what you get when you don't lock your door," Noelle said when she finished.

"Nobody locks their door in Garrison."

"That's a very good policy, don't you agree?"

"I couldn't agree more. What time is it?"

"I don't know. Five."

"How long have you been … busy with me? I thought I was in a dream."

"I knocked, but who could hear anything over that?" Noelle cocked her head toward the fan.

"How did you know I was home? I usually work till five on Saturdays."

"I thought so, too. William said he saw you coming out of Archie's a little after twelve, and heading here instead of back toward Caplan's."

"William."

"Yes. He's off to a sales convention in Boston. He won't be back till tomorrow night."

"What about little Teddy?"

"My mother's watching him. She'll keep him overnight if I ask her."

"I don't know, Noelle. I feel funny, you know, in Laura's bed and all. You know how it is."

"We'll go to my place. I wouldn't feel funny there and neither should you. All's fair, and all that." Noelle had on a pair of short shorts and a halter-top that revealed a lot of breast. I suddenly felt self-conscious of my nakedness. I tried to pull a corner of sheet over my front.

"Don't be modest, Paul. You've got nothing to be ashamed of. I like your body. I like your face, too. It's such an interesting face."

"That's what all the girls say to ugly guys."

"You're far from ugly, Paul."

"How far?"

Noelle reached for my cock. I turned away. She started to tickle me. I hate being tickled almost as much as I hate being bitten and "hickeyed" by women.

"Cut it out, Noelle, for Christ's sake." Noelle giggled like a lunatic. "You're out of your freaking mind."

"This is the thanks I get for sucking you off?" She got off the bed and smoothed the bottom sheet with both hands. "Come for supper at seven-thirty. Plan to spend the night. A bottle of red wine would be nice."

"Liquor store's closed."

"Then we'll have to open one of William's." Another loony giggle issued from her throat. William fancied himself a wine connoisseur and gourmet cook. In fact, he did all the cooking when he was home, or if he deigned to allow Noelle in the kitchen, he would supervise her carefully, like the head chef of a five-star restaurant. We had been to their place often for meals. I had to admit, grudgingly, that the guy knew his way around a recipe. I also knew he kept a good-sized stock of wine on hand. He wasn't shy about lecturing us on whatever vintage he had so scrupulously chosen for the meal he was preparing. I was used to drinking the kind of wine that came with screw caps, not corks, although I would never admit this to William. My food tastes were fairly parochial as well, so I was always slightly apprehensive when they had us over for a meal, fearing he might spring a dish on us that concealed an internal organ. The truth was I could have happily dined at William's table any day of the week. I could have learned something about the gastronomic world from him if he wasn't always so predictably unpleasant. Now, here I was being unfaithful with his wife.

"Noelle, I have scruples. It's one thing to bang a man's wife, but to drink his wine ..."

"You can replace it on Monday if you're so conscience bound."

"What does he pay for these wines of his?"

"Who knows? Plenty. I've got to run. Seven-thirty. Don't be late."

The guilt I felt the instant Noelle was gone did not center on William, because William could not have cared less what his wife did with me or anyone else. He was a shameless philanderer, and he made no effort to conceal the fact from his wife. No, what I felt was profound disappointment in myself. I thought I truly believed in marital fidelity, and I knew Laura felt the same way, even if her views on most other social institutions bordered on subversive. I began to have serious misgivings about this evening's assignation with Noelle. I was angry at myself for letting her toy with me. Finally, I decided that I would not go to Noelle's tonight. For what had happened this afternoon I could hardly blame myself. Hadn't Laura described Noelle as a predator? This self-deception lasted for only as long as it took me to draw a bath. For an hour, I soaked in the tub in a troubled state of mind.

The phone rang at eight o'clock. It had to be Noelle, though it could just as likely have been my wife calling. In any case, I didn't answer it. I wouldn't have put it past Noelle to come looking for me. I locked the front and back doors. The phone rang again fifteen minutes later. I let it ring. Then I began to feel guilty for standing up Noelle. What if she had actually prepared a meal? The likelihood was small, but that didn't make my behavior any less craven. I dialed Noelle's number intending to apologize to her, to explain that I'd had a change of heart and couldn't go through with it. There was no answer at her end. If she had decided to come looking for me she would have been here by now; their apartment was no more than a five-minute walk away.

J. Alfred's cage needed cleaning. He perched obediently on my shoulder while I removed shit-splattered newspapers and replaced them with an old edition of the *Garrison Record*. The headlines carried news of the signing of the nuclear test ban treaty by the U.S., U.S.S.R. and Great Britain.

"Show them what you think of their treaties, J. Alfred." He nuzzled his crested head in my ear. I loved his musky smell. I rewarded him with a few sunflower seeds fed from my lips. Twenty minutes passed and there was no sign of Noelle. I tried her number again with the same result. Now I found myself regretting not going to her place for food and sex, and realized, perhaps for the first time, that I had married much too young. I should have given my hormones more time to ripen. I wanted my wife back, too. I apparently wanted too much.

SIX

Sid had a look for me when I punched in Monday morning.

"Embry," he said, before I could get past his little cubbyhole of an office made to look even smaller by the presence of an enormous oak desk, which faced the corridor.

"Yeah, Sid?"

"You punched out early Saturday. Am I right-or-wrong?" Sid had a peculiar way with this phrase. "Right-or-wrong" came out with the same inflection, as if it were one word.

"That's right, Sid. I was feeling sick at my stomach." I wondered if he caught on that I was mocking him with "sick at my stomach," which was another one of his odd expressions, as if he had been brought up in the South, instead of Perth Amboy, New Jersey.

"Why didn't you say something to me, or to Chessy?"

"I was in a bad way, Sid." Of course, I wasn't sick at all, unless you counted how I felt about Sid Caplan and Chessy Chessman.

"What?"

"I felt like I was about to lose my breakfast, and I didn't want to deal with that in your place of business. So I left. Sorry."

"Next time tell somebody." And with that Sid dismissed me, inserting a cigarette between his lips. He hadn't actually lit up a cigarette in ten years. All the same, he went through a carton of Chesterfields a week. He was doing penance for leaving a live butt on the edge of an ashtray, and then closing the store. The lighted cigarette found its way into a wastepaper basket and burned his store to the ground. Since that time, he would just put the unlighted cigarette in his mouth, and leave it there until it got soggy before replacing it with a fresh one. A carton a week; it was only one among his many idiosyncrasies. I was surprised to hear "next time" come out of his mouth. Part of me expected to be shown the door today. Even if I was ambivalent about my job, the employment scene in Garrison wasn't that promising. I should have been more concerned about holding the job I had, as disagreeable as it had become.

Justin was already in the office. I saw no sign of Chessy, and nobody was in Tommy Laroche's office either. My basket was empty. I feared another day of make believe awaited me. I made up my mind to have it out with Chessy.

"Is Chessy around?" I asked Justin.

"Haven't seen him." His reply struck me as pointedly indifferent.

"How long have you been here?"

"Not long."

"Did you, by chance, take work from my basket?" Justin glanced at me. I could see now that his hair was most definitely dyed. Nature would never have made hair come out that yellow. Not human hair.

"I wasn't aware that it was your personal in-basket." Chessy came through the door.

"I'd like a word with you," I said. "In private."

"It will have to wait. I've got work to do out front." He swirled out the door, leaving me to wonder what had brought him into the office in the first place.

"Horse's ass," I said to Chessy's back. If he heard me it didn't impede him on his mission to do his "out front" work. "Insufferable son-of-a-bitch." Justin had suddenly become intent on his posting.

"Nobody likes an ass kisser, Justin," I said, and stalked out of the office. I headed for the store's smelly toilet, no bigger than a coffin, not because I had to use it, but because I needed to be completely alone. It was occupied, of course. Tommy Laroche said it wasn't large enough to fit a full-grown man and a whole roll of toilet paper at the same time. If you needed to sit down to take a crap, your knees would be jammed against the door, and there were a couple of cracks in the wooden seat that could give the backs of your thighs a pinch. It had an overhead tank with a pull-chain flusher.

Ernie Golding and old Harry Lamb sat on metal stools at their sloping metal-top desk getting ready to put up orders for shipment.

"I don't suppose it has escaped your notice what a first-class asshole Chessy Chessman is," I said to them.

"Better not let Sid hear you talk about his fair-haired boy," Ernie said, extinguishing a cigarette in a howitzer shell case he used for an ashtray.

"Yeah," Harry added, "he'll have your balls cut off. Either that, or let Chessy fondle 'em."

"Chessy probably can't do much about who he prefers having sex with, but anybody, if they want to, can make an effort to be less of an asshole." It was the first reference I had heard from anyone in the store about Chessy's homosexuality.

"Kid sounds bitter," Harry said to Ernie.

"The kid is bitter. Hey, maybe you guys can use a hand out here in shipping. There's nothing for me to do in the office since the boy with the yellow hair arrived on the scene. What do you make of him?"

Ernie thought he seemed like a nice enough young man. Harry had no opinion. He never acknowledged a new man's existence until he'd been at least six months on the job.

"We got things pretty much in control back here," Ernie said. "Besides, it would be up to Sid to send you back here, not us." Ernie had thinning black hair, and a receding cleft chin beneath which his big Adam's apple moved up and down like a piston. Old Harry was stout and gray-haired. His glasses had a way of slipping down his nose, especially when he got sweaty. Harry was quick to anger, a tendency the salesmen exploited by goading him until he would explode. This would be what the salesmen wanted to see. And hear, because when Harry got boiled he would just say funny things, even if he were not really trying to be funny. He once called Arty Knox an Ethiopian motherfucker. Harry was a mouth-breather and a wheezer. His wheezing was never more acute than when he was coming down from one of his outbursts. He'd storm out of the shipping area leaving wheeze in his path.

Ernie made an effort to come to work every day with a new dirty joke. He also had what he thought were funny things to say about the parts he shipped out. "Autolite but it don't," was one of his favorite sayings. I would have preferred working with these guys than with the likes of Chessy Chessman and his new best friend.

"We got to turn to now, Paul. Harry, let me have a look at that clipboard," Ernie said.

"What, no joke today?"

"Come by after dinner. I got a doozy."

Sid intercepted me on my way back to the office. "Embry, what's the idea, you giving Chessy a hard time?"

"Hard time? I asked to have a word with him. He was too busy for me. What hard time?"

Sid popped a fresh Chesterfield in his mouth. There was sweat on his upper lip, above his gray pencil-line mustache. He looked past my shoulder when he spoke. He had a reputation for not looking you in the eye, especially when he had something unpleasant he wanted to say, and my gut told me Sid had something very unpleasant he wanted to say to me.

"Chessy said you swore at him."

"I called him a horse's ass. I thought that was generous considering what I really wanted to say to him."

"Embry, I'm going to have to let you go. You know how I mean?"

His words took me off guard, given what I thought was the amnesty I got from him this morning after punching out early on Saturday.

"You hear me, Embry? I'm going to have to let you go."

"I hear you." I had begun to tremble. I couldn't find any words to express the rage I felt.

"Have Tommy cut you a check. I'll pay you through this week. No overtime, though."

"Wait," I said, as Sid was about to walk away from me. "Don't you think you owe me an explanation? For almost four months I've been treated like a freaking leper by your ..."

"Watch what you say, Embry. Don't make trouble."

"Trouble?" My voice rose. We were in the corridor outside the offices. I knew that the countermen out front, and whatever customers were in the store, could hear us. "I've only been trying to do my job. Why have I been treated like this?"

Sid whirled around to face me, eyes averted. "I don't like my workers bettering themselves on my time; you know how I mean? You want to go to college, go to college. You want to work for me, you work for me. You know how I mean?"

"Yes, Sid. I think I know perfectly well *how* you mean. It's *what* you mean that's got me confused."

"You trying to be a wise guy?" At this I laughed out loud. All of it was as I had suspected all along. Chessy resented me for my harmless little interludes with French verbs. It was more likely that he was jealous of the fact that I was looking beyond Caplan's Auto Supply for a future, something that apparently was out of his reach. Sid, of course, thought I was laughing at him.

"Get out of my store, Embry, before I call the cops."

"With pleasure," I said, bowing deeply. "And you can keep your crummy week's pay. Keep it and shove it in your favorite orifice." Sid retreated to his little office and closed the door. The countermen pretended to be busy with their catalogs when I headed for the door. I felt like giving them a parting shot, but kept my mouth shut.

I hadn't walked the two blocks to Archie's store before it hit me that I had just burned a bridge. I was trembling, hyperventilating. Then it occurred to me that this would be just the kind of thing Laura would approve of. Cutting all ties to Garrison was her mission for us. If this realization should have been a source of comfort, I would have been hard put to explain why it wasn't.

* * *

Archie was poring over the racing form. He let the bookmakers use the store's public telephone to take bets. For this he was paid a pretty good fee. He spent a fair amount of time at the track with Doc, too. There were more ways to turn a buck in Garrison, New Hampshire, than peddling beer, cigarettes, and rancid meat. Archie had a number of things going for him, all of them nefarious. Now that my main source of income had dried up, I was tempted to ask him if he could put me on to some of his action. I knew I would never be able to carry it off. I was far too law-abiding for the underworld, which was to say too chicken of getting nabbed and jailed.

"Look who's here. You're starting to keep banker's hours," Archie said, reaching in the ashtray for his dead stogie. There were no customers in the store, nothing to distract Archie from his betting strategies.

"Sid the squid just canned me. Threw me out of his place. Threatened to call the cops."

Archie laughed. "What'd you do to get that kind of treatment?"

"He doesn't like his employees bettering themselves on his time."

"He didn't give you a week's notice? Just like a fucking Jew."

"He offered to pay me for the week. I told him to stick his week's pay in his ass."

"That's the ticket. Let's have a beer."

"It's not even nine o'clock."

"Call it a celebration.' Archie started for the beer cooler.

"I can't seem to get in a party mood with unemployment as a theme. Nothing for me, Arch. I'm going to have to start pounding the pavement."

"Come on down back. It don't look good drinking out front."

"You're right. Appearances are important." I was wasting my irony on Archie. I followed him to the back room. The odor of urine was still powerful. There was no end in sight of the heat wave even if the temperature had dropped to seventy today.

"Keep an eye out for those little fuckers," Archie said, sliding into his recliner. This was apparently a favorite time of day for the guttersnipes to come in the store to swipe penny candy.

"Be thankful they don't have their eye on your beer and cigarettes."

"Only a matter of time. What else can you expect, the kind of home life they got? Parents probably already drunk on their ass," Archie said, and swallowed some beer. His round face was clean-shaved today. He shaved maybe twice a week.

"I suppose I'm going to have to get on my knees at the unemployment office. I thought I'd seen the last of those pricks in '61."

"Job outlook ain't that bright, Paulie. I can give you a few more hours, you want."

"Thanks, Arch. I'm afraid I might have to take you up on it. At least for a little while. Shit, I don't know what I'm going to do. I'm in a spin."

"You'd have to work a Saturday night or two a month. That a problem?"

"What's Saturday night to me? It's like any other night."

"I thought maybe with mama gone you'd want to kick up your heels a little."

"It takes dough to kick up the heels, not to mention the toes."

43

"It ain't much, Paulie, but I got to give Duane some hours. He ain't exactly living high off the hog with what he makes at Biddle Press."

And Duane had a wife and two young kids to feed. I told Archie to forget it. I'd make out. I could be in California next week for all I knew; my fate seemed now to be in my wife's hands.

"The offer still stands, you know, for poon tang. I can get you Candy, you want. Only take a phone call."

"Candy?"

"You know, the Black Dahlia. That's her name. Candy. You didn't think …"

"No, of course not. I don't think so, Arch. I'm in negotiations with the wife. If things work out we could be back together again."

"Be careful with these 'negotiations.' You know how women are. You ain't careful she could have your balls in a paper bag."

"I'm embarrassed to tell the unemployment gnomes I was fired."

"Happens every day, son. Nothin' to be embarrassed about."

I left the store feeling oddly buoyed by my little talk with Archie. He sometimes had that effect on me. For a guy with only a fourth grade education Archie Cahill was a pretty savvy guy.

It hit me, when I got back to my apartment, that I had forgotten to give Mrs. Pappas the July rent. It was already well into August and she had said nothing to me. I shouldn't have been surprised. Laura had said more than once that Mrs. Pappas was as close to a saint as anyone could get. I went into our accordion-like budget folder that Laura used to organize our bills and found seventy dollars in the rent compartment. That was the only cash left in the folder. I now regretted my hubris with Sid in declining his offer of severance pay. I wondered if he was bound by a law of some kind to pay me. I was ignorant of the law. I was ignorant of a great many things.

* * *

I took off my shoes and tiptoed around the apartment so Mrs. Pappas wouldn't know I was there and take it in her head to knock on my door, wondering why I was home so early. She'd worry that I might be ill, and with Laura away there would be no one to look after me. Then I would have to explain to her the real reason I was home early. Of course, she would find out in time anyway.

I was grateful for the brief respite from the heat wave today. It seemed as though the temperature had not fallen below eighty degrees all summer long, since the middle of June. I had no need to turn on the fan; that would surely get Mrs. Pappas's attention. I sat on the edge of the bed, put my sweaty face in my hands, and tried to comprehend what was causing my life to come unraveled in such a short space of time. It was as if I were being made to pay for unspeakable sins I wasn't even aware of committing, sins I couldn't name, or perhaps ones I'd forgotten about. Could it have something to do with what I had done in my youth?

My youth. Here I was barely twenty-four years old, and contemplating youth. Yet it seemed so very remote at this moment. It was as if there were only the here and now, that I had never had a previous life. I seldom, if ever, indulged in nostalgia, or dwelled on the past. Laura was actually contemptuous of the tendency to speak fondly of the past. She considered it maudlin self-indulgence, a kind of corruption of reality. Now, I had to admit that since I had known her, her opinions had subtly influenced my way of thinking. I admired her intellect as much as her beauty. I was in awe, in fact, of her mind. Someone had once told me that a marriage was doomed to failure from the start if the woman was smarter than the man. Laura often insisted that I was far brighter than she was, if not as educated. That was why she was so insistent on my taking night courses at the university until we had saved enough money for me to matriculate full time. She had me believing that she truly believed herself that I was brighter than she was, even if I knew in my heart that it wasn't true. She had mentioned a trust fund when we talked last week. It was the first I had ever heard of such a thing. Not that I would have allowed her to pay my way, no matter how long I had to work to save enough for school. But why had she never mentioned it?

Laura had quit the university on impulse in the middle of the second semester of her senior year. She had been an English Literature major. She claimed the university had become fraudulent and hypocritical; furthermore, she was weary of being required to put on what she referred to as a social veneer just to get along with people she despised. The fact that for all its fraudulence, hypocrisy, and demand for veneer she still found it acceptable for me, I let pass unchallenged.

As a youth I had never imagined myself as a married man. Most of my friends in high school took it for granted that they would marry and raise a family. It was simply never a part of my thinking. In retrospect, I was never one to project myself into any kind of future. It was as if my motto were "live for the moment." With such an attitude toward life one would have thought I'd be more spontaneous.

I had my first date with Laura a week after my father's funeral. I had been home only a couple of weeks before my father suffered a fatal heart attack driving his car to work in the predawn. He died at the wheel, and the company car he drove slammed into a concrete bridge abutment. Only a month before his death he had been promoted to general manager of the bakery where he had worked since graduating from college. The promotion brought with it longer hours, greater responsibility, greater pressure to put up bigger sales figures. His annual physical revealed an aneurysm; he never had a chance to get scheduled for surgery. He was forty-five years old.

As I said, I knew virtually nothing about Laura. She was, as the words in the song went, "a face in the misty light." In fact, what details of this face I recollected from high school I would not have been able to put with the face of the girl sitting alone in a leatherette booth in Leggett's Tea Room. I had ducked in for a cup of coffee and a Danish before setting out on my daily job-hunting ordeal. I had a view of the booth she occupied from the reflection in the big mirror behind the counter. We made eye contact briefly. Then she was at my elbow.

"You're Paul Embry, aren't you? I fell in love with your I.Q. when I worked in the principal's office at Garrison High, junior year." She was tall and slender, and her straight brown hair hung to the middle of her back. She had large brown eyes that bore no makeup, and a slightly dimpled chin. I was disarmed by her words.

"My I.Q.?"

"Yes. I snooped through everybody's files. It was either that or go mad with boredom. Most of your classmates were dolts, in case you hadn't noticed. So, you've been away."

"Yes, but I'm back now." I couldn't bring myself to ask her who she was. The fact that she knew who I was, and had knowledge of my being away, made me think I should have known her, and to ask who she was would have been embarrassing, even rude.

"Hi, I'm Laura Sargent. Nice to meet you, finally." She offered her hand.

"I've heard of you. Didn't you used to have short hair?" She laughed and flipped a handful of hair behind her shoulder.

"You like foreign films?" Foreign movies were all right with me if they were dubbed. I was no fan of sub-titles.

"Sure."

"La Dolce Vita is at the Colonial. Come see the first show with me. We'll come here for coffee and a critique afterward."

"All right."

* * *

La Dolce Vita turned out to be the kind of foreign film with subtitles. No matter, because all I remember about the flick was the huge statue of Christ suspended by cables from a helicopter flying over some Italian city, Rome, I guess; paparazzi on Vespas, and Anita Ekberg and Lex Barker going into a fountain pool fully clothed. Lex Barker I recognized as the pretty boy replacement for Johnny Weissmuller in the Tarzan movies. I didn't bother looking at the subtitles; my mind was totally occupied with Laura, sitting inches away from me, her scent—the smell of her wool sweater, and freshly shampooed hair—washing over me. She spent the entire film on the edge of her seat, completely engaged by the images on the screen.

Later, over coffee in Leggett's, she recalled details of the film that I, in my deliberate inattention, had failed to notice. She critiqued the symbolic meaning of each for me. At the time, I wasn't dead sure what was meant exactly by the term "symbolism." It had never been used by any of the teachers in my high school English classes. As she lectured me on the significance of the opening scene—the Christ statue, beautiful but unreal, with the closing scene of the sea monster, ugly but real—I felt my ardor waning.

She was perceptive enough to notice. "You don't care about any of this, do you, Paul."

"That's not true. It's just that ..." It was just that I didn't care about those things at the time. It didn't take long for Laura to make me care. She tutored me in poetry and literature, art and classical music, philosophy and religion. By the time we were married and I started the first semester of English at the university extension, I had a leg up on my classmates. Most of the males were ex-GIs like me.

My father left behind a maroon '57 Desoto in mint condition. My mother didn't drive, my older brother Kenneth had moved to Pittsburgh, and my younger sister Janice had married right out of high school. The car was mine for all practical purposes, and some impractical ones. I had been looking, unsuccessfully, for work for the past nine days while the State Unemployment Agency processed my application for unemployment benefits.

Laura would have no part of the residential life of the university. She lived at home and depended on a boy in the neighborhood, a friend of the family and a new freshman, for a ride to school. I offered to pick her up after her last class and take her home. She told me that I was very "gallant." After that, I don't think a single day went by that we didn't see each other. We were married in St. Paul's Episcopal church across the street from Garrison High School a week short of the anniversary of our first date.

*   *   *

I lay my head down on the pillow and fell instantly asleep. When I awoke four hours later from another erotic dream there was no Noelle to affirm it. I found myself feeling disappointed that she had not tried to contact me since I stood her up Saturday night. I assumed she was angry with me. She had every right to be. I thought about calling her, but it was only a little after two o'clock. She'd be at work. I would never call her there. Besides, William was bound to be home from his sales conference by now, so there was no point in my thinking about Noelle. Yet she stayed in my brain as I wandered around my tiny apartment trying to figure out what I was going to do next.

Then, Charlie's soft knock was on the door. He must have heard me moving around. I'd forgotten that I was supposed to be at work this time of day. I didn't answer the door. He kept knocking, in his uncoordinated way, for maybe two or three minutes more before I heard his slow, heavy steps down the stairs. Ten minutes later, Mrs. Pappas called from outside my door.

"Paul, is that you in there? Are you all right? Paul?" I sighed and opened the door.

"Hello, Mrs. Pappas. I'm fine, really. I wasn't feeling so hot at work this morning, so I punched out early. It's nothing, really. I slept. I feel much better now."

"Are you sure, dear? Laura's not here to look after you. Is there anything I can get you? Some Sal Hepatica?"

"Thanks, no. Oh, there's something I can get for you, though." I got the budget envelope out and handed my landlady the late July rent. "I don't know what got into me. I never forget these things."

"Oh, please don't worry. I'd forgotten myself. I don't have my receipt book with me." Mrs. Pappas searched her apron pockets as if to convince me that she was not packing her rent receipt book.

"I can get it later."

Mrs. Pappas took the bills and shoved them in her apron pocket without counting them. She lingered, not looking at me directly. She wanted to talk, to find out what was going on with me. I stood there in awkward silence.

"Well, I better see to supper. Would you like to join us, Paul? Nothing fancy, but you're more than welcome to share our meal."

According to Laura, Mrs. Pappas had given up Eastern Orthodoxy for Adventism and the bizarre dietary baggage that went with it. I wasn't eager to subject myself to whatever it was she was concocting in her kitchen tonight.

"Thanks a lot, Mrs. Pappas, but I've been invited to a friend's for supper. I appreciate the offer, though."

"Are you sure you're all right, dear?"

"Yes, Mrs. Pappas. I'm sure."

* * *

When I wasn't escaping my condition by sleeping at inappropriate hours, I was soaking it away in the bathtub. I ran a bath, sniffed the gas stove, and went into the living room with the intention of putting on a record while I waited for the interminable time it took the tub to fill. Everything in our collection reminded me painfully of Laura: Beethoven's *Nine Symphonies*, *The Brandenburg Concerti* with Wanda Landowska, Offenbach's *Tales of Hoffman* were a few of the recordings Laura brought to our marriage. The very first gift I had ever bought for her was The Modern Jazz Quartet's *Fontessa*. I also had a scratchy LP of *Jazz at Massey Hall*, and even scratchier 45-RPM recordings of the Mulligan/Baker Quartet. Together, we collected a number of Nina Simone albums, and a four record set of Rubenstein playing Chopin. One of our first purchases was a hi-fi whose speakers and turntable folded into what was made to look like Samsonite luggage.

I returned to the bathroom without putting anything on the turntable. I had all but tuned out on the world; I had watched maybe a half hour of TV since Laura's disappearance. The small radio we kept on the kitchen table fetched only the local station and the local station's programming was abysmal: top forty songs and local advertising; a one-hour program after supper called "Open Mike" where Garrison's crackpot element vented their spleens over issues ranging from fluoridation of the drinking water (they were against this obvious communist conspiracy to contaminate our water supply with enervating chemicals designed to make us susceptible to commie doctrine), to their virulent hatred of JFK.

I stepped into the bath and was no sooner prone than I fell asleep again. Devlin's voice at the kitchen door awakened me.

"Paul, you in there? Come on out and enjoy the cool air. Supposed to be around for the next few days."

"Give me a minute."

The air was cooler, indeed. Cool enough to need a long-sleeved shirt, something I had not had on since early June.

"Autumn's in the air," Devlin said, as I sat down on the step beside him. He had a bottle of beer ready for me. "And you know what that means."

"Yeah. Winter can't be far off."

"No, Paul. The World Series. Yankees in five. Sure you can't use a shot to wash that down?"

"I'm sure. This has been some day."

"You telling me?" Devlin ran a shaky hand through his hair. I told him about losing my job. "Christ. I'm sorry, Paul. That's too bad, especially these days. Listen, there's a guy at work, brother has a small outfit, cleans offices and the like. He might be able to use some help. It

49

would be only part time, and it's night stuff. It probably won't pay much, but it'll be under the table."

Cleaning offices lacked a certain appeal, but I was what you might call desperate. "Hey, anything I can get. I'd appreciate it, Dave."

"I'll talk to him first thing in the morning. Maggie," Devlin shouted at his kitchen door, "you hear that? The little hebe fired Paul."

"I'd just as soon Mrs. Pappas not hear about it. Not right now. All right, Dave? If you don't mind." Devlin's voice was loud enough for Mrs. Pappas, maybe even the whole neighborhood, to hear. Maggie came out on the landing to commiserate with me. Devlin told her about the guy at work whose brother operated an office cleaning service, as if to validate the story he'd given me.

"I'll swing by the unemployment office first thing in the morning. What a time to be without a car."

"Have you heard anything from Laura?" Maggie asked me.

"Not for a few days. I'm half expecting her to call tonight. I can't wait to give her the good news." I didn't explain to Devlin and Maggie that it would be just that to Laura. Good news. There would now be nothing to hold me to the native sod. This fleeting thought made me feel inexplicably melancholy. Devlin noticed. He put his veiny hand on my knee.

"Cheer up, my boy. This won't be forever. Believe me."

"It's beginning to feel like it already."

"You poor dear," Maggie said.

"All right. Enough self-pity," I said.

"Maggie, they need any help in the office? You can type, right, Paul?"

"About twenty words a minute on a good day. I'm like lightning on a ten-key calculator, though."

"Hear that, Maggie? What about it?"

"They ain't hiring, Devlin. Don't go getting Paul's hopes up over nothing."

"There's not much hiring going on anywhere," I said. "Archie offered to give me a few more hours. With that, and the forty bucks a week I'll get from unemployment, I might be able to squeak by for awhile."

"Is that all they give you? How the hell do they expect anybody to live on that? Goddamn government," Devlin said.

"Nice talk," Maggie said.

"That's what they were offering the last time I drew. In '61."

"It's got to be more than that now. How do they expect a man to eat, to feed a family?" Annoyed with government—any government, local, state, or federal—Devlin finished off his shot and brought his glass down hard on the step.

"Calm down, Devlin," Maggie said, and went inside. I sipped some beer. Devlin's brand tasted bitter in my mouth. He must have been already slightly torched because he started to mutter under his breath, as if he were not aware that I was sitting there beside him.

"How's that, Dave?"

"Goddamn women."

"What goddamn women?"

"At work. You got no women where you work, right?"

"Where I worked. No."

"You're lucky."

"How's that?"

"They're taking over, Paul. The young ones, especially. They sashay around in their thin dresses, their mini-skirts. Bend over, you might as well be looking straight up their ass."

"You're complaining?"

"It's more than that. Everything's for the women these days. Watch the TV sometime. You might learn something."

"Sure."

"Don't look down your nose at the TV, my boy. It's a mirror on the times."

It was not the first time I had heard Devlin's rant on women in particular, the "youth culture" in general. In his estimate, the young had seized the economy by the throat, and were squandering our wealth on conspicuous consumption of useless goods. Women were infiltrating (his word) the work force, undermining male dominance. He would use Maggie's obstinacy (for example, when she refused to bring him his whiskey) to illustrate his point. The fact that she was constantly sassing him reinforced his theory. Something told me that this was always the way it had been with Devlin and Maggie, and therefore it hardly represented a change in the social order. He would have to do better than Maggie if he wanted to get weight behind his views. He would have a better model in my wife, although I would never suggest such a thing to him.

"If that's the case," I said, referring to TV as a "mirror" on the times, "then the times are in a bad way."

"I'll drink to that." But Devlin's glass was empty. "Maggie."

* * *

I went inside, jumpy in anticipation of the call from my wife I sensed was coming. Nine o'clock came, but no call. I didn't know what to do with myself. I wasn't in the mood to listen to music, and despite Devlin's assertion that TV had something important to offer sociologically, to me it was so much banal noise. I could take a walk uptown, see what was going on, maybe stop around Frenchie's and shoot some pool. I hadn't done anything quite so independent in a very long time. I was out of practice. And if Laura called while I was out she would no doubt think the worst. She might even believe that I'd succumbed to Noelle's sexual blandishments. The thought of Noelle caused a stirring in my groin. I tried to put her out of my mind. The phone rang. I literally jumped out of the kitchen chair.

"Sid fired me today." Laura didn't answer. "Did you hear me?"

"Paul, I'm so sorry. He's an evil man. And so is that other person, what's his name, Chubby?"

"Chessy."

"You must feel just awful. Paul, think of it as an opportunity. There's nothing to hold you to Garrison now. Not that there was really anything before, but now the tie is cut. Now we can make plans."

"Somehow I knew you'd say something like that."

"What do you mean? Is Honcho back yet?"

"Don't you think that's the first thing I would have told you?"

"I don't think I like your tone. No, I don't really like your tone at all."

"I'm sorry about my freaking tone."

"Do you have to be vulgar?"

"Sorry. I haven't gotten over the fact that, that turd …"

"I know, hon. Let it go. It's for the best. You'll see."

"Sure."

"Paul, we're going to have to be patient for a while. I'll have to find a job and an apartment before I send for you. It wouldn't make any sense for you to come out now. I've got a few leads, and Andrea has been very helpful. Hillary, too."

"Hillary?"

"One of Lydia's friends. She lives in the same building. I should have something in a couple of weeks, a month at the most."

"I hope the job scene's better in San Francisco than it is here. Aren't I lucky? I get to call on my good friends at the unemployment office again."

"Oh, don't bother, Paul."

"Don't bother? I just handed over my last seventy bucks to Mrs. Pappas. What do you mean, 'don't bother'?"

"Didn't Sid give you severance pay? I'll send you enough to take care of expenses. It won't be that long, Paul. Trust me."

"Did it ever occur to you that I might not want to go traipsing off to California? You know I got no use for big cities. At least to live in. Did it

ever enter your head I might have something to say about where we
live?"

"There's that tone again. Paul, I'll hang up. I mean it."

"Let me save you the trouble." I hung up loudly. A minute or so
later the phone rang. I let it ring. It rang for a long time. In fact, it was
still ringing when I went out the door.

SEVEN

Last night was comfortable enough to sleep without the roaring fan. I slept poorly, nevertheless. The phone call from Laura had put me in a rage. I left the apartment and walked aimlessly for the better part of two hours. I walked all the way to the hospital, a couple of miles north of the lower square, and back again at full throttle, talking under my breath to myself every step of the way. Today, I walked the same distance in the opposite direction to file for unemployment compensation, and to get a feel for the job market. The hard truth was that I wasn't very marketable. I had been a supply clerk in the Army, responsible for the financial records of my company's supply transactions. In other words, I was a not-so-glorious glorified bookkeeper. Government bookkeeping practices bore no resemblance to civilian ones, however, so my army experience counted for nothing. As I said, I could type a little, operate a ten-key calculator and was, as one of my supervisors had once described me, "a quick learner." Try telling a prospective employer that you might not be able to do squat, but you were a really fast learner. See where that gets you. There was more money to be made in stoop labor anyway, but the construction season was winding down. I had heard talk in Caplan's that companies weren't hiring.

When I showed up for work at Archie's he reminded me of his offer of more hours. "You give it some thought, Paulie? Like I say, I can give you a Saturday night or two a month, you want."

"I appreciate it, Arch."

"What say to this Saturday night?"

"Sure."

"I've gotta go home and change. Doc's down back. Tell him I'll be back to get him in half an hour."

"Off to the Rock tonight?"

"Yeah. I'm feelin' lucky. Hit the trifecta yesterday. I'm on a streak." Archie took a handful of bills from the cash register, lifted the cover for a look at the day's receipts, grabbed a package of White Owls off the cigar rack, and was out the door. There were no customers in the store.

Doc was stretched out in the recliner, nursing his vodka and milk cocktail, his nose in the *Garrison Record*.

"What's new, Doc?" Doc let the paper drape over his chest. He raised his glass to his lips.

"They got almost three million in that train heist in England. You hear about that one?"

"No. I've kind of shut the world out lately. Three million? I wouldn't mind a piece of that."

"What's new with you, Paul? Any word from Laura?"

I told Doc about my getting fired.

"That's too bad, Paul. You need some dough?" Doc reached in his pocket and came back with a thick roll of bills. Both Doc and Archie liked to carry around large sums of cash, and they wouldn't hesitate to flash it every chance they got. Doc once told me he earned fifty thousand dollars last year. He'd been drunk and had gone on about how I shouldn't believe in the myth that money can buy happiness. I found it hard to imagine myself ever earning that kind of money. At Caplan's I had made a buck seventy-four an hour. I sorely wanted to take Doc up on his offer, but I had my pride.

"No thanks, Doc. I'll be all right." Doc shrugged his heavy shoulders and put the money back in his pocket. "So, you and Arch headed for the track tonight?"

"Yeah. Big-balls is feeling lucky. He hit the trifecta last night. Thinks he's on a winning streak. We'll see. Loretta's pleased." Doc smiled ruefully.

"Excuse me for saying so, but what does he see in Loretta?"

"You could just as well ask what Loretta sees in him."

"He gives her things."

"He gets things in return."

"She's kind of … unattractive, to put it politely."

"Yeah, and Archie's Gregory Peck."

"He said he'd be back in half an hour."

"You got any skills, Paul? You good with your hands?"

"I can't do much. Finding a job isn't going to be easy."

"Which is exactly why you should be going to school full time. Get a college education, Paul. You're at a dead end without one. Take a look around."

"I'm broke, Doc. I'm already at a dead end."

"What about the G.I. bill?"

"I joined up between wars. It expired maybe a year before I enlisted. Maybe if Vietnam heats up …"

"Get yourself a loan. Banks got liberal policies these days on student loans."

"I got no credit. Laura wants me to come out to California."

"So, you have heard from her. How do you feel about that, California?"

"I don't know how I feel. I want to get back with Laura, but …"

"Get off this dead end street, for Christ's sake. San Francisco's as good a place as any. What's your problem? Why the ambivalence?"

"If I knew that … maybe I don't like being jerked around. Maybe I'm no different than Archie where women are concerned." Doc laughed. "I'm joking."

"Give this some serious thought, Paul. Listen to your wife. She did the right thing. I know it's hard to swallow. Believe me, she knows what she's doing." Doc hoisted his bulk out of the recliner. He brushed the wrinkles off the front of his shirt, and hitched up his trousers. "What, you want to end up like Archie? Like Whitey and Ray? I repeat. Listen to your wife." Doc slapped me on the shoulder and headed for the front of the store to wait for Archie.

I found myself annoyed at Doc for the way he had characterized Archie, even if I knew he meant well. I was acquainted with a number of successful people who had been born and reared in Garrison. Where did Doc get off calling Garrison a dead end street? I could have asked him if the place was so dead end what kept him here? I could have asked, but I already knew the answer. His wife is what kept him here. It never occurred to me that he had children. If he did, he kept the fact quiet. Frankly, his remarks about Archie and the others took me by surprise. I guess I was naïve enough to believe that he really did care about these guys, that his apparent friendship with them was genuine. Maybe there was a touch of the fraud in the good doctor.

When I returned to the front, Doc was gone. There wasn't much business tonight, and the evening seemed to go on forever. The radio Archie kept blaring all day and night from on top of the beer cooler got on my nerves. I climbed up on a milk crate and turned it off. By ten o'clock I had seen only a few beer and cigarette customers, and a bunch of the urchins had come in to redeem empty soda bottles for penny candy. They brought in three shopping bags full of bottles that fetched them two cents apiece. They were hoping I would haul them down back after the count so they could fill their dirty pockets with candy while my back was turned. I was wise to their tactics. I watched them carefully as they placed their Tootsie Rolls, Bazooka bubble gum, and the like on the counter until they had bought up their eighty cents worth of redeemable bottles.

One of them, the ringleader by the way he was treated by the others, was a filthy little towhead. He was about twelve or thirteen. I had been taken by surprise one day at the university art gallery to see a black and white photo of the kid. He wore his navy watch cap at a rakish angle, and had a street-wise expression on his face that got viewers' attention. Laura was charmed by the photograph, if not by the kid himself in person. She was put in mind of Dickens, she had told me. All I could see in front of me tonight was a dirty, emaciated little boy, slightly retarded, looking for the chance to heist Archie's penny candy.

"Okay, guys, you've done your business, now be on your way." The head urchin gave me an insolent smile; he made no move to leave. His three companions held their ground as well. "Out." I made a move toward them.

"You lay a hand on us, mister, we'll have the cops on your ass," the head urchin said.

"If you don't get out of here right now I'll have the cops on your skinny little asses. Out." I came from behind the counter; they scrambled for the door, laughing. As they exited, Eddie Flanagan came in for his nightly Orange Crush. Eddie was the youngest of a large Irish family that lived in the neighborhood. Chronologically he was sixteen, but he couldn't match those years in intellectual development. He had quit school the day he turned sixteen, not having made it past eighth grade. He was a sweet kid afflicted with a bad case of stammering. I noticed that when he was alone in the place with me, after a few minutes, his stammering lessened.

"How they hanging, Eddie?"

Eddie swallowed audibly, trying to summon the appropriate words for reply. "Goo ... goo ... good. You?"

"Not bad, Eddie. What have you been up to tonight?" Eddie's cousin, Duke, was a self-employed window washer. He had the storefront accounts on both sides of Center Street. He took on Eddie as a part-time helper after the kid quit school. Eddie was a good worker, according to Duke. I was on casual speaking terms with Duke, who was about five years older than I was. Eddie just shrugged his shoulders at my question to inform me that nothing much was up with him. Was there ever anything up in his life? He was a fairly rabid Red Sox fan, so I asked him how his team had fared tonight.

"Good," he replied, gulping air. "They did... did... didn't play." Eddie at least had a sense of humor about the Boston Red Sox, which is more than I could say for a lot of the Sox fans among Archie's customers.

"Duke working you hard, Eddie?" Eddie grinned, shook his head in the negative, and took a swig of his soft drink. The Black Dahlia came in wearing a black mini-skirt, and white satin blouse cut low in the front. Eddie's mouth fell open.

"Is Archie down back?" she asked me, her eyes rimmed with liner, lashes thick with mascara. She must have known Archie was not in; his car would have been parked in front of the store.

"Nope. He's at the track with Doc. I don't expect him back tonight." She glanced at Eddie and turned back to me as if Eddie were invisible.

"You heard anything from your wife?" Her question caught me by surprise. It shouldn't have. As soon as I let the news out in Archie's store, I should have known the whole neighborhood, maybe even the whole town, would hear about it.

"What do you mean?"

She smiled coyly. "Nothing. Let me have a pack of Old Golds. Archie started a tab for me."

"It's Candy, right?" I asked, pulling the cigarettes from the rack behind me. I doubted if I'd find "Black Dahlia" written on the spines of any of the charge booklets.

"Yes."

"Right. There a last name?" I flipped through the booklets in the drawer below the cash register.

"No. Just Candy."

"Here it is." There were no entries on the page. I penciled in thirty cents for cigarettes. "Anything else?"

"Why don't you call me some time," she said on her way out the door.

"Hubba hubba," Eddie said without the slightest stammer.

"You like that, Eddie?" Eddie made his eyebrows go up and down to indicate that he liked the Black Dahlia ... a lot.

"You should find someone a little more wholesome. She's not your type, Eddie." I detected a trace of lechery in Eddie's grin.

EIGHT

I rolled out of bed at seven-thirty, not eager to hit the streets again in search of gainful employment. Yesterday, Archie had loaned me his car to follow a job lead out of town; a lead that led nowhere. I couldn't keep asking to borrow Archie's car every time I had a job opportunity beyond walking distance. Garrison offered no bus service in or out of town. Some of the places I had circled in the want ads were either in other cities or on the outskirts of Garrison, farther away than I cared to walk. I couldn't afford to hire a cab. Devlin's office cleaning lead never panned out.

Western Electric had a transatlantic cable subsidiary near Portsmouth that was advertising for temporary help loading ships with cable. The plant was maybe nine miles south of Garrison. I hadn't thumbed a ride since high school and was in no mood to take up the practice again at my advanced age. It was undignified. Besides, what did "temporary" employment mean? Even if I could get out there to apply for the job and got hired, how would I get to work day in, day out?

I caught a break in the form of Leo "Fat" Grenier. He was two years behind me in high school, six-foot-three inches tall; by the time he was a senior he weighed about two hundred eighty-five pounds. All State tackle his junior and senior years at Garrison High. I hadn't seen him since before I went in the Army; that is until this morning when I ran into him at Lord's Snack Bar on Fourth Street. I stopped in for coffee and a maple square before hitting the pavement, and there he was, bigger than life, as it were, all alone on a stool at the counter.

"Embry. Long time no see."

"Yeah, a long time, Leo. Where you been hiding?"

"You're the one been hiding. I hear you got hitched."

"Let's not talk about that. Okay?"

"I hear you."

It turned out that Leo was also out of work, and was on his way to check out the Western Electric ad. Leo had wheels, a two-tone '58 Chevy convertible. We drove to the wire and cable division, Leo's radio blaring "Heat Wave" at full volume. They were offering two weeks work on the first shift at a pretty good hourly wage. The work involved laying cable in the holds of ships designed to string the stuff across the bottom of the Atlantic Ocean. The cable came in several diameters ranging from the size of a garter snake to that of an anaconda. The cable would be fed from the warehouse down to the ship's hold. Our job would be to guide the cable in the hold, layer upon layer in concentric circles, until it was full. You had to walk backwards while you guided the cable. It proved to be dirty, exhausting work. I experienced vertigo on my first shift, and nearly hit the deck, as it were. It was so disorienting, walking backwards in circles, that we were allowed to work only a one-hour shift followed by one hour of rest. So, an eight-hour day really consisted of four hours of actual work. Nevertheless, I was as tired at the end of my first day as I had ever been in my life.

On Friday, our second day on the job, Leo left me off at the drugstore in the lower square after work. My apartment was only a five-minute walk away. I saw Noelle across the street a block away from my house. She was pushing little Teddy in a stroller. I crossed the street.

"Hello, Noelle." She looked up, startled, as if a stranger had accosted her. Then she squinted and said,

"Paul? Is that you?"

"In the flesh."

"My God! You're so … dirty. I barely recognize you." Little Teddy began to cry. I brought Noelle up to date on my latest misfortune. "Where did you get so filthy?"

"Western Electric. It's only temporary. I've filed for unemployment. Sorry, you know, about last week. I …"

"Oh, don't worry." Noelle waved away my apology. "I knew you wouldn't come. If you feel that contrite why don't you come for supper tomorrow night? William's preparing his famous *bouillabaisse*."

"I don't know about that, Noelle."

"Please. You know William. Do you think he cares what I do?"

"I'll give you a ring tonight. Let you know."

"Just come at seven tomorrow. There's no need to call."

"Can I bring anything?"

"Bring some beer if you like. You don't have to. Teddy, stop crying. He won't hurt you. It's only Paul. He's just dirty, not evil." Teddy cried harder. "Please bathe before you come to supper." Noelle pushed off with her wailing baby.

* * *

I had no sooner settled into the bathtub than the phone rang. I ignored it for five or six rings, then, knowing that it was probably Laura, and she would let it ring forever, I hauled myself out of the tub and answered it naked and dripping wet.

"I was in the bath. I started a temporary job today at Western Electric. You wouldn't believe how dirty I am at this moment."

"I'm so angry at you, Paul."

"I'm sorry to hear that. What is it you have to be angry about?"

"Please, spare me the sanctimony. I would have thought you'd be happy that somebody made a decision. God knows I couldn't depend on you to make a move."

"It appears I don't share your sense of urgency, honey."

"Don't honey me. That's the problem. You don't sense anything. You're perfectly content to …"

"I thought we had a plan, Laura. I thought we had worked this all out before we got married. What happened, Laura? What happened to the plan?"

"It wasn't realistic, Paul. Not in that place."

"So, where you are everything's different, everything's possible, right?"

"Yes, Paul. Exactly. And I can tell from your tone that you can't accept it. You've been out in the world. More than I have. How can you be so obtuse?"

"Can we possibly stop arguing for once? Can we maybe start talking calmly about this?"

"As I told you before, I have a few job leads. Apartments aren't easy to come by, at least not decent ones. Lydia's been a saint, not pressuring me, or anything. But Floyd is a problem. That's Lydia's boyfriend. He's an accountant."

"An accountant? I thought accountants were guys in their forties. Is Floyd in his forties?"

"He resents having me and Andrea around the apartment. We'd really like to find something. The sooner the better."

"We? I thought you were looking for something for us. When did it become we?"

"You wouldn't believe what they're asking for rent in the city."

"You expect me to come out there to share an apartment with Andrea who I can't bear to be around for more than ten minutes at a time? Is that what you expect, Laura?"

"It would be only temporary. Andrea and her boyfriend will find something together eventually."

"Now it's Andrea and her freaking boyfriend! Have you lost your mind?"

"Listen to yourself. You sound so … Garrison, New Hampshire."

"And for that I suppose I need to apologize."

"What you need to do is to open up your mind, Paul. Do you want to be with me or not?"

"Of course I want to be with you. Why do you have to ask such a question?"

"I miss Honcho so. And J. Alfred."

"Hauling them out there should be a treat."

"Are you saying that Honcho has come home, Paul?"

"Not yet, but he will. It's only a matter of time. You know cats."

"How can you be so sure of that? You haven't done as I asked, have you. You haven't put up a sign. You haven't knocked on doors and ..."

"I walk the street every night calling for him. He'll show, believe me."

"You are so ... irresponsible."

"Right. I should take your lead. If the going gets tough I should just take off, leave my problems behind for someone else to deal with. Right?"

This time it was my wife who did the hanging up. Except I couldn't call her back, not knowing this Lydia's number.

The bathwater had cooled off. I turned on the hot water faucet. I got only lukewarm. I had wanted to linger awhile in the tub, to try to sort out the confusion that raged in my head. The water temperature was not to my liking, so I climbed back out and pulled the stopper, not feeling a whole lot cleaner than when I went in, even if the black scum left behind in the empty tub was evidence to the contrary.

I was dog tired from going around backward in circles all day, and it was my night to work at Archie's. There was nothing to eat in the house and I was starved, hungry enough to take a chance on a bologna sandwich with Archie's rancid meat. I would have to ask Archie for an advance in pay, too. He would oblige cheerfully, but I hated asking just the same. I had about twelve dollars to my name. I didn't want my wife wiring me money for "expenses." She said it might be as much as a month before she "sent" for me. I didn't like the sound of that, either; I didn't like being sent for. Talk about your life taking a left turn.

* * *

By the time I went on duty at Archie's I had worked myself into a headache. The radio on top of the beer cooler blared "Wipeout," which did nothing to improve my head condition. Archie was stocking the cigarette rack, his back to the counter. He had on a clean white shirt, and when he turned around he presented a clean-shaved face.

"Going to the ballet tonight, Arch?"

"Nah. Loretta's been hounding me to take her out to eat. Takin' her to the chinks. Gonna cost me plenty."

I wondered if he ever took Betty out, but I knew the answer. Who in his right mind could they get to look after their brood while they went out for an evening? Their oldest child, Archie junior, was only thirteen. I doubted that Betty would leave the young ones in his charge. I spotted

Whitey's ball-capped head peeking out the back room door. He grinned at me and raised his beer bottle in greeting. I waved.

"Who's down there with Whitey?"

"Doc and Ray. They're already drunk as skunks. I'll shoo them out before I leave." Archie meant he'd shoo out Whitey and Ray. There would be no "shooing" out of Doc Robinson. Doc came and went as he pleased. He could stay as long as he wanted.

"Paulie, you mind hauling up a couple cases of Knick and maybe a couple more cases of Bud, a case of Schlitz? I think we're okay with everything else."

"No problem."

Archie "shooed" Whitey and Ray out the door, then left to collect his fair Loretta. In the meantime, I was kept busy with typical Friday night beer customers, and a few of the regulars who did their grocery shopping on Fridays, such as groceries were in the store. For an hour and a half they kept me hopping. If nothing else, it made the time pass quickly, and took my attention away from my headache. When it quieted down, I went down back to organize the redeemable bottles that had accumulated the last few days. Doc was asleep in the recliner, mouth wide open, snoring noisily. I tried to be quiet, but quiet wasn't easy when you were handling a lot of glass bottles. Doc woke up with a start.

"Shit. Didn't mean to wake you."

"Don't worry about it." Doc reached in his jacket pocket for his cigarettes. "I covered rounds for Doc Azziz last night. Didn't get much sleep."

I didn't imagine that pounding vodka-milk cocktails all afternoon compensated much for his sleep deprivation, either.

"It's been so busy I forgot you were down here. I see Archie has a dinner date with his princess tonight."

"Yeah. He'll feed her, fuck her, and be back here to play in a couple hours. You got a light?" Doc searched all his pockets for matches and had come up empty. I was surprised he didn't own a lighter.

"Got some up front. Be right back."

"Don't bother going all that way. I keep forgetting, you don't smoke."

"Seven months now." Just then, Honcho emerged from the cellar and sidled up to me, purring and rubbing his chin against my leg. "I'll be goddamned. Where have you been, you bad cat?" I reached down and picked him up. He felt considerably lighter than he did the last time I'd hoisted him. "I've been worried sick about you, you mutt." I said to Doc, "He's been missing for ten days, for Christ's sake, as long as my wife."

"Don't let him jump on me," Doc said. "I got no use for cats."

"He's skin and bones. He must have been locked up somewhere. Honcho, you all right?" I held him at arm's length, looked him over for injuries; I felt his stomach and groin, palpated his joints. His fur was matted and dull, but I could find no evidence of wounds or broken bones. I'd have to get him to the vet for confirmation, me with twelve bucks to my name. "You must be starved, you poor kitty." My own hunger I'd forgotten, along with my headache. "Doc, can I give him some of your milk?"

"Help yourself. Just don't let him jump on me."

I found a dirty plastic bowl on the shelf above Archie's cluttered desk. Archie sometimes ate soup out of it. I poured milk into the bowl and set it down on the floor, away from Doc. Honcho slurped voraciously.

"Listen, I'd like to get him home and get some solid food in his stomach. You mind keeping an eye on the place for ten minutes, Doc?"

"Go ahead. I'm just waiting for big-balls."

NINE

As odious as the prospect was of spending an evening in the company of Noelle's husband, William, it was mitigated somewhat by the knowledge that I would finally be eating a meal that didn't come out of a can or a cold meat package.

In the meantime, I had decided to put my wayward cat under house arrest. Now I would have to accommodate his toilet needs in the apartment. I picked up a bag of cat litter and a stack of beer cartons from Archie's. Finding an appropriate place for a litter box in the tiny apartment was a challenge. The choices were few, and I finally settled on the space between the toilet bowl and the bathtub. It seemed a fitting place for a cat latrine. I would have to be mindful of it when I got in and out of the tub, but there was really no other suitable place for it.

Honcho had always been an outdoor cat. That meant he would have to be trained to use the box. I breathed deeply, picked him up and placed him in the box, expecting him to bolt and head for one of his hiding places. Instead, he scratched at the dusty litter with his paw, moved a large pile of the stuff to a corner that suited him, and squatted as if he had always done his shitting in a litter box.

"Way to go, Honcho. I should be such a quick learner."

* * *

"Puff the Magic Dragon" was playing on Noelle's hi-fi when I arrived. I handed her my offering of a six-pack of beer.

"Well, you look a little cleaner than you did yesterday. My God you were filthy!" Noelle put her hand on my crotch. I backed away.

"Jesus Christ, Noelle!" I whispered.

"William's in the living room. I'll be right in." Noelle carried off my beer to the kitchen.

I found William stretched out on the living room floor, reading a newspaper. His shoes were off; he wore argyle socks. Noelle had once remarked that William was the only man she had ever met whose feet didn't stink. It was one of several reasons she gave for detesting him.

"What do you say, Paul? Enjoying the bachelor life again, I hear." According to Noelle, William was not supposed to know that Laura had left me. On the other hand, how would I explain her absence tonight? Noelle had no choice but to tell him.

"Yeah. You never know what you're missing until it's gone." William laughed at my double meaning, in his harsh way. Noelle appeared with a tray of cheese and crackers and three bottles of the beer I brought. "Puff the Magic Dragon" ended; "Stewball" started to play.

"Noelle, enough PP and M already," William said, taking the needle off "Stewball." Noelle was a rabid folk-music fan. William was partial to jazz and made it a point to give his wife a hard time about her "simple-minded" tastes in music. "Did you check on my *bouillabaisse*? You best not screw it up, Noelle."

"I turned the heat down to low just as his highness, James Beard, instructed me to do," Noelle replied. "Paul brought some beer." Noelle offered the tray to me, then to her husband.

"Paul, how can you drink this dinosaur piss?" William said, inspecting the bottle with an expression of mock distaste.

"I happen to prefer the taste of dinosaur piss. Beats horse piss by a mile," I said, and took a swallow. William laughed and raised the bottle to his lips. Noelle drank from the bottle, too, like one of the guys. "Where's the baby?"

"Mother's got him for the evening," Noelle said.

"Spoiling him rotten," William added. "Noelle, you had better check on the *bouillabaisse*. It shouldn't be left unattended." Noelle looked like she wanted to tell William to check it himself, but she merely sighed and left the room to do as she was told. William shook his head. "She'll never learn to cook properly. Thank God she gives good head. Don't you agree, Paul?"

I could think of nothing to say. I don't suppose I should have been surprised that Noelle had told her husband about us, but hearing William speak of it so baldly caught me off guard.

"Hey, Paul. You're not a baseball fan, are you?"

"Not really."

"Neither am I. We have so much in common, Paul." William had on a pair of gray dress slacks and a white shirt with starched collar. He dropped to the floor and executed five one-armed push-ups on the right side, then five more from the left. I hadn't done a push-up since Army boot camp, and I could never bring it off one-armed.

"That looks difficult," I told William when he'd finished.

"It is if you're not in shape." William propped himself on an elbow, his chin cupped in his hand. He smiled at me like a man with inside information. Noelle returned.

"You'd better taste it," she told her husband. "It seems fine to me, but I don't have your refined palate."

"You can say that again." William rose to his feet gracefully, pulled a comb from his back pocket, and ran it through his wavy brown hair before heading for the kitchen.

William and Noelle's living room was almost as sparsely furnished as my own. Noelle couldn't have been bringing home much of a paycheck as a social worker, but William sold insurance, and I always believed that insurance was a lucrative business. William was a natty dresser and liked sporty cars. At present, he drove a red '63 Corvair convertible. Their combined incomes were obviously not spent on house furnishings.

I wondered how Laura would like being married to a man like William; would she have been so ready to flee to California? I disliked William, yet I had a grudging admiration for any man who had the kind of control over a woman that William seemed to have over his wife. Even if I felt inclined to, I would never treat Laura the way William treated Noelle. Laura had told me more than once that Noelle was William's "doormat." He was four years older than Noelle. They had met her junior year in college. William had a reputation as a womanizer and a smooth operator. He was a born salesman, and had been married once before. He sired a child from that union, a child that was in its mother's custody without objection from William. He had attended college for one semester. Even if he was very intelligent, at times intellectual, William was no scholar. The lure of money was greater than his thirst for knowledge. In fact, William valued money and the pursuit of women equally. Noelle had once confided in me, when she'd had enough to drink, that William would not need much provocation to belt her across the face with the back of his hand.

As I knew it would be, William's *bouillabaisse* was delicious. It was the first good meal I'd had since the last time I dined at their table. I ate with gusto, the way Honcho had eaten when I got him home last night. But William wore his enigmatic smile throughout the meal. What he had said in the living room had put me off balance, and I felt that the smile was his way of taunting me. Noelle seemed not to read anything in his manner, or, if she did, not to care. It was a well-known fact that William and Noelle had what they termed an "open" marriage. Nevertheless, I was uneasy with William's knowledge of my intimacy with his wife. But, as Laura had lately reminded me, I was just another provincial from Garrison, New Hampshire. Whatever I was, I cast about in my mind for a way to excuse myself from William's company.

"Noelle, why don't you put on some music," William said. "Please, no more PP and M." Noelle rose from the table and hurried out of the room.

"Did you enjoy the *bouillabaisse*, Paul?"

"Very much. You are truly a wizard in the kitchen."

"What about a dessert? Why don't we say a nice *ménage `a trois*."

Michael Burns

"That was a really good wine." I inspected the label on the long-necked bottle. "German. I thought only the French made good wine."

"I can't find my Kingston Trio album," Noelle announced, on her return to the kitchen.

"Ask Paul why he's blushing like a schoolgirl," William said.

"You wouldn't have thrown it out, would you, you bastard?" Noelle's fists went to her hips; she thrust her jaw in her husband's direction.

"How could you think such a thing?" William's smile was playful, but cruel. "Go ahead, ask Paul why he's so red in the face."

"You are such an ass, William." Noelle turned and left the room in a huff, her husband laughing obscenely after her.

"Christ!" I said, smacking my forehead with an open hand. "I cannot believe this."

"Can't believe what, your good fortune? As soon as she finds her precious Kingston Trio album we can get down to business."

"Sorry, buddy, but you're going to have to go it without me. I just can't freaking believe it. I was supposed to work for Archie tonight. Jesus."

"So, you blew it. Nothing you can do about it now. Might as well stick around and play. We'll make it a tag team for three." William found this enormously amusing, and laughed so hard I thought he would choke.

"Thanks for the great meal, William. I've got to get over to the store and explain to Archie or whoever got stuck working tonight." I got up from the table. Noelle was back in the room, the Kingston Trio album in her hand. "Thanks for having me over, Noelle. I've got to be going."

Noelle shot a dark look at her husband. "Why, Paul? It's early." I explained to her how I'd forgotten that I had duty tonight at Archie's. "It's not that at all. It's his doing."

"Noelle, don't blame me," William said, pointing his forefingers at himself. "I offered Paul dessert. All he managed to do was blush. You need to train this lad better. You'd think he just fell off the turnip truck."

"Oh, just shut up, William." Noelle turned to me and laid her hand on my sleeve. "I'm sorry, Paul. Don't think badly of me." William giggled and went into the living room.

"Really, Noelle. It's true what I said about missing my shift tonight. Not that I would have anything to do with what he suggested."

"He's sick, Paul. I don't know how much longer I can bear it."

"Hang in there." I patted Noelle's arm and got the hell out of there.

70

TEN

Duane was on duty when I showed up at Archie's on the run last night. When it was clear to Archie that I was a no-show, he called Duane. I apologized all over the place to Duane (it was about nine-thirty) and offered to finish up for him. He insisted that it was no big deal; it gave him an excuse to get out of the house, away from the wife and kids for a few hours.

Now I had to face Archie this morning when I went in for my shift at eleven.

"Don't worry about it. I should've reminded you Friday. You ain't used to working Saturdays. Don't worry about it. Wont no harm done."

"Thanks, Arch. I'm sorry. What a jerk."

"I said forget about it."

"You want me to work next Saturday?"

"Duane's on for next Saturday. Why don't you plan on the week after that. Look, I got to get going. Takin' the wife and kids to the beach today. How lucky can I get, right?"

"Don't get a sun burn."

* * *

I hadn't talked to Laura since Thursday. She'd been gone almost two weeks now. It felt like two months. I lay around in bed last night tormented by my overactive brain. I must be slow because I still couldn't fully understand why my wife had ditched me the way she did. And all her talk about finding a job, getting an apartment (with Andrea and her boyfriend) sounded less plausible the more I thought about it. Was it possible that she was just toying with me before she finally gave me the heave ho? I never thought of Laura as having a perverse streak.

I slept fitfully; at 2:30 a.m. Charlie woke me up with his howling, and not long after that the phone rang. Thinking it might be Laura, I bolted out of bed, but when I picked up the receiver I heard only a dial tone. I tried reading *The Naked and the Dead*. I must have read the same paragraph four times before giving up and turning out the light.

Ménage `a trois was probably what William considered wholesome fun. A roll in the hay with Noelle wasn't an unpleasant idea, but not with William along. I was apparently too provincial to get any mileage out of that concept. I woke up at ten with a headache, probably from William's German wine.

* * *

Business was uneven on Sundays in Archie's Corner Grocery. There would be periods of an hour or more when I'd run my butt off back and forth between the grungy meat slicer and the cash register; I'd have customers three deep at the counter. Then, nothing. Of course, time went by a lot faster when I was busy. Another bad feature of the slow periods was that my mind would get busy and get me into a black funk.

Doc showed up around four-thirty, during one of the slow periods. He pulled a carton of milk out of the cooler and produced a pint bottle in liquor store wrapper from the inside pocket of his suit jacket.

"I'll be down back. Want a taste, Paul?"

"No thanks, Doc."

"Well, come on down and talk. Looks dead around here."

"Comes in waves." I followed Doc to the back room. Archie kept a sleeve of paper cups on his desk. Doc got himself arranged in the recliner, unwrapped his pint, and poured himself a vodka-milk cocktail.

"Sure you won't have one?"

"I don't touch hard stuff, Doc. Even if I did, that combination wouldn't be my first choice."

"It would be if you had my ulcer. I need the milk."

You wouldn't need the milk if you passed up the vodka, I thought. "Archie spent the day at the beach with his wife and kids. He didn't seem pleased at the prospect."

Doc chuckled and his big belly rippled. "Big-balls is not much of a family man."

I wondered if I would be much of a family man myself. Laura had never said so out loud, but she let me know, in subtle ways, that she had no interest in having kids. "I love kids," she would say to people who asked us if we planned to have a family, "Other people's kids." Or, "Noelle and her suckling child are coming over in an hour. Is that fair enough warning?" As I said, Doc never mentioned having kids of his own, and if he thought that Archie was no family man, what did that make him?

"I've been thinking about what you said about applying for a college loan. You say the banks have liberal policies on these loans. How liberal? What if you're unemployed?"

Doc looked at me as if he didn't understand the question. "Don't you think most students are unemployed? That's the point. The most you should do is get something part time. Something that pays a little more than what big-balls gives you. You'd be making a big mistake if you tried to hold down a full-time job while you were going to school."

"I've heard stories about guys who went to school full time and worked a forty hour a week job."

"That's crap."

"Was medical school demanding?"

Doc laughed and shook his head. "That would be putting it mildly. Being married and having a small child didn't make it any easier." Doc crossed one big leg over the other, and raised his cup to his lips. A small child. So Doc *was* a family man. Something stopped me from asking him about his child. I had the feeling it was a sore point with him.

"And then there's the intern thing and all that."

"Oh, yeah. You wouldn't believe the hours. You considering pre-med, Paul?"

"It's crossed my mind. I was always pretty good in math and science. Laura wants me to be an English major."

"What, and give up your citizenship?"

It took a second for Doc's joke to reach my brain. "I guess that would be more of a sacrifice than I'd be willing to make. Besides, I never ranked higher than PFC in the American Army."

"California has the best system of higher public education in the country. You couldn't do better. Listen to your wife, Paul. She's a sharp cookie."

"So you've said." I heard voices from the front of the store. "Excuse me, Doc. Duty calls."

I was into another busy spell for the next hour. During that time Doc finished his drink and left. When the rush ended I was left alone with my troubled thoughts. Doc had once asked me why I was ambivalent about joining my wife in California. It was a fair question, not deserving of the evasive answer I'd given him. The truth was, I couldn't pin it down at the root. I couldn't deny the strong pull in the westward direction I felt, simply because I wanted to be back with Laura. There was also this invisible force that resisted it. This I couldn't explain. If I could stay on the line with my wife for more than a minute and a half without quarreling maybe she could help me come to grips with it.

* * *

Eddie Flanagan came in the store working a yo-yo.

"Hey, you're pretty good with that thing. Let me see the cat's cradle." Eddie obliged.

"Say, Eddie, you think you could do me a favor? Could you run down to the Greeks and pick me up a chicken salad roll and some fries? I haven't eaten all day."

Eddie nodded agreeably. I gave him two bucks and told him to keep the change. Eddie performed an around the world with his bright red yo-yo before going off on my errand.

I wolfed down my chicken salad roll and fries while Eddie nursed an Orange Crush. Eddie didn't like Sundays. There was nothing to do on Sundays, he complained. I had the feeling Eddie didn't have a wide circle of friends, and his many siblings went their separate ways. Eddie was a lonely sixteen-year-old who carried a torch for the Black Dahlia.

When I was that age I had my driver's license and a car that ran like a top. I had lots of friends and an after school job in the bakery, thanks to my dad, which put more cash in my pocket than most guys my age. All of my friends drank a lot. It never occurred to me that they hung around with me because I had wheels and didn't drink except for the occasional beer. I took their friendship at face value. A couple of guys I used to hang out with were really serious boozers. Nobody could hold a candle to Jack Scanlon and George Stacy when it came to drinking. Jack Scanlon sat behind me in homeroom, junior year. Sometimes he'd bring a pint of Early Times to school with him. He'd lift the cover of his desk up and take a nip before the first period bell rang. He'd carry the bottle around with him for whatever part of the day he decided to attend classes, nipping from behind raised desktops. Teachers had no clue about what he was up to; kids thought Jack Scanlon was extremely cool. If you considered the ability to handle your liquor as a principal criterion for being cool, George Stacy would qualify too. He was cool, but not as cool as Jack Scanlon.

Jack had a pretty good game of pool too. We had some good games in our day. We would clash in straight pool--one hundred twenty-five pointers. I could beat Jack more often than not, but he was a competitor. I once ran forty-nine balls on him, my personal best. I walked around for a week thinking I was another Willie Mosconi.

I remember a warm night in the summer of 1956. Five of us piled into my 1940 Mercury convertible, and headed for Wells Beach, Maine. Among them were George Stacy and Jack Scanlon. They brought along a case of beer each, and shared a fifth of vodka. If we had got stopped by the cops, that would have been the end of my driver's license. Even if the court didn't take it away, my dad would. I was plenty worried but I didn't let on that I was. To worry was not considered cool.

At the time, a few Air Force guys from the new SAC base used to hang around with us, contriving, through us, to get into the pants of the high school girls. They soon found out that they could accomplish this without any help from us. In fact, they got a lot further in that endeavor than I, or any of my friends, did. There were two guys in particular who had attached themselves to us. One kid was a country boy from Virginia, the other a big city wise guy from Pittsburgh, Pa. The Virginian's name was Carl Bolton; the wise guy from Pittsburgh had the unlikely name of Francis Francis. His middle name was also Francis. He was a Catholic and had taken on the name Thomas for his confirmation. Francis Francis Thomas Francis was the way he signed his name.

Carl Bolton had a slight build and a flattop, DA hairstyle. Francis Francis was stocky and wore his hair in a crew cut. They enjoyed drinking, dancing, fighting, and chasing after girls. George and Jack shared two of these pursuits with the Air Force boys. Fighting and dancing were not part of their repertoire. They preferred to talk when they drank, to discuss music (they were both jazz enthusiasts), philosophy, literature, and movies. That night they were all together with me in my car:

"We gonna get us some hot Canadian chicks and rumble with the local boys down at that Wells Beach, Maine," Carl Bolton declares before chugging a whole twelve ounce bottle of beer. He belches loudly and blows his breath in Francis Francis's face. Francis Francis returns Carl's belch with a robust one of his own. Bolton is missing his two front teeth. He lost them in a brawl in a Garrison beer joint last week. He is only nineteen, but he has a doctored military I.D. card. He is known to pick fights with grown men in the local beer parlors. Francis Francis is twenty and also a brawler. In Jack's opinion, Francis Francis is a sadist who takes pleasure in inflicting pain on the people he picks fights with. He is very tough. Even the tough grown-ups in town think twice before they get into it with Francis Francis. I feel sorry for the poor bastard in Wells Beach who catches Francis Francis's attention.

Bolton wastes no time finding a rumble opportunity. In a game arcade full of guys around our age, Bolton deliberately tilts a local boy's pinball machine.

"Just what the fuck do you think you're doing?" the kid says, squaring off to face Bolton, his hands loose and at the ready. He is flanked by three of his buddies, tough looking country boys with big shoulders and thick necks; their heavy legs rise into their Bermuda shorts like monoliths.

"Picking a fight with you, hick. That's what the fuck I'm doing."

"Those clowns with you?" The kid motions toward Jack, George, and me who are uneasy spectators at this dangerous scene.

"This is between you and me, fuck stick," Bolton says. "So why don't we just bring it out in the street?" Bolton turns on his heel and heads for the sidewalk, followed by the kid and his companions. As soon as Bolton sets foot on the pavement, he wheels around fast and lands an uppercut under the big kid's jaw. The kid looks more surprised than hurt. Before he can counterpunch, Bolton assails him with a flurry of blows, his arms moving like a windmill, landing his tightly clenched fists all over the kid's face and shoulders. The kid goes down on one knee.

75

Bolton grabs him in a headlock with one arm, and punches his face with his fist. The kid's buddies jump on Bolton and tear him off their friend.

"He's had enough," the biggest one says to Bolton. "Why don't you get lost now before we hurt you?"

"I'll take you all on, one at a time. What do you say?" Bolton's eyes are wild, his breathing fast.

"Yeah, and have the cops on us like flies on shit. Just get your skinny ass out of here or you'll have to deal with all of us at the same time. These pussies with you don't look like they got the stomach for fighting." He has that right. I haven't come to Wells Beach to trade punches with the local toughs, even if Carl Bolton and his sadist comrade have. Francis Francis had split off from us when we arrived, and had gone in pursuit of two girls in tight shorts and thin blouses. He will be disappointed when he hears about the action he missed. "You gonna go, or are we gonna have to stomp a knot in your ass?" Bolton shrugs off the boys who hold him, reaches in his back pocket and comes back with a long comb, like the kind barbers use. He proceeds to groom his hair in front of them. The guy Bolton has vanquished is down on one knee spitting up blood on the street. Passersby give the combatants a wide berth; they move quickly, heads turned toward the scene on the street. Bolton's hair combing is more than the big guy can take. He lunges at Bolton and wrestles him to the ground. They flail at each other, rolling around on the sidewalk while the rest of us watch. One of the kids spots two policemen headed our way.

"Knock it off, you guys. It's the fuzz." Bolton and his opponent break apart. Everyone starts running in different directions. George, Jack, and I run together. We run for a long while, and eventually find ourselves on the beach, out of breath. There are no policemen in sight. A little later we run into Bolton and the kids he'd fought with. Bolton has his hand extended to the first kid he'd assaulted.

"No hard feelings, all right? I got nothing personal against you guys. You know how it is." They apparently do know how it is. Suddenly they are all shaking hands and laughing it up. Jack, George, and I discreetly part company with them.

Jack and George have stowed their beer and the bottle of vodka in the trunk of my car. We fetch a case of beer, the vodka and a blanket, and look for a secluded piece of beach.

"I told you Bolton was a psycho," Jack Scanlon says to George."

"Yeah, but not as big a psycho as Francis Francis Thomas Francis. Paul, have a beer. One won't kill you." I refuse George's offer. If I have to drive I don't want to be impaired, or get stopped by the fuzz with the smell of booze on my breath. My driver's license is important to me. Besides, I don't care for the way beer, or any alcohol, for that matter, tastes. Neither George nor Jack ever tries to push booze on me the way some of my friends do. For this I am grateful.

"Let me have one of those beers," a voice behind me says. "And I need a smoke. Let's have a cigarette," Francis Francis says, snapping his fingers for someone to hop to. Francis Francis is used to getting his way. He uses his menacing physical presence to get high school kids to give him money, cigarettes, anything it takes to satisfy his immediate need.

"How'd you find us?" Jack Scanlon asks, handing Francis a bottle of beer. George holds out his pack of cigarettes to him. Francis doesn't take the church key Jack offers him; instead he bites the cap off with his teeth, which is another one of his intimidation tactics.

"I followed the smell. Why don't you assholes gather up some driftwood, light a fire? It's fucking dark out here. No fucking moon."

"We don't want to draw attention," I say, and tell him about the rumble at the arcade.

"Shit. Where's Bolton at now?"

"With his new buddies, I guess," George says. "What have you been up to? We saw you trailing after those two chicks."

Francis Francis puts his "pussy" finger in George's face. George turns his head away. "I've got to find Bolton. I'll catch you assholes later." Francis Francis disappears into the darkness.

"Too bad," Jack says. "I would have enjoyed another fifteen seconds of his company."

"I'm not waiting around for those guys," I say. "If they're not here when we're ready to go, I'm taking off without them."

"Francis Francis won't like that," George tells me.

"Screw him."

"It's a nice night," Jack says. "Why don't we sleep here on the beach, pull out in the morning? What do you say, Paul?"

"My mother would worry."

"You can take off if you want to. Don't worry about us. We can find our way back tomorrow. Make sure you leave the beer, though," Jack says with a laugh.

"I'll stick around for a while."

"Good," George says.

Jack leans back on his elbows, his hand around the vodka bottle. The case of beer is on the blanket between Jack and George. They pass the vodka back and forth, take short nips, and chase it down with swallows of beer.

"Miles Davis is at Storyville this weekend," Jack says. "You want to come with us tomorrow for the matinee, Paul?"

"I'm not doing anything tomorrow. Why not?"

"Do you mind driving? We'll chip in for gas."

"No, I don't mind."

"We can park in Everett and take the MTA if you don't like to drive in town," George says.

"I don't mind driving in town." It's true. I find it a lot of fun to drive in Boston. It's definitely a challenge.

"It's just that it costs an arm and a leg to park around Copley Square. It's only about a half a buck to park in Everett."

"Okay. Everett. It makes no difference to me," I say.

"Who's Miles got with him these days?" George asks.

"Coltrane, Philly Joe Jones on drums, Red Garland on piano, and a new kid, Paul Chambers, on bass. *Downbeat* says they're dynamite." None of these names, except for Miles Davis, is familiar to me.

"Sounds good," I say.

"Good. We should leave around noon," Jack says, lying back on the blanket. He holds his beer bottle on his chest with both hands.

"Can you believe that psycho?" George Stacy says, referring, I assume, to Carl Bolton. "He looks like a sissy with his pretty blond hair. And he's built like a girl, a skinny girl. Who'd think he was such a tiger?"

"He's sure got an unorthodox way of fighting," Jack adds. "I wonder how he'd do against Francis Francis?"

In my opinion Francis would destroy him. I say this out loud.

"Yeah," Jack says, "the guy's a bull."

"And a sadist if I ever saw one. What do chicks see in these guys?" George wonders.

"They know how to dance," I offer. "Girls like nothing better than guys who can dance. And to Garrison High girls, these guys are kind of exotic, not to mention older and in the service."

"I've been thinking about enlisting in the Navy after I graduate," Jack says. "I've had it up to here with Garrison." He puts the back of his hand under his chin.

"What are you talking about?" George says. "What about college? You're talking crazy."

"I've got to get out of here. I'm suffocating."

"I know what you mean," I say. "It's the perfect word for the way I feel, too. Suffocating. My parents would be really disappointed if I didn't go to college. But I know exactly what you're talking about, Jack." This is a lie, and I don't know why I tell it. I don't feel at all suffocated. Maybe I'm just being ingratiating. I don't like myself for it.

"I'm not looking back. I owe this town nothing." Jack speaks of Garrison, N.H., not Wells Beach, Maine, where we are on this warm, dark night in July before our senior year in high school.

* * *

"Young man. Paul?" Mrs. Laughlin said to me, breaking my reverie. "You appear to have been daydreaming," she said, smiling her kindly smile. Over by the soft drink cooler, Eddie stifled a laugh.

"I guess I was. Sorry, Mrs. Laughlin. What can I do for you?" She was an elegant old woman who lived in the large yellow Victorian house above the railroad tracks, in the "good" section of Washington Street. She was a regular customer of Archie's, an incongruity that I could never figure out. She was from obvious wealth and good breeding. That was clear from the clothes she wore, the way she spoke, and, of course, from the house she lived in, alone, since she was widowed several years ago. I wasn't sure of her age, but I would guess she was over seventy. Her mind was young, her wit nimble.

"I asked Archie to order some cigarillos for me last week. Do you know if they have arrived, Paul?"

I looked over the stock on the cigar rack. No cigarillos. I rummaged around in the shelves underneath the counter. Among several boxes of condoms I found a few packages of Swisher Sweets but no cigarillos.

"I don't see them here, Mrs. Laughlin. How long ago did you ask Archie to order them?"

"Oh, I don't know, last Wednesday. Or it could have been Thursday. I think it was last week. Perhaps it was the week before, or perhaps it was only yesterday." Mrs. Laughlin shrugged her shoulders and smiled. "It's not important. I'll come by another time. How are you, Paul? Starting another semester at the university in the fall?"

"I haven't decided yet. It kind of depends on how a few things go."

"That sounds cryptic enough. I won't pry, but I think you should make every effort to continue your education."

"Thanks. I intend to. How is the Portsmouth project coming along?" Mrs. Laughlin was a strong financial supporter of a major restoration project in the old part of Portsmouth. She called it the "Strawberry Banke" project.

"Splendidly. We are making good progress despite the expected voices of opposition. We shall prevail! Good evening, Paul. And good evening to you, Mr. Flanagan," she said, bowing her head to Eddie on her way out. Eddie nodded back, tongue-tied as always when addressed by Mrs. Laughlin.

"Classy lady," I said. Eddie shook his head in the affirmative.

ELEVEN

"So, how you doing with the transatlantic cable?" Devlin asked me on the back steps. He had poured himself another shot from the bottle of rye he kept close by his side. No more would he ask Maggie to wait on him. I wondered if Maggie had her own private stock beside her on the kitchen table as she put together another one of her many jigsaw puzzles. She had started a new one tonight, fifteen hundred pieces of a Jackson Pollack painting. Good luck with that one, I said to myself.

"Hasn't left the dock yet. Today we loaded on this really thin stuff. It's easier to handle than those big numbers. A lot faster, too. I really hate this work, Dave. Thank Christ it'll be over in two days. I'm whipped, I don't mind telling you."

"How's the money?"

"Buck ninety an hour, but no overtime. Who knows when we'll get paid?"

"Why don't you ask?"

"I'm not sure who to ask. There's a foreman who supervises the loading, but when Leo asked him about our money he played ignorant."

"You better get some answers, son, before your ship sails off into the sunset. I don't like the sound of it." Devlin raised his glass to his lips, threw his head back and quaffed his double. He ran his tongue over his lips, savoring the taste before chasing it away with a swallow of beer. I nursed the beer he had insisted I take. As I said, I didn't like Devlin's beer anymore than William liked the "dinosaur piss" I'd brought to his dinner party Saturday night.

"You're right. I'll check it out first thing tomorrow. Jesus, I'll be glad when these two days are over."

"Goddamn cold last few nights," Devlin said. "Need a friggin' blanket." Devlin put his bony elbow in my side and gave me a nudge. "Can't get any warmth from the bag of bones I'm sleeping with."

"Maybe you'd be warmer on the couch," Maggie riposted from the kitchen. "And you're not my idea of a hot water bottle yourself."

"Beats sweating. Beats not being able to breathe."

"Me and my old girl like it hot. Don't we, old girl?"

"I can hear you, Devlin," Maggie said, "and so can the whole neighborhood."

Devlin waved his hand in dismissal. "Bah. Women. You got no women where you work. Right, Paul?"

"You mean at Western Electric? Down in the hold? No, Dave, not that I know of. But we get so dirty, who could tell for sure?"

"I mean over at Caplan's."

"Are you drunk already, Devlin?" Maggie yelled, sounding none too sober herself. "Paul lost his job at Caplan's the same way you're losing your mind."

"You better watch your mouth, old woman."

It was time for me to take my leave. "I've got errands to run, Dave. Thanks for the brew. See you later, Maggie."

"Don't old woman me, you good-for-nothing."

I slipped away into my kitchen. I could have gone to sleep right then and there. I had nothing else to do. As I was about to crawl into bed the phone rang.

"Have you got over your pique?" my wife asked me.

"Before you go any further, I've got something you might like to hear." I told her about Honcho's dramatic return.

"Oh, Paul, that's just wonderful."

"I don't know when I'll get the chance to bring him in to the vet. Probably not before Saturday. I might not last till Saturday." I told her about how tough my job was at Western Electric.

"Didn't I tell you I'd send you money? Quit that dreadful job and look after Honcho."

"It's only for a couple more days, and didn't I tell you I don't want you to send me money? I'm capable of paying my own way. Speaking of jobs, how are things looking where you are?"

"I went to three interviews Friday, three more today. I got the don't-call-us-we'll-call-you treatment."

"Why don't you try waitressing?" I was trying to be funny. Laura was on record as loathing waitressing more than any other occupation on the planet. She once told me she'd rather scrub floors on her hands and knees twelve hours a day than waitress for fifteen minutes.

"I'll find something. Trust me. You need to be patient. It could take a month, maybe more, but I promise you something will come up."

"Come home, Laura. They'll take you back at the bank. I can find something steady eventually. Come home. I need you. We all do."

"You still don't get it. I'm never going back there."

"Even if it means us splitting up?" Laura didn't answer right away. The long pause gave me a moment of panic.

"There's no need for it to come to that, Paul. If you loved me ..."

"You have to know I love you."

"Then stop talking nonsense. This will work out, Paul. I'm going to wire you five hundred dollars ..."

"I won't accept it, Laura. I mean it."

"You are so ... exasperating. What do you plan to do when this so-called temporary job is over?"

"I'm entitled to unemployment. That should hold me for around four months."

"You can't live on that, not that you'd have to do it for four months."

"I'll make out. Don't waste your time sending me money. I'm serious."

"Have you seen Noelle? Is she still in pursuit?"

"No." Telling my wife about Saturday night's events would have been more complicated than my fatigued brain could handle over the telephone. She would twist it and turn it and find a way to put me in bed with Noelle. That she wouldn't be far from the truth was beside the point.

"I don't believe you. You're sleeping with her. I suppose I can't blame you, but please, sweetie, get over it. You're only acting out of hurt."

"What are you talking about? I'm not sleeping with her out of hurt or anything else. I told you I haven't seen her since the night she was here, the night you called."

"You're not good at lying, Paul. Just be careful."

"Maybe it's you who's doing the sleeping around."

"You know me better than that. I've got to hang up now. Andrea needs to use the phone. I love you, sweetie. Don't worry. Everything is going to be fine, just fine."

"I love you, too."

Don't worry. I love you. I'll send you money; I'll send for you. Be patient. You're not good at lying. A couple of months at most. Laura's words ricocheted around my brain until I felt like my skull would crack open. Five hundred bucks would probably get me to California with money to spare. I could simply turn up there unannounced. It shouldn't be that hard to track her down; my guess was that Noelle knew her address. I had to wonder how that would sit with her, my showing up out of the blue. Something told me that there was more going on here than met the eye. I had a strong urge to get on the phone to Noelle. I hesitated because if William answered, no matter how much he professed not to care what his wife did with other men, I'd feel uneasy. The image of Noelle's pliant body was in my head now; those full lips and nearsighted green eyes.

TWELVE

Archie handed me the keys to his car. I thanked him, went home and packed Honcho into a beer carton with flaps. He caterwauled all the way to the vet. The doctor gave him a thorough going over, found nothing wrong with him, and charged me twelve dollars. Archie had advanced me twenty, but the vet's bill nearly tapped me out. Then, on the way home, distracted by Honcho's throaty crying, I took my eyes off the road long enough to run head on with a Chevy Impala driven by an elderly man at about eight miles an hour.

Archie's left front fender and grill crumpled like tinfoil. Honcho ended up on the passenger side floor. He scrambled out of the box, jumped out of the convertible, and disappeared behind a nursing home on Union Street. The Impala suffered little damage: a broken headlamp and a wrinkled fender. The old man behind the wheel looked out of it. The cops arrived; I handed over my license, and managed to find Archie's registration among the junk in the glove compartment. The accident was clearly my fault, but apparently that wasn't so obvious to the cops. There were cars parked on both sides of the narrow street, so there was an even chance that the old man could have veered into my lane. I didn't tell them about my cat. At the moment I was more concerned that I'd cracked up Archie's car. The accident happened not far from my apartment. I could only hope that Honcho would find his way home this time, and not end up in somebody's basement or in Archie's stinking cellar.

* * *

"You'd better step outside, Arch. I got something to show you, and it's not pretty."

Archie inspected the damage, his stogie moving from side to side in his mouth. That moving stogie said it all. He'd never express it to me out loud, but I could tell that he was steamed.

"I'm sorry, Arch. What can I say?"

"Don't worry about it. I'll take it up to P&E. They'll have it patched up good as new. It steers all right, don't it?"

"Yeah. I got here from Union with no problem. I feel like shit about this. What can I do to make it up? Why don't you let me work a couple nights for you, Archie?"

"You don't have to do that."

"I mean it, Arch."

"Don't worry about it."

* * *

I got home to find Honcho eating from his bowl in the kitchen. My back door was open. "Honcho, how did you get in?"

"I couldn't stand to listen to him howl, so I took the liberty of letting him in," Devlin yelled from his kitchen.

"Thanks, Dave." I reached down and stroked my cat. "You are a very good kitty."

"What say to a drink?" Devlin called. It was not yet noon.

"I don't think so."

"Young woman knocking on your door a little while ago. I told her you'd gone to the vet with your cat."

"What did she look like?" It had to have been Noelle. But there was no note on the door, and Noelle was a compulsive leaver of notes.

"Real easy on the eyes. Had on tight shorts; long black hair."

"Oh, yeah. A friend of Laura's." Devlin came out on the landing and stood in front of my screen door. He had a mischievous grin on his face. "What?" I asked.

"Friend of Laura's? Do I look like I was born yesterday?"

"You got it wrong, Dave."

"Sure I have."

"Come on. I mean it."

"Let's have a drink. I promise to keep my lip zipped. It's a nice day. Your kind of day, Paul. Cool."

"I should be out looking for work."

"Slim pickings out there, my boy. You're going to need some luck."

"Look, an hour ago I thought I'd lost my cat again, and here he is. How much luckier can you get?"

"Come on over for steamers and corn on the cob tonight. What do you say?"

"I say you're on. You sure Maggie won't mind?"

"She won't mind. Five o'clock."

I doubted that either one of them would be conscious by five o'clock if they uncorked the bottle now. Honcho finished up what was in his bowl. He looked at me as if he had something he wanted to say.

"What do you say to a refill? You've had a lot of excitement so far today." He let out a trill. Laura always insisted that he understood our language.

* * *

"Were you looking for me a while ago?"

"I was in the neighborhood, so I knocked on your door. Sorry I missed you."

"Me too."

"William's off on another trip this weekend."

"How nice for him."

"It can be nice for us, too. Come over for supper. Don't worry, I'll order take-out."

"Can't. Dining with the neighbors."

"Come afterwards. I'll have dessert waiting."

"I'm tempted."

"I'll expect you. Whenever you get here is fine."

I hung up, conscious of my heart galloping under my shirt. "Oh, my lord," I said. Honcho looked up at me, blinked, and went back to his bowl.

Somehow, Devlin and Maggie managed to stay conscious long enough to put supper together. They were feeling no pain when I joined them at five o'clock, and they continued to put away the rye and beer right through the meal. By the time we finished eating, Devlin was barely coherent and Maggie looked ready to pass out. I ate heartily even if my attention was less on the food than with the prospect of what lay ahead of me this evening with Noelle. There would be no backing down this time.

* * *

"I knew you'd come, but what a nice surprise anyway," Noelle said.

I stood at the door swinging a six-pack of beer at my side. "How about a brew?" I moved into the room. Noelle put her arms around my neck and kissed me for a long time.

"What about a brew afterward?" she whispered. Then she got busy with the zipper of my fly.

Later, as we sipped beer from bottles in the living room, the hi-fi's volume on Sinatra's "Only the Lonely" turned low so as not to wake little Teddy, Noelle asked me to stay the night.

"I don't think so."

"Why not? Don't worry about William."

I felt guilty enough for coming to Noelle's bed after my righteous denial to my wife that I had been seeing her again, without compounding it by spending the night with her. As if there were a moral distinction between the two kinds of conduct.

"I shouldn't have come here in the first place. I'm weak."

"No, you're not. You're just not sure yet what it is you want. Let me help you, Paul," she said, sliding onto my lap.

Noelle was correct. I apparently didn't know what I wanted. She seemed determined to convince me that she was aware of at least one thing I wanted. We made love again on the living room floor, the floor that William liked to stretch out on when he read his newspaper. I had never experienced such sexual spontaneity with Laura. Her bohemian nature didn't include adventures in sex.

"Are you going to confess your sins to Laura?"

I pulled myself up and got into a cross-legged position. I sighed. For the first time in the eight months since I'd quit smoking, I craved a cigarette. Noelle had quit, herself, and this was one craving she would not be able to help me with.

"I could really use a smoke. Did William leave any around?" Noelle was behind me, on her knees, her arms wrapped around my neck.

"You don't want a cigarette, Paul. Not after all this time."

"Oh, yeah. Then what do I want?"

"You want me, Paul." She fell on her back alongside me and giggled.

"Aren't we playful." Even in the poorly lighted room I could see her expression change.

"That's William's tone of voice," she said, rising to her feet, picking up her bathrobe off the sofa. "You want coffee?" Noelle headed for the kitchen without waiting to find out whether or not I wanted coffee.

I got into my clothes and left Noelle's apartment without saying goodnight.

THIRTEEN

"I slept with Noelle." It was out of my mouth before I could think. I knew instantly that I'd made a mistake, a big mistake. The silence on my wife's end of the line confirmed it. "I'm so sorry, Laura."

"How could you, you bastard? You pathetic, weak bastard. Noelle's my best friend. You did this to punish me."

"That's not true."

"Of course it's true. You are always looking for ways to punish me. Why do you think I left?"

"I don't know what you're talking about. Why would I want to punish you? I love you."

"After what you've done, you have the nerve to say you love me?" She began to cry. I was tempted to remind her of her so-called best friend's behavior since she'd been gone. Not to mention how cavalier she had seemed about Noelle's tactics with me. That would only compound my mistake. "Why did you have to tell me? You stupid ..."

"I had to. I couldn't live with it."

"Oh, just shut up. I hate you so."

"Laura, please." But the next thing I heard was the dial tone.

I drew a hot bath and stayed in the water so long my fingers began to wrinkle. Honcho came in to use the litter box; he put his front paws up on the tub and regarded me in a way that made me wonder if the cat knew what was up with its owner.

"Yeah, I know. I'm a complete idiot." Honcho's ears went back, and he left the bathroom in a hurry, as if he had some particular place to go. My wife had a good point. Why did I have to tell her? It wasn't as if I had a highly developed sense of morality, or a passion for truth telling. What I did have was an overactive conscience, and a low threshold for feelings of guilt. Who did I have to thank for that? It would have come out eventually, perhaps when I was back together with my wife. I would have had a better chance for damage control if we were actually together. Now, I held out little hope of reconciliation. There was a good chance that I might not ever hear from her again.

I heard Devlin on the other side of the wall, hawking and gagging. I slid down in the bath water until my head was submerged. By the time I came up for air, Devlin had finished. Devlin and Maggie. Two more pathetic human beings I couldn't imagine. Yet they had stuck with each other for more than twenty years. I couldn't make it to my first wedding anniversary. What if Laura were correct about me, about my wanting to punish her? The idea had never crossed my mind. If I couldn't be described as introspective, I believed that I possessed at least a degree of self-awareness. I liked to think I would be able to admit to myself motives as dark as those my wife accused me of if I harbored them. No, I did not set out deliberately to punish my wife, although the thought had crossed my mind more than once that Laura was exacting some kind of revenge on me. I would not know how to broach such a subject to Devlin, or to anyone else I could think of, not even Doc. Noelle would have her opinion, but at the moment I could think of no one I would care less to confide in than Noelle. I was finished with her. I would call her and tell her what I had done. She had flippantly asked me if I had confessed my sins to my wife.

The phone rang. I pulled myself out of the bathtub, and in my haste to get to the phone, stepped in the cat litter box and Honcho's fresh deposit. In the time it took me to clean off my foot, the phone had ceased ringing. I just knew that it was Laura calling back. To tell me what? To tell me that we were through, that was what. I sat at the kitchen table, a towel around my loins, and waited. Something told me she would try again. The ringing of the phone startled me.

"Paul, I'm sorry for the way I talked to you. I know it wasn't your fault. I've always known what Noelle is. I won't pretend not to be hurt, but I understand what you must have been feeling. It's not the first time she's done something like this. I know this is all my fault. Can you forgive me, darling?"

"It's nobody's fault. Please come home, Laura."

"Oh, Paul, how many times do I have to say it? I will never go back there. It would be impossible for us to make a life in that town. Something will break soon, Paul. Have patience."

"That's beginning to sound familiar."

"Do you think you could stay away from Noelle? For me, Paul?"

"I'll never see her again. I promise."

"Take care of yourself for me, darling. Hug Honcho and J. Alfred."

FOURTEEN

It was only last week that I had thought about Jack Scanlon and George Stacy, my erstwhile high school pals, when I hadn't thought about either of them in years. Now, there was Jack Scanlon framed in my doorway.

"You won't believe this, Jack, but I was thinking about you only last week. You and George." Jack grinned and shrugged his shoulders. He had put on a little weight since I'd last seen him. We had spent a fair amount of time together the summer after we graduated from high school before going our separate ways: Jack into the Navy, just as he had predicted, me into the Army, not at all what anybody, least of all I, had predicted.

"I hear you married Laura Sargent. How did a dork like you end up with a dish like that?" When I told Jack that Laura had left me exactly one month ago to the day, his face went slack with embarrassment.

"Jesus, Paul. I'm sorry. What an asshole I can be without even trying. Listen, why don't we go around The Cantina for a meatball sandwich and some beers? We've got some catching up to do."

I learned that Jack had gotten out of the Navy around the same time I was discharged; he got his papers in San Francisco while I was finishing up my time down in Monterey, at Ford Ord. In the meantime, George Stacy's family had moved to San Diego. George went to live with them while he spent a semester at San Diego State. For some reason he quit, came back east where he met and married Elaine Osgood, and matriculated at U.N.H. Jack had spent some time with George's family after his discharge. It was there that he met Katie Durand, one of George Stacy's kid sister's high school friends. As Jack told it, this Katie Durand may have been only seventeen, but she was a well-practiced temptress, a regular Lolita with blue eye shadow. The long and short of it was that Jack knocked her up, and was forced (more by his own conscience than from any pressure from Katie or her parents) to marry the girl. He took a job at an automobile factory on the assembly line, and he and his new bride lived with her parents in their tiny house until the baby was born. Neither Jack nor Katie liked living with her parents. In the time they spent there together they also discovered that they didn't like each other very much, either.

So Jack had come back east to look for work and a place to live. He wanted to work full time and go to school nights, preferably at U.N.H. The university was giving him the bureaucratic shuffle about transferring credits he'd earned at a junior college in California, however. He had a lead on a factory job outside of Boston that he was on his way to check out.

"I've been staying with George and Elaine for about a week now. She's ready to throw me out on the street. Thinks I'm a bad influence on her husband. Imagine that?"Jack's laugh was sardonic. "Can you picture George married?"

"About as much as I can picture you married with a kid. Or me."

"Glenda," Jack called the waitress. "How about another round over here?"

"Not for me, Jack. You know how I am."

"Come on. This is a special occasion. We're both free ... at least for the moment. You'll be back with your wife, and, God help me, I'll be sending for my wife and kid." Jack's year-old daughter was named Lucy.

"You don't sound pleased."

"We hate each other, Paul. We have not one thing in common. It's only for Lucy's sake we stay together, believe me. I made a real mess of my life, Paul. Maybe we all did. George won't admit it, but he's not that crazy about being married. And look at you."

"I thought I was doing the right thing marrying Laura. It seemed right at the time. I'm still not sure what went wrong. This got me on the blind side, Jack."

"I was you, I'd get my ass to the West Coast. San Francisco is where it's at, pal. If you ask me, Laura's the one got her head on straight. It's you who's fucked up, if you ask me."

"Thank you very little."

Jack squeezed my arm. "Have another brew, for Christ's sake. That's always been your problem. You need to let it go once in a while. Take up drinking. There's still time."

"I should introduce you to my neighbors."

"You know, Paul, I'm tempted to just disappear, vanish without a fucking trace. Start over fresh, somewhere nobody knows me from shit. I can't deal with this family crap, Paul. Understand?"

"Yeah, sure." I didn't really understand Jack Scanlon, and never had. I don't think I would feel the same way in his place, not with a child to bring up, no matter how I felt about my life. I didn't think I could say this to Jack. And what good would it have done either of us for me to say it out loud?

"What's going to become of us, Paul? All of us. I take that back. I don't really mean all of us. I mean me. You guys at least married intelligent women. I ended up with a twit, a fluff-head. And a slut to boot." Jack drained his glass and brought it down hard on the table. "Glenda."

"Laura doesn't think I have the guts to leave Garrison. She thinks I'm a prisoner here."

"Do you, Paul? Do you have the balls to get out of here? Tell you the truth, I was surprised when you went against mommy and daddy's wishes and joined the Army. Best thing you ever did. Now you're back here. I can't figure you." Jack shook his head. He was slightly wall-eyed. And when he drank a lot, it became more pronounced.

"I had my reasons. And am I seeing things, or is that you across the table from me? I'm back here. Now you're back here. There's a difference?" I knew it was the alcohol talking through Jack, but his words stung, nevertheless.

"You're wrong about my being back here. If I do come back it will only be for a little while, until I can get a degree. I've got something going in Boston, I told you. Paul, you've got to get out of here while the getting's good. Garrison will suck the life out of you." Glenda was back with another glass of beer for Jack.

The Cantina's horseshoe shaped bar was in the middle of an enormous room. There were booths along all four walls, and tables occupied the space between the bar and the booths. Beer on tap and in bottles was all you could get in the way of alcohol in The Cantina. University students made up the majority of The Cantina's clientele. A blue pennant with white lettering that hung over the entrance to the kitchen declared: "When Better Women are Made, UNH Men Will Make Them." Pennants identifying all the fraternities and sororities hung from the walls as well. The place was packed to capacity on Friday nights. It could seat maybe two hundred. With the first semester about to begin, the room was filling up in a hurry. I recognized a few faces that came through the door even if I couldn't put names to them. Across from me, my former high school pal counseled me about love and life even if his own love life was in shambles. I suddenly felt dreadfully sad. To Doc Robinson, and now Jack Scanlon, the path I should take was clear. To me, the way was anything but clear. I envied the college kids, envied them their energy, their cocky buoyancy; I was jealous of the way they carried themselves, the way they dressed, the way they talked. I wanted to be among them, to be one of them. Instead, I was a "townie," and now I felt like a stranger in my own town.

"I think I'll take you up on that beer. And how about letting me bum a cigarette?" I drank another beer, and smoked Jack Scanlon's cigarettes, the first smoke I'd had in about eight months. I drank another beer. We drank beer, in fact, until The Cantina closed at midnight. Jack wanted me to go with him to George's apartment, to continue drinking and talking. I had already had more to drink than I could remember, and on the sidewalk in front of The Cantina, I discovered how much it had affected me. The pavement undulated, and so did my stomach. I said goodnight to Jack and stumbled the three blocks to my apartment. As soon as my head found the pillow the room went into a spin. Then I was on my knees in front of the toilet bowl, with one hand in Honcho's litter box, which needed changing badly. I lost my meatball sandwich, and everything I'd had to drink followed. I made two more trips to the bathroom before sleep overtook me.

* * *

I woke up with the first hangover I'd had since that bout of shot swapping my last night in Inchon, Korea. It was only the second hangover in my entire life. I vowed that it would be the last. On the up side, I wouldn't have to face a day at Sid's inhaling gasoline fumes from the machine shop. It was my night to work at Archie's, but I had the whole day to recover, to get "well," as Jack Scanlon and his drinking buddies used to refer to the process. I examined my haggard face in the bathroom mirror and decided that it was not the kind of face that would have any luck in the job hunt today. So I lolled around the apartment, reading and listening to music. At two o'clock I put my head down intending to take a short nap. I was awakened at ten after six by the telephone.

"It's a good thing you called. I was about to sleep through my shift. I don't think Archie would take kindly to my missing another one." I told my wife about forgetting to show up for work a couple of Saturday's ago. I didn't put the story in the context of Noelle and William's dinner. I also told her about drinking with Jack last night, and my hung over condition this morning.

"So you drank too much. And you napped during the day. These things don't sound like you."

"If it ever turns out we see each other again you probably won't recognize me. I keep doing these things that don't *sound* like me."

"Paul, please don't start. I'm doing the best I can. It's a bad economy. Jobs are scarce. You must be patient."

"You had a good job here until about a month ago. But you don't need me to remind you."

"Don't make me laugh."

"I should be getting my unemployment check in the next week or so. Want me to wire you some cash?"

"Very funny, Paul."

"I'm sorry. How are you doing, sweetie? You meeting new people? What do you do with yourself nights? You having any fun?"

"I've met several interesting people. Artists, poets, musicians. What are you doing with yourself?"

"Hey, my social calendar is full. If I'm not having cocktails and dinner with Devlin and Maggie, then it's a *soiree* in Archie's back room, or maybe an evening in Frenchie's billiard emporium. I can't keep up, Laura."

"Or Noelle's bedroom?"

"That was a little below the belt, even for you, Laura."

"Since when has the truth been ruled a low blow?"

"I thought we settled this. It's not the truth, Laura."

"As I've said before, Paul, you're not a very good liar."

"Last time we talked you all but forgave me, remember?"

"And you took that as permission to keep on with Noelle?"

"There is nothing going on between us. I swear." It occurred to me that my wife might have been in contact with Noelle. Who knew what Noelle could have told her? "What, have you talked to her? And you'd believe her before you'd believe me. Is that it?"

"I haven't talked to her. I don't have to. Goodbye, Paul."

FIFTEEN

Another heat wave was into its third day. The line at the unemployment office extended all the way to the corner of Locust and Maple. I must have been outside, with the sun beating down on me, for a half hour before the line began to move. It was another half hour before I crossed the office's threshold. All that standing in line got me a ten-minute interview with a dour lady with the personality of a Burroughs ten-key calculator.

"Did you seek employment last week, Mr. Embry?"

"Yes, ma'am."

"What places of employment did you visit last week, Mr. Embry?"

"Let me see. I went out to Epping to a place called Circle Brick. That was Monday. They only employ eight workers. The brick business seems to be slow these days. They weren't hiring Monday and probably won't be in the foreseeable future. That's what the guy told me."

"And where else did you inquire, Mr. Embry?" She had a pencil in her fingers, and was checking off items on some kind of form.

"Well, on Tuesday a friend drove me over to the Navy Yard. I put in an application for an office job, thinking my military service might give me a chance of landing a G.S. spot. They've actually been laying off workers at the Yard lately, but I guess I don't have to tell you that." Her dour expression remained fixed as she checked off little boxes on her form.

"Did you inquire anywhere else, Mr. Embry?"

"Yes. On Wednesday I tried all the shoe factories in the area. Same story everywhere. Nothing doing, unless you have experience. Now, if I were a bedlaster, whatever that is, they might be able to use me. They have no interest in providing on-the-job training in the shoe industry, is my guess." She paused and studied the form in front of her, as if she'd forgotten I was sitting there. "What about you folks?" I asked her. "Have you got anything in your files that might help me?"

She looked at me over her spectacles as if the question were impertinent. She opened a file cabinet next to her desk and flipped through several folders, and selected one. She lifted it halfway out of the drawer and slipped her glasses down to the end of her pug nose.

"There's a seafood restaurant in Portsmouth that is looking for a busboy and a dishwasher. Hours would be noon to eight."

"Portsmouth? Sorry, I have no means of transportation."

Again she regarded me over the top of her glasses, and her expression conveyed skepticism. Instead of eyebrows, she had painted black lines over her eyelids. "Did you not say that you inquired at the Portsmouth Naval Shipyard, Mr. Embry?"

"Yes, ma'am, I did."

"And how did you think you would manage your transportation had you been offered employment there?"

"I have a good friend who works there and lives here in Garrison. He's the one gave me a ride over there Tuesday," I lied. I was grateful there were no pearl diving opportunities listed for Garrison. She showed me her sour puss and resumed her search through her drawer of file folders.

"Have you had any experience surveying, Mr. Embry?"

"Afraid not." I had filled out a form listing my job qualifications. She could have consulted that and saved us both some time.

"I have here an opening for a tree pruner for a landscaping firm in Garrison. It's only part time, and seasonal, however."

"Well, you see, I'm not very good with my hands, and I was hoping for something full time, because I really need full-time work. General office work and the like."

"There is nothing available in that area at this time, Mr. Embry. I would point out to you that at times like these one can't afford to be too particular. If you refuse to accept a reasonable offer of employment, or if you fail to actively pursue gainful employment, your benefits could be curtailed. Do you understand, Mr. Embry?"

"Oh, yes. Perfectly. I'm trying my best, but when you're without a car …"

"We'll see you next week, Mr. Embry," the fat lady said and swiveled away from me.

So, not much had changed at the unemployment office since 1961. Benefits had increased by three dollars a week, and I was eligible for six, not four, months of compensation. That is, if I "actively" pursued employment and was offered only unreasonable jobs. Six months. Surely my wife would land something in that time. I would either be lining up at an unemployment office in San Francisco, being supported by Laura, or she would have kissed me off and I would be left to face the fat-faced gorgon every Monday morning for six months. Given the last conversation with my wife, the latter scenario seemed more likely.

What would become of us? Jack Scanlon had wondered in The Cantina Thursday night. There was always the option of re-enlisting in the Army, or the Navy. I'd once fantasized about sailing around the world as a merchant mariner, of having a girl in every port and being carefree, carefree, carefree.

* * *

Mrs. Pappas had not caught on that I'd lost my job at Sid's. I made it a point to get out of the house early in the morning to look for work. If I got discouraged in that endeavor, or just ran out of leads, I would sneak up the back steps after making sure Mrs. Pappas wasn't in her kitchen with its view of the back landing. Then I'd have to take off my shoes and tiptoe around the apartment until I'd just give up and fall into bed and find refuge in sleep. I couldn't keep this pretense up much longer. The rent was due and I didn't have enough to cover it. She deserved to be told that I no longer held a full-time job. When my unemployment checks started to come in regularly, along with what I made at Archie's, I'd be able to scrape by. I had no doubt that Mrs. Pappas would let me slide. I just didn't want to face her with the news because it would have to include the truth about Laura's absence.

After my ordeal at the unemployment office I paid Mrs. Pappas a visit. She sat on the middle cushion of her overstuffed sofa, her lap full of needlework. Charlie was away for part of the day at the Great Bay School for the Mentally Handicapped. He attended from ten in the morning until two in the afternoon four days a week.

"You're home early, Paul. Aren't you feeling well, dear?"

"I feel just fine, Mrs. Pappas, but there's something you need to know. Have you got a few minutes?" And I laid it all out for my landlady, including the whole story about Laura and me. As I suppose I knew she would be, Mrs. Pappas was sympathetic, so sympathetic that I began to feel like an even bigger jerk for withholding from her in the first place. She invited me to stay for a cup of tea. I don't normally drink tea, but there was no way I was going to refuse her kind offer.

That week I went twice more to Mrs. Pappas's for tea. She had begun to tell me the story of her life. Even when Charlie was home from the school, never was he in the room with us. I wondered if Mrs. Pappas had finally sensed my aversion to the boy, or if Charlie himself was afraid of me, the way wild animals are afraid of humans instinctively.

Mrs. Pappas was born in Albania to poor parents. The austere life she described in that place, the bleakness of the outlook for the future, filled me with pity. She was fortunate, in a way, as the oldest daughter among six children, to have been summoned to America to fulfill a marriage agreement with Harry Pappas, a Greek, a man fifteen years her senior. Harry Pappas was a silent, bitter man who worked fourteen hours a day in the woolen mills that were once Garrison's principal industry. In the past twenty years, shoe factories that manufactured cheap shoes for women had replaced the woolen mills. Harry made his wife go to work in the mills, too, until they had saved enough money to buy the house we sat in now. Then she stayed home and began to raise a family. The neighborhood was different in those days. There were no young thugs roaming the streets day and night, turning over garbage cans, ringing doorbells, bullying young children and old people. And there was hardly any automobile traffic on the street. Her life with Harry Pappas was filled with silence and sorrow. She pulled her bathrobe tightly around her.

"My robe of sorrow," she said with a little smile. I was flattered that she felt comfortable enough with me to appear in anything except the black dress I had always seen her wear. The only joy she took was with her children, two daughters, both married now and living in California with children of their own. Then Charlie was born. Harry was an old man when Charlie arrived, and he blamed his wife for producing a defective child. He died seven years later without ever acknowledging his son's existence or speaking again to his wife. He died as silently and as bitterly as he lived. She had been glad to see him go, even if it made her tremble with fear now to admit it.

A year after Harry's death, Mrs. Pappas discovered she had diabetes. Her biggest fear now is that she will go before Charlie, leaving him alone in this terrifying world. Neither of her daughters would take him. Of that she was reasonably sure. They seldom called and never wrote. I found myself wondering if Mrs. Pappas had pinned her hopes for Charlie's future, for his safety, on Laura. I wasn't above using this notion as a bargaining chip. Laura truly loved the boy, and it was my guess that she would do just about anything to keep him from harm or unhappiness. And for Charlie's part, he had not given up his ritual climb up the stairs to my door to ask "Is Laura home?" On the other hand, Mrs. Pappas didn't look ready to check out just yet.

* * *

"Well, finally you're seeing Mrs. Pappas for what she really is. You were missing a lot, Paul. Now, if you could get to know Charlie, really know him, you'd understand how I felt about them both. I was very angry at you for the way you were with them, Paul. Very angry."

"I couldn't help how I felt, Laura."

"You could have made an effort. You knew how much I loved them. You could have pretended."

"That would have been a little dishonest, don't you think?"

"Since when has honesty meant anything to you?"

"Is this your reason for calling? To lecture me on honesty and morality?"

"You could stand some instruction on morality, since you bring it up."

"So now you're speaking from a position of moral superiority. That's kind of laughable under the circumstances, Laura."

"I wasn't the one who fucked your best friend."

"That's a pretty way to put it. Maybe this wouldn't have happened if you didn't take it in your head to just walk out on me."

"I love your use of the word maybe."

"Mrs. Pappas is worried that if she dies before Charlie there'll be nobody to look after him. I think she's counting on you, Laura. What do you think about that?"

"I think that for you to resort to this kind of blackmail is … well, pathetic."

"Why did you call, Laura? I haven't heard from you in a week. You've been gone for almost six weeks. What's the occasion? It wouldn't have anything to do with the fact that today is our anniversary, would it?"

"That's one reason I called today. Not to wish you a happy anniversary, of course. I've been thinking about us a good deal, Paul. And I've been talking with people—Andrea, Lydia, and their friends. I have to say it to you now, Paul. We made a mistake a year ago. At least I made a mistake. Being out here these past weeks has finally opened my eyes. Everyone is so different here, so self-actualizing. I'm not convinced you would thrive in this environment, Paul. It saddens me to have to say this to you. I think there's a part of me that loves you dearly."

I'd had dreams lately in which my wife used words like this. I had awakened from them troubled, and I would be in state of despair for hours. I deliberately avoided thinking about the possibility that she would arrive at this state while we were apart. Hearing it straight from her mouth, even from a distance of three thousand miles, had a paralyzing effect on me. I could not find my voice.

"Do you think you could say something to me, Paul?"

No, I couldn't answer. I tried, but I couldn't make my voice work.

"Paul, are you all right?" I moved my lips but no sound came out. Finally, she said I was being tiresome with my little drama. Then she hung up on me.

* * *

"Maybe what your wife had to say scared you speechless," Doc said, raising his paper cup to his lips. "Minor strokes can result in temporary loss of speech. I doubt very much you suffered a stroke, not at your age. No, I'm staying with the scared speechless hypothesis." Doc was smiling in a way that made me think he was making fun of me. I should never have confided in him, or anybody else.

"Don't despair, Paul," Doc said, not smiling this time. "You know women. She was probably trying to bust your balls, get you on the ropes. She'll call back and tell you she's sorry. Everything will work out. Wait and see."

"Maybe. Have you ever heard the expression "self-actualizing"? Laura used it on me. I'm not sure what she meant by it, but she made it sound like a good thing."

Doc shrugged his shoulders. "Sounds like the kind of thing you'd hear out of the mouth of a psychology type." Doc had no use for "psychology types." He considered psychology pseudo-science, and their practitioners one rung on the professional ladder above a chiropractor. In retrospect, I remembered that Laura had taken out a few books from the library on the subject, books by authors like Erich Fromm and Carl Rogers. I never heard any psychology jargon come out of her mouth, however.

Doc and Archie took off for Rockingham racetrack; I was alone in the store on Friday the thirteenth, on my first wedding anniversary, waiting for something even more dreadful to happen. It was too early for the college beer business, so I would have to be by myself for a while, alone with my black thoughts.

* * *

Back in '61, after our first date, as I said, I started seeing Laura every day. I'd drive her to the university in the morning, and drive her back home after her last class if she decided to hang around that long.

One day at the Memorial Union cafeteria, we joined some of her classmates from the philosophy course she was taking. They were slouching in canvas chairs, drinking coffee out of paper cups. There were no introductions, and the only attention any of them paid me was when they were asking for my cigarettes. They were intellectuals, I guessed, since nothing they said made any sense to me. I sat in a mire of verbiage for over an hour. At one point they argued earnestly, even angrily, over the question: does a tree falling in the forest make a sound if no one is around to hear it? They were very much taken with the work of an author they referred to as "Ann Rand," but the paperback book on the table entitled *Atlas Shrugged* bore the name Ayn Rand. Where they got *Ann* out of *Ayn* I chalked up to my own ignorance.

Laura's father and I disliked each other at once. He owned a small hardware store, was a staunch Republican, and missed no chance to recite his philosophy of self-reliance and states' rights. Next to him, I felt like a subversive. My own father had been as staunch in his support of the Democrats as Mr. Sargent was of the Republicans. Laura's mother was a stay-at-home wife who, in the summer, tended her flower garden, sipped tea with her bridge club three afternoons a week, and spent her evenings in front of the TV knitting sweaters and socks, or braiding rugs. Trade journals and the *Reader's Digest* were conspicuous in the house, but the serious literature was confined to Laura's room. She majored in English, minored in philosophy, and when I met her she was in her Russian phase, as she called it: Dostoyevsky, Tolstoy, Gorki, Pasternak. Her father was convinced that if she weren't an actual card-carrying communist she was at the very least a dupe and a sympathizer. He and other right-minded people like himself knew that the university was a haven for communists, socialists, and every other species of social deviant. Her mother assiduously censored her daughter's bookcase for filth. Laura claimed she had destroyed nine copies of *Lady Chatterley's Lover.*

The day I went into the hardware store to ask Laura's father for his daughter's hand in marriage the old man was taking inventory at a bin of elbow joints. He never once looked at me, and all he had to say was, "I assume you realize that you're getting the better end of the bargain." I replied that I realized that, and left. Laura's parents appeared at the wedding long enough to see the ceremony through. Then, with his wife in tow, her father hurried away. They refused to set foot in our apartment although it was in a respectable part of town, on a tree-lined street not far from the Episcopal Church where we were married. I was just as stubborn in my refusal to visit them. Laura made a few solo visits to her parents, but soon diagnosed the relationship as sham and pretense. She stopped seeing them, ending her relations with her family as easily, it seemed to me, as she had dropped out of school.

I had just lost my father, and my mother, a taciturn woman, had little in common with Laura. She visited once or twice out of courtesy, and after that we saw her only if we went to the house in Portsmouth she'd moved to after my father's death. Laura admitted to not feeling comfortable in my mother's presence, and seemed relieved when it became clear that she would be an infrequent visitor. So, virtually cut free of parental ties, Laura and I began our marriage in three commodious sun-filled rooms. The first week, Laura served me breakfast in bed every morning. The next week, I did the same for her, rising an hour earlier than usual so that I could do it and get to work at Sid's on time. It wasn't until the third week that we discovered that neither of us cared for breakfast, in or out of bed. Coffee was adequate in the morning.

Laura had no talent, and no inclination, as a cook. Even so, in the beginning she tried to see to it that our evening meal was a civilized experience. I would come home from work to find her amidst a clutter of measuring cups, mixing bowls and saucepans, (after an eight hour shift at the dry goods store where she worked) painstakingly following a cookbook recipe. She would have covered the kitchen table with a crisp white cloth, set out the plates and silver so that when we sat down we faced each other along the long axis of the table. There would be candles, and Brahms playing on the hi-fi, a bottle of wine breathing on the counter. But this was not really Laura's style, and when she said so, I quietly assented. I got used to the TV dinners and cold sandwiches eaten on a bare table. I secretly missed her cooking, however bland, while she worked the *New York Times* crossword puzzle with the sound of Miles Davis's muted horn issuing from the hi-fi. I thought she would be impressed that I had actually seen Miles, and Coltrane, and the rest of the quintet at Storyville in 1956. She wasn't even mildly impressed.

The landlord was a queer duck. He went around in bibbed overalls, and a gray fedora whose soft brim kept his face in shadow. He was a little man, thin, wizened, and full of energy. He kept the long driveway clear of snow with an old-fashioned wooden hand-plow. He was suspicious of everybody and everything, and made excuses to nose around our apartment on the pretext of checking radiators, plumbing, electrical fixtures, and the appliances that came with the rent. He seemed always to be sniffing around. One Sunday morning we woke up to find him peering in our bedroom window. He claimed he was checking the storm windows.

One day, we took a shower together and realized too late that the bottom of the curtain was outside the tub. The bathroom floor flooded, and water leaked down to the landlord's ceiling. He gave this as justification for evicting us. He told us we were as irresponsible as puppies. Laura maintained that his real reason for giving us the boot had more to do with the fact that all we had for furniture was a brick-and-board bookcase and a hi-fi in the living room, and that her hair was long, and that she had gone to the university. This made her, in the landlord's eyes, she reasoned, a beatnik and a communist. She was furious, but there was nothing we could do.

It was January, and we walked the frozen streets for two days looking for a place to live. Mrs. Pappas's apartment we looked at as a last resort, not wanting to move to that part of the city unless we were forced to. Rents were scarce that time of year, and in the end we had to settle for Mrs. Pappas's. Laura didn't actually complain about the apartment, but it was easy to see that she despised it. Every night that first week her crying awakened me. She said it was nothing, only the humiliation of being evicted, the upheaval of moving.

Laura looked for a better paying job, and bumped up against employers who wouldn't hire her unless she cut her hair. She finally landed a job at Garrison Savings Bank at fifty-five dollars a week without having to sacrifice her hair. I went to work for Archie to supplement our income. We survived the first winter of our marriage equably.

With Laura's income, we were able to afford the "sweet" '55 Chevy. Over my protestations, my mother had sold my father's Desoto. In the spring we would take long rides to the beach, or on country roads, enjoying the freedom all Americans who owned a car enjoyed. Then the car suffered a cracked block and I couldn't drive it unless I wanted to feed it a quart of oil every five miles. An engine job, or another used car, were financially out of the question. Since June we had been without transportation. Confined in the three tiny rooms, we started to get on each other's nerves, and the summer heat, which began in June, did little to improve our lot.

* * *

Four urchins burst through the door and fanned out in a semi-circle in front of the counter as if they meant to launch an assault. The dirty towhead, the ringleader, stepped forward and dropped a quarter from his grubby little hand on the counter. "Twinny five cints worf pinny candy," he said, a demented grin on his pale face. Now, Archie had told them, as he had told me, in no uncertain terms, that they were not to come in the store anymore. I supposed I was being tested. Their usual method was to swarm the penny candy display, help themselves, and then bring their pickings to the counter. This is when you had to watch them carefully, because they would be watching you, looking for their opportunity to fill their pockets. By asking me to choose their candy for them, perhaps they believed that this could be construed as an acceptable alternative to their outright banishment.

"Sorry, guys. You know what Archie said. He no longer desires your business, so you had better run along." The towhead started to give me guff, and the others began to spread out. I made my move from behind the counter, and they took off running out the door.

Twenty minutes later they came back. The only customer in the store was a skinny guy, a regular from Sigma Beta; he was looking over the beer selection.

"I thought I made it clear to you guys that you weren't welcome in here anymore," I said, moving behind the counter. The towhead stepped forward, while the others stood behind him elbow to elbow. They were a little comical in their defiance. "Shoo," I said. "Get your little asses on out of here."

The towhead reached behind him down the back of his trousers and came out with a handful of his shit, which he proceeded to hurl in my direction, before all four of them bolted. I'd never in all my life had shit literally thrown at me. My reflexes were good enough to avoid a direct hit in the face, but I took enough on my chest and arms to consider myself a serious casualty. The surprise and horror of the act rendered me temporarily paralyzed, the way my wife's phone call had done earlier. Instead of taking after the little bastards and putting some hurt on them, I just stood there behind the counter in a semi-catatonic state. The Sigma Beta guy, apparently oblivious of what had just happened to me, came to the counter with two six-packs of Blackhorse Ale.

"Jesus! What the fuck happened to you? You look like somebody shit all over you! Oh, Jesus." He recoiled from the smell.

I had pulled a dirty towel from under the counter that we kept to wipe up spills. I dabbed tentatively at my soiled shirt. A lot of it ended up behind me, on the cigar display and on the wall. "Look, do me a favor and get your brew somewhere else tonight. I got to close for awhile."

"No problem. Holy shit!" Sigma Beta man hurried out the door.

I locked up and headed for my apartment on the run; I tore off my shirt on the way and threw it in an empty trashcan on the sidewalk.

As I soaked in the bathtub, the stench of the towhead's ordure strong in my nostrils, I turned over in my mind what kind of terrible revenge I could exact on those despicable children. Maybe there was something to this Friday the 13th business after all. Archie wouldn't like it if he found out I closed the store this early on a Friday night, the best beer sales night of the week. I'd tell him that a buck an hour was hardly enough compensation to take the kind of shit, as it were, that I took tonight. Then my conscience got the best of me, and after I'd scoured myself for a good half-hour, I went back and opened up the store.

SIXTEEN

"You got anything to drink?" Jack Scanlon said, pushing past me into my living room.

"Sorry, Jack."

"Of course not. What am I thinking?"

"How did you make out in Boston?"

"I start Monday. Consolidated Blowers in Waltham. Five grand a year. Not bad, eh?"

"Way to go, Jack. That's great. Finding a job, any job these days, is a feat. Congratulations."

"Let's go around The Cantina. We finally got something to celebrate." I told Jack about the price I had to pay for my last visit to The Cantina. I had no wish to repeat that experience. "So drink a Coke, eat some spaghetti and meatballs. It's my treat. Hey, this is my last day of freedom. George takes me to Watertown tomorrow; I've got to get my new apartment ready for Katie and Lucy. They'll be coming in about three weeks. Then my shoulder's to the wheel."

Jack Scanlon treated me to spaghetti and meatballs while he poured one glass of beer after the other down his throat. He became more garrulous with each round.

"Aren't you going to eat something, Jack?"

"Not while I'm drinking. With me it's one or the other. Food ruins the taste of beer, in my opinion."

"Most people say that beer enhances the taste of food. Some food anyway."

"Not this kid."

"So you're going to be living in the big city. How are you going to like that?"

"Watertown's hardly a big city. But it's close enough to Boston. I like the city anyway. Always have. Beats living in Garrison and places like it. Small town America's not for me. Small towns go with small minds, Paul. You should know that by now. I don't know how you put up with it. No wonder your wife hit the road."

"So you've said."

"Come on, Paul, don't get testy on me. I'm trying to straighten you out, so enough with the hurt feelings already."

"You're not hurting my feelings, Jack. Besides, it's all over between Laura and me." I told him about Laura's phone call. Jack shook his head sympathetically and drained his beer.

"At the risk of sounding insensitive, my friend, I envy you. You're a free man. You got absolutely no reason to stick around this one-horse town a minute longer. Free at last, as the man said. Did you see King's speech on TV a couple weeks ago, Paul? What an orator."

"No. My TV doesn't come in half the time. I've been kind of out of touch with the world since Laura took off."

"It's time you got back in touch with it. Shit is happening, Paul. In a big way. Surely you've heard about all the hell that's broken loose in Mississippi and Georgia. Glenda." Jack raised his empty glass when he had the waitress's attention. "My God, that woman is ugly!"

"Yes, but she's one hell of a waitress."

"I can't argue that point, but wouldn't it be nice if the boys could hire a competent waitress who was also a looker? Is that breed so rare? Stacy says Glenda's got the kind of face that makes him want to drive nails into it."

"What about your Katie, Jack? She pretty?"

"I used to think she was. That was before I got to know her. A bad personality can nullify physical beauty in a hurry. She's small, only five-one; she's got a turned up nose and a smallish mouth. It was her sweet ass that got my attention in the first place. She knew how to use it, too. Christ, Paul, how did I make such a mess of my life? What a schmuck I am. Believe me when I tell you, pal, I envy the living shit out of you."

"To be honest with you, Jack, I don't find much comfort in your envy. Remember, Laura was the one who walked out on me. I want her back, so don't waste your envy on me. My life at the moment is anything but enviable."

"Don't get sore, Paul. You know what I'm talking about."

"Just find somebody else to envy. Envy George Stacy. Didn't you tell me he married an intelligent woman?"

"Yeah, but intelligence isn't everything. She makes a lot of demands on George. And nobody's happier than Elaine that I'll be moving to the Boston area. She would have preferred that I go back to California, but she'll settle for Boston." Jack laughed. It had an edge to it, though. I think he was bothered by the fact that Elaine Stacy was eager to be rid of him and his influence on her husband. When George and Jack got together there was no way of predicting what would happen. I sympathized with Elaine Stacy.

SEVENTEEN

"I admit it. All right? The shit slinging unnerved me. Now can we drop the subject?"

"Look on the bright side, Paul," Doc said. "At least it took your mind off your marital problems for a little while."

"Yeah. I feel better already. Thanks."

"I should get a fan for behind the counter," Archie offered, lighting up his cigar stub. "That way, next time the shit starts flying it'll hit the fan instead of Paulie." Ray Duffy found this very amusing.

"Paul," Ray said, "Now you know what it's like to be shot at and missed, shit at and hit. At least the shit at and hit part."

The urchins had been conspicuously out of sight since Friday. I knew they were around; the tipped over trashcans along the sidewalk from Green Street to Kirkland Avenue attested to that fact.

"I tell you guys, it's going to take a supreme act of will to keep me from tracking down that smelly little bastard and kicking his ass to kingdom come," I announced.

Doc laughed. "Jail could be a good experience for you, Paul. Full-time employment; all the male companionship you could ever want. No wife to look after. Yes, jail could be the answer to all your problems, son."

"Thanks a lot."

"I'm joking, for Christ's sake. Can't you take a joke?"

"I'm better at taking a joke when I'm not the object of it."

All the needling I was getting from Archie and the boys made me less inclined to share the incident with Devlin. He would have his own wise-ass comments to make, and since he never frequented Archie's store it was unlikely that he would hear about it from another source.

* * *

It turned out that Doc's prediction came true — at least in part. Laura called around eleven-thirty my time. Her tone was very businesslike as she informed me that she had decided to begin divorce proceedings, and that I should expect to hear from her lawyer in due time. Once again I was struck speechless by her words. This time, however, she refrained from making any cracks about my theatrics, and expressed none of the exasperation I was getting used to hearing from her. No, she merely said what she had to say, and hung up.

Well, she could initiate divorce proceedings until she turned blue in the face. I had no intention of responding to them. The law didn't compel me to. Or did it? Maybe I should consider hiring a lawyer of my own. What a joke, considering my financial circumstances. I confess that, until recently, divorce was not a concept that I'd had much experience with. Nobody in my family that I knew of, either on my mother's side or my father's side, had ever been divorced. The parents of my friends remained so steadfastly married that I wouldn't have been surprised to learn that there had never been a divorce case in the city of Garrison. Now, it seemed, divorce was suddenly in vogue. Just the same, I never imagined it would ever come to that with Laura and me. But, as Laura would be sure to remind me, there were a great many things I was incapable of imagining.

I had been put off balance by her timing. I had even come to accept, or believed that I did, Laura's arguments for my pulling up stakes in Garrison and heading west. What now? There was no one I could talk to. Jack Scanlon would tell me that I had cause for celebration; he would envy me even more now that my estrangement from my wife was practically *official*. Doc would tell me to play the waiting game, that Laura would snap out of it eventually. Archie would commiserate but he would not comprehend. My mother was still in a state of mild depression over my father's untimely death, and to be truthful I was never able to confide in her about my personal life. The same was true of my sister and brother. I had no use for religion; I was of the same opinion as Doc on psychology and psychologists; I didn't believe in magic, palmistry, or astrology. I didn't frequent bars, so that left out bartenders as a potential source of counsel. What I was, I realized, was isolated; high and not so dry, surrounded by water in which swam sharks and piranha. The situation called for sleep.

* * *

"One good thing, I suppose, about not having a pot to piss in is that the divorce shouldn't be too complicated, or expensive. You can't have a tug of war over who gets what when there's nothing to get," I said to Devlin on the back steps. The weather had been pleasant today, with temperatures in the high sixties. I nursed a beer while Devlin took down more shots of rye than I could count. I had to work a shift at Archie's tonight for Duane.

"Suppose she'll want your cat and bird?"

"Yeah, probably."

Devlin laughed from deep down in his phlegmy throat. "Women," he said, shaking his head.

"Dave, thanks again for the tip on the job. I'm kind of desperate. Even if it only lasts for three weeks or a month, it'll keep my head above water."

"Sorry I couldn't be more helpful, Paul, but times are tough. You don't need me to tell you." Devlin had spotted an ad in last Friday's paper for temporary help in a traffic survey the city was conducting. It paid a buck seventy-five and hour and it was estimated that the actual survey would be conducted over a period of three weeks. If you were chosen to help with the processing of the data, they could use you an extra week. My unemployment benefits wouldn't be affected either. I planned to go the temporary headquarters of Tibbets, Abbot, McCarty, and Stratton first thing in the morning and put in an application.

* * *

As luck would have it, I would have no need to apply for the job in the morning. It was slow in the store, and no one was drinking in the back room. I stepped outside for a breath of cool evening air. I leaned against the telephone pole, my head for once void of thoughts of divorce, marriage, the meaning of life and death. I was so absorbed in nothing at all that when Sid Caplan pulled up to the curb he took me completely by surprise, because if I had seen him coming you can be sure I would have retreated into the store. Sid lowered his window and inserted a fresh cigarette between his lips while I just stood there as if my feet were cemented in their tracks.

"Nice weather," Sid said. "Cool. Way it ought to be this time of year." I didn't reply. "Listen, Embry, I don't blame you for being sore. You got a right. I just want you to know I realize now I was wrong. You know how I mean, Embry?"

"Not really, Sid."

"Let me explain. It was that Chessy. He was poison. It took me a long time to find out. He was clever; you know how I mean? It was there all along and I didn't see it. A lot of people didn't. Tommy, Kaiser, Gil Freese, a lot of people. You hear he got beat up bad? You hear that?"

"Chessy? No." I removed my hands from my pockets and took a step toward Sid's car.

"Yeah. In Rochester. He tried to pick up a young boy, and the kid went and told his older brother and his friends. They went to Chessy's house and waited for him to come home. They put him in the hospital, Embry. That's when the stories started to come out; even the guys in the store had things to say about him. He was a vindictive man, Embry, but I'm not telling you anything you don't know. I couldn't see it." Sid shook his head in disbelief at his own inability to see the real Chessy

Chessman. "Hard to believe, a guy with a wife and kids. I can't understand people like that; can you, Embry?"

"Why tell me all this?" Even if Sid's words sounded like sweet music to my ears, I was dubious of the source. Part of me, a large part of me, didn't trust Sid any farther than I could have thrown him.

"I just want to set things straight, Embry. I figure I owe you at least that much. I had to let him go, of course. That Justin, what's-his-name, quit right after I got rid of Chessy. They were pretty close."

"I figured that."

"I'm asking you to come back, Embry. I'll raise your pay a half a dollar an hour. You work hard, I'll make you inventory and purchasing manager, just like Chessy. Forget what I said about bettering yourself and all that. I was out of line. You should get your education; you're a smart kid."

"I don't know what to say." I didn't know what to say. It was becoming a chronic condition with me, not being able to respond to people—like my wife, and now Sid Caplan—when their words touched my emotional tender spots. I was all at once conscious of my heartbeat, and my palms were all slimy with sweat. I wiped them on my trousers.

"Take your time. Think about it. I'd appreciate it, though, if you'd get back to me one way or the other as soon as you can." And then Sid was gone, his long black Cadillac moving slowly down Washington Street in the direction of his store.

* * *

My ambivalence must have been showing when Sid greeted me the next morning. He invited me to follow him to his tiny office. I had stopped outside the store for a look through the double-paned windows into the office where I once worked. Phil, the crippled boy, was seated at the inventory trays.

"You don't look sure, Embry. You know how I mean? You don't look like you know for sure."

"I can't help how I look, Sid, but I know how I feel. I want to come back to work. I mean it."

"You sure, Embry?"

"I'm sure. Maybe I should ask if there's any work to come back to."

"Business was slow there for awhile," Sid said, turning his eyes this way and that, avoiding eye contact with me as was his habit with everyone he talked to. "Things are starting to pick up. It goes in cycles; you know how I mean? You'll have the office to yourself. Tommy's doing Chessy's work, on top of his own. I'll have him show you the ropes. A month or two you'll know as much as Chessy did. I got to know you're sure, though, Embry. I got to be able to count on you."

"You can count on me, Sid. When can I start?"

"Tomorrow? Can you come in tomorrow?"

"Will there be any overtime?"

"All you can handle. It comes in cycles. You know how I mean?"

Sid's handshake was moist—soft and tentative. In spite of the insincerity I suspected was lurking in Sid's heart, I felt my own heart pounding in my chest as I left Sid Caplan's Auto Supply store.

EIGHTEEN

"What'd I tell you, Paul? Didn't I tell you the Yanks would clinch?" Devlin reminded me for about the third time since the New York Yankees actually did clinch the American League pennant maybe three or four days ago. The first time he gloated about his prediction come true, he followed, as an afterthought, with news of the Birmingham church bombings in which four Negro kids had been killed. The news put me in mind of what Jack Scanlon had said to me only last Saturday. His words, now, struck me as prophetic. Maybe he was right, maybe it was time I got back in touch with the world, if I had ever been in touch with it. I wondered what Laura, with her highly developed social conscience, would make of the bombing. It wouldn't surprise me if she packed up and headed south to march and protest, and make a general pain in the ass of herself.

"I expect the Dodgers will clinch their pennant in a few days. Then we'll see who's the best team in baseball." Devlin raised his shot glass, as if to offer a toast to major league baseball.

"So, which team do you like, Dave? You lean toward the Dodgers if I remember correctly." I was careful to needle Devlin before he imbibed too many shots and chose to take offense at my kidding.

"Yankees in five. I'll wash and wax your car if I'm wrong. That's a promise."

"Don't forget the new engine."

"Hah."

"I'm going back to work for Sid tomorrow. What do you think of that, Dave?" I filled Devlin in on my encounter with Sid.

"Ain't that something?" Devlin shook his head, as if in disbelief, a wry smile on his lips. "Imagine the nerve of the little hebe ..."

"Well, I think it must have taken some courage to come to me and admit he'd made a mistake. It was the last thing I would have expected him to do. You have to respect him for that."

"I don't have to do shit. Ask yourself this, my boy: what's in it for him? Those people don't give nothing away without there's strings attached to it. There's always something in it for them. Mark my words."

"He gets the benefit of my employment." I meant it as a joke, but Devlin apparently didn't have his irony detection unit turned on this evening.

"Just watch your ass with that little chiseler, Paul. You know his reputation. Everybody in town knows about Sid Caplan. Shake hands with him, you better count your fingers afterward."

Remembering Sid's mushy grip, I couldn't imagine him removing fingers from my own hand. Besides, where did Devlin get his information on Sid Caplan? Devlin didn't even own a car.

"You got another letter returned today, Devlin. When you going to learn?" Maggie shouted from the kitchen.

"Ah Jesus! Goddamn government with their numbers. What's this zip code crap supposed to accomplish, can you tell me that, Paul? As if we haven't got enough numbers to keep in our head already, they have to invent more? Before you know it we'll all be just numbers. Goddamn government. Goddamn Kennedy. Country should've known better'n elect a Catholic. Next thing, we'll be taking our orders from Rome."

I'd cast my absentee ballot for the "Catholic" in 1960. It was my first vote for a political candidate. I remember feeling secretly proud and enfranchised. I planned to vote for Kennedy in 1964, no matter who ran against him. I liked the man's style; I liked the way he handled the Cuban missile crisis last fall. I also knew better than to reveal to Devlin, or to any of my co-workers at Sid's, my feelings about Kennedy because the anti-Kennedy sentiment among these people bordered on virulent. If I argued with Devlin for Kennedy on the virtue of his actions during the Cuban missile affair he'd hit me with Bay of Pigs. I'd learned that political arguments with Dave Devlin were best avoided. And I didn't want to admit that I had no idea what "zip code" referred to.

"Get used to it," Maggie said. "Either that, or let me pay the bills."

"You're more than welcome to pay the bills, my dear. You are the bookkeeper in the family. What do you say to some TV, Paul? New show supposed to be starting tonight. Something called "The Fugitive" or some such thing. Sounds pretty good from the ads."

"Don't think so, Dave. Got bills of my own to pay."

"Yeah, well don't forget to write down the goddamn zip code on your envelopes." Devlin shook his head in exasperation.

I bid my neighbors goodnight, and returned to my apartment to find J. Alfred Prufrock dead on the bottom of his cage. I sat down on my rock hard love seat, buried my face in my hands, and actually wept. Honcho rubbed against my legs until I picked him up and held him to my chest. When I finished crying, I wrapped the bird in an old *Garrison Record* and buried him in the back yard near one of Harry Pappas's hemlocks.

Later, I asked myself where this powerful feeling of sorrow had come from. My wife's leaving and subsequent announcement that she was after an actual divorce hadn't produced as much emotion in me. I wasn't up on psychology, but I could just hear Laura on the subject: Prufrock's death acted like an emotional catalyst for me by finding an outlet for the pent up grief that resulted from my wife's abandoning me. Yes, that sounded like the kind of nonsense I'd get from her.

Then I began to feel guilty, putting the blame for the bird's death on myself because, since Honcho's return, I had neglected the thing. I never took it out of its cage anymore to perch on my shoulder, to nuzzle its musky head in my ear, to wander down my arm to dip its beak in my beer glass. I picked up Honcho; he purred loudly into my chest.

NINETEEN

I returned to my old job at Caplan's Auto Supply to find a large volume of work to post to the inventory cards. Phil had been trying to keep up with inventory and do his own job at the same time; the way Tommy was doing double duty, with Chessy gone. Work for me was tonic; it kept my mind off the things that troubled me.

"Check a number for me, will you, Paul," old Harry Lamb from Ukiah, California said, standing in the doorway in his gray work smock.

"What have you got, Harry?" Harry recited the stock number for a leaf spring.

"Good to see you back on the job, Paul."

"Thanks, Harry. It's good to be back. Card shows two in stock."

"Couldn't find 'em. Better look again. Eyes aren't what they used to be."

"That ain't all," Tommy Laroche piped in from the next office.

"And you can kiss my arse," Harry replied, starting to grow red in the face, and to breathe heavily, "you Ethiopian ..."

"Now, calm down, Harry. Remember your blood pressure, you old goat," Tommy said, as if he were talking to a child.

"I got your blood pressure," Harry said.

I held up a stack of sales slip that hadn't been posted. "Maybe it's in here. Let me go through them before you waste your time looking again, all right, Harry?" But Harry stalked off muttering to himself before I could finish. I said to Tommy, "How would you like to be responsible for giving Harry a stroke or a heart attack?"

"Harry can take it. He been taking it for twenty-two years. Phil, get me accounts receivable, will you?"

I was dying to ask Tommy Laroche about the Chessy Chessman incident, but I didn't quite know how to broach the subject. For all I knew, there could be hard feelings among some of the guys in the store, hard feelings over Sid's decision to let Chessy go. I had always assumed that Tommy and the rest of the guys had a lot of respect for Chessy, at least for his competence as a worker if not for the man himself. For this reason I was reluctant to bring up the matter. Still, I was eager to know everything; part of me wanted to savor whatever vindication might come my way as a result of Chessy Chessman's great fall.

Phil's legs were in braces, and he needed to strap those aluminum canes on his wrists every time he got out of his chair. To get up and cross the room to the file cabinet to fetch Tommy's accounts receivable ledger took a great effort for him. Why Tommy Laroche couldn't get off his butt and get the ledger himself baffled and infuriated me. I kept my mouth shut; at the moment I didn't need more conflict in my life. Phil, uncomplaining, clop-clopped across the room on Tommy's errand.

"So when is it you plan to teach me everything that's worth knowing about purchasing and inventory control?"

"Soon as I finish accounts receivable I'll be over to give you your first lesson. Pay attention 'cause there'll be a test."

"I appreciate it."

"No problem."

* * *

Gil Freese, one of the countermen, and a golf nut, especially on the subject of Arnold Palmer, came into the office to check a part number. Before I was fired, Freese was constantly after me to join him for a round of Sunday afternoon golf. Laura considered golf a *bourgeois* pastime. She expressed disbelief when I showed a mild interest in going out to play. The truth was I secretly wanted to go out to the links with Freese, not because I had any interest in golf so much as to do something that did not involve my wife. But as usual, I deferred to her. Now, here was Gil Freese bringing up the subject of golf again.

"Hey, this time of year's perfect. No fucking bugs, not too hot. Come on, for Christ's sake. The snow'll be flying before you know it."

"All right. Why not? Can you pick me up? My car's not running."

"Sure thing. How's eleven o'clock?"

"Yeah, sounds good," I said, not remembering, until Freese had left the office, that I had to work at Archie's on Sunday. I'd ask Duane to cover for me for the afternoon.

* * *

I had a set of rusted old Ben Hogan irons, and a two-wood with a deep gouge in the clubface, in a cloth bag stored in the shed in back of Mrs. Pappas's house. The irons were all odd-numbered, and the grips were dry and starting to peel off the handles. I could find nothing in the set that resembled a putter. I pulled the two-wood out of the bag and made a few practice swings. I hadn't held a golf club in my hands since before I joined the Army. I had played maybe five times in my entire life. As a kid, I'd caddied at the Garrison Country Club where I developed a strong aversion to the sport, mainly because of the pompous, self-indulgent, materialistic, and dishonest people that I encountered on the job. All of these traits I came to associate with the game, so when Laura expressed her opinion about golf I was in no position, in my own mind, to argue for its virtue. What lure there was for me to accept Gil Freese's invitation now, I could not explain. Maybe he would have a spare putter I could borrow. I'd have to pop for some used balls, too, because the ones in the pocket of my ratty bag all wore big smiles.

* * *

The Glen Lea Golf Club was a nine-hole public course that got a lot of play, especially on weekends. It was wide open, featureless, and appealed to the lower tier player, of which Gil Freese and I were clearly members. As fanatic a golf enthusiast as Gil Freese was, he managed only three or four rounds a season. By anyone's definition, of course, I was no golfer. Despite the infrequency of his play, Gil Freese had high expectations for his game today.

"I feel a good round coming on," he said, as we turned into the parking lot in his Ford pickup. "Today's the day I break a hundred. I feel it right here." Freese pointed in the direction of his belly, or maybe it was his groin he pointed to.

"I'd consider it a personal triumph if I broke a hundred for nine," I said. "What do they get for greens fees?"

"Four bucks. We should be able to get in eighteen if it's not too crowded. I gotta get back by five."

"What do they want for used balls?"

"Don't worry about balls. I got a bushel basket of them in my garage."

"You wouldn't happen to have an extra putter."

"No. Share mine. What fucking century do those clubs belong to?" Freese said as I pulled my cloth bag of rusty clubs from the back of his pickup. "I can feel it, Embry. Right here. Right in the gut."

There were three foursomes ahead of us. The third group offered to let us tee off ahead of them. Freese declined; he didn't want the worry of a twosome holding up a foursome. It could ruin his concentration. As anyone might have predicted, another foursome arrived behind us just as we were ready to tee off.

"Put them out of your mind, Gil," I counseled. "Concentrate on your own game." Nothing should be allowed to distract Gil Freese from his mission to break one hundred on this fine September day.

Freese's tee shot curled right in a vicious banana-shaped trajectory. The first fairway was so wide, so amorphous, that he was still in play even if he was farther away from the green than he had been from the tee. I dribbled my ball off the tee with a mighty swing that caused me to lose my balance enough to nearly bring me to the ground. My ball came to rest behind the women's tee box.

"You know what this means, don't you, Embry?"

"Yeah, it means I've still got a long way to the green. Not as far as you, though."

"That's not what it means, Embry."

"What are you talking about?"

"I guess you don't know nothing about golf etiquette, do you. If your drive doesn't make it past the ladies' tee you have to play the rest of the round with your dick out."

I laughed. "That sounds like high etiquette, all right. I suppose this is in the rule book."

I flailed at the little ball nine more times before finally arriving on the first green of the par four hole. Twice I had outright fanned. The only good shot I produced was my last five-iron, which I struck solidly. I two-putted with Gil Freese's ancient putter (and he had the nerve to comment on the vintage of my clubs) for an eleven. Gil had not fared much better, finishing the hole with a nine, after four-putting.

"We'll get it together next hole," Freese said, undaunted. But the next hole was only slightly better than the first. I tried to summon the address, stance, and swing that had translated into that solid five-iron, but it was no good. When I wasn't whiffing, I was chunking, shanking, and topping the ball. The only place I enjoyed any success was on the green. By the fifth hole, Gil Freese had run his score up to thirty-five; I'd stopped recording my own score after the fourth hole. He was in a serious funk by the sixth hole, a short par three with a shallow stream running halfway between tee and green. Gil chunked his tee shot into the stream, and then hurled his seven-iron into the stream after his ball.

"That's fucking it," he screamed on the eleventh green after four-putting for about the fifth time. He broke his putter in two over his knee, and left the pieces next to the flagstick.

"Gee, this is really a lot of fun," I said.

"Let's get the fuck out of here."

We left Glen Lea Golf Club, Gil Freese's bag several clubs lighter, and headed back to Garrison. Gil had little to say on the ride back. I vowed never to set foot on a golf course again if I lived to be a hundred.

TWENTY

"Hey, Arnie," Tommy Laroche said to me as I came in the office, "I hear you broke the course record over at Glen Lea yesterday. You and Julius."

"I never pretended to be a golfer."

"Right. But I hear around that you're some kind of a pool shark."

"Where did you hear that?"

"I got my sources."

"Sure you do, Laroche."

"Well, just how good are you, Embry? I've always heard that good pool players were good golfers, so I gotta wonder just how good of a pool player you really are."

"I have no idea where you got the connection between playing pool and playing golf, but my guess is that I'm at least better than you are. I'd guess that you wouldn't even have to be a 'pool shark,' as you put it, to be better than you."

"You hear that, Brother James? Mister Embry guesses that he's better than me. Those are pretty strong words, don't you think, Brother James?" Tommy Laroche snapped his chewing gum between his teeth as his fingers danced over the keys of his calculator.

"Maybe you ought to have a game," Brother James said, sounding bored, as he licked his fingers and turned the pages of a parts catalog. "Then there'd be no doubt who was best, would there?"

"Hey, I'm not about to play some pool shark even," Tommy said. "I'd need to be spotted."

"What if I spot you twenty-five balls in a fifty pointer?" I said without thinking, and realized that Larorche had got under my skin, had made me angry.

"Twenty-five? You're on. Let's say for twenty bucks. How's that sound to you?"

"Just say when and where." I had no idea how good a player Tommy Laroche was. It seems I had let my anger and my pride corner me. I didn't like to think about having to cough up twenty dollars to anybody, let alone Tommy Laroche.

"All right. Tonight. Frenchie's; ten-thirty."

"Why so late?"

"I got to watch my shows."

"All right. Ten-thirty."

* * *

I arrived at Frenchie's a half-hour early to get in a little practice before I'd have to clash with Tommy Laroche in a game of straight pool. What had I been thinking of to offer the jerk a twenty-five point spot? I hadn't played seriously since I got married.

A couple of old timers were playing one-ball on table six; there were no other customers in the house. I had hoped that there wouldn't be an audience for my match tonight. Frenchie sat behind the counter reading a fuck book. He logged me onto table one without a glance in my direction. Table one, where the titans clashed. I didn't feel very much like a "titan" at the moment. My stomach was already aflutter, and Tommy Laroche wasn't even on the scene yet. I broke open the rack and played a few long shots, some acute angle shots, and shots with the cue ball flush against the rail. My hands shook badly. I miscued twice in my first three tries.

Tommy Laroche came through the door at ten-thirty on the nose, carrying a narrow leather case. He unzipped it and assembled his cue stick. I could feel the sweat standing out on my forehead, and starting to course down my sides.

It had been about this time in September, six years ago, when Jack Scanlon and I had the good fortune of bumping into Dick and Don, two door-to-door vacuum cleaner salesmen who were working Garrison and the seacoast area for a couple of months.

* * *

Jack and I are tied at one hundred-twelve in a hundred twenty-five pointer, when these two older guys, each dressed in sports jacket and tie, walk through the door. Frenchie assigns them to table four, next to ours. One of the guys is about my height with wavy blond hair; I think he's maybe twenty-five or thirty years old—I'm no good with people's age. The other guy is a good six feet tall; he is beefy, and his jacket is too small for his frame. He wears his brown hair in a crew cut. They start up a game of eight ball.

Jack has a perfect angle for a shot in the corner pocket that can break the rack wide open. He breaks the rack to smithereens but misses his easy shot, and I run thirteen balls to win the game. Jack makes a big show of slapping a ten-dollar bill on the table to pay me off; we didn't have a bet on the game. Before I can say anything, Jack winks at me. I don't know what he has up his sleeve. He tilts his head toward the guys at the next table, who have had their eye on us.

"So you guys like to play for money?" says the blond-haired guy.

"As long as it's friendly," Jack says.

"Well, how about a friendly game of nine ball, then?"

"You guys wouldn't be hustlers, would you?" Jack says with a sly grin. The big guy laughs and explains that the only hustling they do is with vacuum cleaners.

"We prefer three-six-nine around these parts. Makes for a bigger pay day," Jack Scanlon, Mister Cool, says.

"So, three-six-nine," the blond guy says. They introduce themselves, hands out to shake. The blond guy's name is Don something; the big guy is Dick something.

Jack puts away the striped high balls except for the nine, and gets the diamond shaped rack from the hook. "Same rules, just three pay balls instead of one. What kind of action were you thinking?"

"What about a dollar a ball?" Don says.

"Hey, we're just high school kids with no means of support," Jack says.

"All right, a half a buck a ball, then?"

Jack looks at me, his eyes bright. I know what he's thinking. He's thinking we've hooked a couple of fish. I don't share his confidence, and all I've got to my name is six bucks. Who knows what Jack has got in his pocket? The ten he gave me belongs to him, but for all I know that's all he's carrying.

After a few games it's clear to me that only one of these guys is a fish. Don shoots a very good stick and he's a cool customer; he never chokes when there's a pay-ball in front of him. The way Jack is signaling me with his eyes I get the idea he wants to team up against these guys; to set each other up whenever the opportunity arises, and in such a way that the door-to-door vacuum cleaner salesmen don't get wise to our game. Jack had made sure, when he dispensed the Kelly pool pills out to determine the order of play, that our turns came in order. That way if one of us has no chance for a pay ball on our shot, we can at least set up the other one for a crack at it. The understanding, of course, is that we will split our winnings.

It's a school night and I have a ten o'clock curfew. Jack Scanlon has no such curfew on him. As ten o'clock approaches, I calculate that we're about four bucks ahead, not much for almost five hours work. I can't bring myself to admit to the salesmen that I, a senior in high school, have to report home by ten o'clock. They have removed their jackets, loosened their neckties, and turned up the cuffs of their shirtsleeves. These guys are just getting warmed up. And I know Jack isn't ready to cut and run for a lousy two bucks apiece. We continue to play.

I sink the three ball on the break, and get hot for a little while, running the first four balls and setting myself up for an easy combination for the six, a pay ball, off the five. Then I sink the five and run the rest of the table for a total of five pay balls. Five bucks in a single rack. I'm ready to rest on my laurels, and I see by the clock behind the counter that it's eleven-fifteen.

"That's going to do it for me, guys," I announce, and head for the cue rack.

"Jesus," says Dick. "You're gonna quit now, you as hot as a firecracker? It's early. Stick around."

"I got homework for tomorrow." I've got no homework. None of the guys I hang around with do homework, or at least admit to doing it. The math I have to do I can get done in third period study hall.

"How about you, Jack? You good for some more action?" Dick asks.

"Hell yes."

I'm not sure how Jack will fare head to head against Don, so I agree to play until midnight. My mother will worry, but she won't question me when I tell her I was studying math at Max's house and lost track of time. She would never dream that her little boy was hustling pool in Frenchie's sinister establishment. My mom's as gullible as they come. My dad would have been asleep since eight o'clock because he has to get up at 4:00 a.m. every morning. I had to keep those hours myself last summer when I worked at the bakery. I discovered last summer that I'm no morning person.

By midnight we have squeezed about nine bucks out of our traveling salesmen. Not a bad night's work for a couple of high school kids.

In the weeks ahead, we get to be regulars at table five as we bang heads with Dick and Don. Jack and I cease our collusion before they catch on to our game. We stop splitting our winnings too; it's now every man for himself. It turns out that Dick is the only one of the four of us who consistently ends the evening losing money. None of us wins big, but poor Dick seems to be losing big. I begin to feel sorry for the poor sap, but Dick is a cheerful loser, always eager to get on with the game because, like every fish I've ever met, Dick doesn't know he's a fish.

One night, after we finish, Don offers to buy us coffee at the Ramble Inn. It is a pleasant enough way to pass a half hour. Don and Dick reveal that their paths crossed at an Electrolux workshop for new salesmen in Newport News, Virginia. Dick is from Scranton, Pennsylvania; Don hails from Dubuque, Iowa.

Jack wants to know if they get a lot of action from housewives in their business. Jack tries to come off like a man of the world, but I know for a fact that he's never gone all the way with a girl. Neither have I, and I'd bet a buck that most of the guys I hang around with have never made it with a girl no matter how much they brag about all the nooky they're getting.

Don and Dick glance at each other and smile knowingly. Don looks more like a ladies' man than Dick, and I'm inclined to believe him when he tells us, in an offhand way, that he once dated Theresa Brewer before she hit the big time. I know that Jack has no use for country singers like Theresa Brewer or Brenda Lee, but he's impressed enough that Don has consorted with a celebrity, even if she wasn't a celebrity, as such, when Don consorted with her. He doesn't reveal his feelings about country music, "hillbilly" music as he refers to it, to Don and Dick who have made no bones about the fact that they're both big fans. Jack Scanlon is not without a certain tact and sensitivity. He wants to know from Don, however, what kind of a fuck she was. In Jack's mind, when an older guy dates a girl, it follows, like daylight follows night, that he's going to get into her pants.

Don just flashes an enigmatic grin, and winks. "My guess is that neither one of you guys has a steady," Don observes.

"Who wants to be tied down?" Jack replies. "We'll all be wearing the ball and chain soon enough. Me, I want to grab all the freedom I can get."

We learn that both Don and Dick are married, with young kids. And they speak of infidelity as casually as if it is axiomatic that a man, by his very nature, is destined to roam. For reasons I can't comprehend, I'm not comfortable with this view. Of course, I say no such thing.

By November, our door-to-door salesmen buddies move on to new territory north of Garrison. Jack and I discover that we miss their company. We took a fair chunk of change out of Dick's pocket, but it isn't the income we are missing; it's more like saying goodbye to a couple of older brothers who we could be ourselves with.

* * *

On impulse, I went to the rack to exchange my eighteen-ounce cue for a seventeen ouncer. I rolled it on the table to test for warp, and chalked up.

"You want to take a few practice shots before we start?" I asked Tommy.

"No. I'm ready."

"Then let's lag for break."

I won the lag. Tommy tried the standard safety on the break by kissing the corner ball with the cue ball. He hit the rack too flush and broke four balls out. I ran them off, but wasn't able to position myself for a shot that would break open the rack. I played a safety, leaving Tommy without a clear shot. My nerves had settled down. Tommy's attempt at a safety resulted in a scratch. I ran off four more balls and stitched my opponent with another perfect safety. By now, I sensed that Tommy was growing impatient with this style of play, as I took a page from Sherm

Hubbard's—Garrison's own local hustler—game book. It became clear to me during the first rack that Tommy Laroche was no pool player, even if he owned a custom cue stick.

I won the first rack thirteen to one. In less than a half hour I won the match in the fifth rack before Tommy could slide sixteen buttons on his side of the wire.

"You're too good, fast Paulie," Tommy Laroche said, laying two crisp ten-dollar bills on the felt. "I'll be home in time for the end of the news, and Johnny's monologue," he said, unscrewing his custom cue stick with the red dragon on the shaft.

"Loser pays for the table," Frenchie said, without lifting his eyes from his book. Tommy laid a buck on the counter in front of him on his way out.

"This cover it?"

"Yeah. You got change coming."

"Keep it. See you tomorrow, Paul." Tommy Laroche, the good loser, said goodnight and left for home and the eleven o'clock news.

"You shoot a pretty nice stick," Frenchie said, coming over to turn off the light over table number one.

"I didn't think you were watching."

"Come around tomorrow night. Tuesdays, there's usually some action."

It had been a long time since I had felt anything except gloom mixed with despair. On the walk back to my apartment on this crisp September night, two smooth ten spots in my pocket, I felt almost buoyant. I was fast Eddie Felsen in *The Hustler*.

TWENTY-ONE

"S'posed to get below freezing tonight," Devlin said, breaking a long silence between us. I think he sensed that I had gone somewhere inside myself, which I suppose I had, and it made him uneasy. I butted my cigarette out in the coffee cup we used as an ashtray. The sun was going down, and the air had taken on a sudden chill after a day of warm sunshine with temperatures in the mid-sixties. It had been over a week since my wife had spoken of her intention to begin divorce proceedings against me. I had checked the mailbox every day in anticipation of that official looking envelope that would change my life in ways that my life had never been changed before. "It's not right, I know," Devlin continued, "but to be honest with you, young man, I'm glad to see you back on the butts."

"It's good to be back. I missed smoking. It's one of the few real pleasures I seem to have left."

Devlin had become animated now that I seemed willing to talk again. "I been smoking cigarettes since I was nine years old and I ain't the worst for it. Nobody I know ever missed a day's work because of their smoking."

I wondered how many days of work Devlin had missed in his life because of rye whiskey.

At work today, Tommy Laroche had made no mention of the fact that, the night before, I had relieved him of twenty of his hard earned dollars in a game of straight pool in which I'd spotted him half the balls he needed to win. It took all my will not to bring the subject up myself. Brother James had either forgotten about our match and our bet, or had been instructed by Tommy to keep his mouth shut. I was tempted to brag to Devlin about my triumph, but something stopped me. Such boasts struck me as unseemly. Now I felt warmed by my own rectitude as I congratulated myself on my restraint.

"You heard anything from the wife yet?"

"Nope. It's like waiting for an execution."

"C'mon, Paul. Don't look it that way. It'll be over before you know it. Then you can get on with your life."

Devlin finished off his shot, and used the handrail to pull himself to the standing position. He wore a brown cardigan sweater over his white work shirt. Devlin looked older in the failing light, as if he had put on ten years overnight. I turned away as he stood there, stoop-shouldered, on the landing. "Sure I can't get you a shot?"

"No thanks, Dave."

"A beer?"

"I'm all set, really." I lit up another cigarette, as if to prove to Devlin that I wasn't a complete ascetic.

"You'll pardon me while I get myself another," Devlin said, shuffling, in his slippered feet, to his kitchen door.

I heard Maggie's voice, then Devlin's voice rise in anger. The battle was on.

* * *

I had just put on the Jacques Loussier record that Laura had bought for me, and I had not listened to yet, when the phone rang giving me a start because it had been silent for over a week. I hurried to the kitchen, thinking that it had to be Laura.

"I missed you," Noelle said. "Can I come over?" I didn't answer right away, taken by surprise by the sound of Noelle's, not Laura's, voice.

"That probably wouldn't be a good idea." I told Noelle about Laura's divorce edict. I argued that I didn't want to advance her case against me by engaging in adultery with her former best friend.

"Aren't you a little late with that concern?"

"I suppose you're right, but why add fuel to the fire?"

"Don't be naïve, Paul."

"I just don't think it would be a good idea."

"Nonsense. I'll be right over." Noelle hung up before I could protest.

Then, in a bizarre confluence, the phone rang as Noelle was knocking on my door and entering without waiting to be invited in. I excused myself and went in the kitchen to answer the phone.

"Oh, Paul. What an absolute bitch I've been. I wouldn't blame you if you never wanted to speak to me again."

"Laura?" And now Noelle was on me like fly paper, her arms wrapped around my waist. I put my hand over the mouthpiece. "For Christ's sake, Noelle, it's Laura," I whispered. "Knock it off." Noelle laughed her crazy laugh, and reached down the front of my trousers.

"Paul, darling? Please speak to me," my wife said. I grabbed Noelle's arm and tried to detach her from me. She resisted, giggling like a teenybopper. "What is it, Paul? Are you there?"

"I'll be waiting in the other room," Noelle said, skipping out of the kitchen.

"I'm sorry, Laura," I said, trying to compose myself. "I guess hearing your voice took my breath away."

"This isn't the first time that's happened, Paul. I'm so sorry."

"How are the divorce proceedings coming along?"

"I deserve that. I know now that I never meant to go through with it. I just wanted to hurt you the way you and Noelle hurt me. I ..."

"Well, you made a believer out of me."

"In case you haven't noticed, I'm not the libertine I make myself out to be."

"I don't seem to have noticed much where it concerns you, Laura."

"Please don't be cold, Paul. I can't bear it. Get angry, scream at me. Just don't be cold." My wife started to sob. What she was hearing from me was more fear than coldness, because I was all too conscious of Noelle's presence, no doubt in my bedroom, in my bed.

"I'm just confused, Laura. You can understand that. I don't know which way is up anymore." Noelle laughed out loud from the other room. I clamped my hand over the mouthpiece again.

"What was that?" Laura asked.

"That was ... Maggie. Devlin must have said something that tickled her."

"Oh, Maggie. I miss them so. Paul, can you get Maggie on the line? I want to say hello."

"Uh, I don't think so, Laura. She's pretty torched right now. You know how they are by this time of night. I think they're getting warmed up for their fight." This brought on another peal of laughter from Noelle.

"So now you've taken her as your mistress? Paul, how could you do this to me?"

"Maggie? Are you insane?"

"Didn't you think I'd recognize Noelle's obscene laugh? Of course, that's what you wanted, wasn't it?"

"Laura, wait ..." I said to the dial tone.

Noelle's slacks, blouse, underwear, and Capezios were in a pile on my bedroom floor. Noelle sat up in bed, sheet pulled up to her naked waist. She crooked her forefinger at me and beckoned, with a salacious grin.

* * *

"So, how long have you had this clairvoyance, Noelle?" I asked her, rolling over. It had to have been something like clairvoyance that brought her to my apartment at the precise moment of my wife's call. She attached herself to my back and slid her hand over my thigh and began to stroke it. "You can't get enough, can you?"

"No, I can't." She nipped at my shoulder with her sharp teeth. "I did it eleven times in one day with four different guys when I was a sophomore."

"High school?"

"College, of course. I was a virgin all through high school. Laura, too."

"Yeah, she claimed that."

"It's true. And all through college; you were her first. Trust me. But what a flirt!" I suppose I should have believed Laura when she proclaimed her virginity; she certainly defended it valiantly during our courtship, despite all my efforts to convince her to give it up. Her ineptitude in bed on our wedding night should have clinched it for me, but there was always a nagging doubt in my mind. As Noelle had said, she was a flirt, sometimes brazen in her coquettishness. Hearing what Noelle had to say about her gave me a feeling of acute longing for my wife.

"You are hopelessly oversexed, Noelle. Whatever possessed you to marry?"

"We girls don't stay young and appealing to men for long. I was afraid of ending up an old maid, manless and sexless. What a fool I was to fall for William."

"Give the devil his due. Hasn't he tried to give you what you need in that department?"

"I don't need perversion. I need tenderness." Her hand found its way to my cock. "Wake up. Get busy. Noelle needs you."

I had nothing against sex as a physical act in itself, but women had a way of taking the fun out of it with their behavior after you were done with it. I was never big on pillow talk and all the other post-coital ritual that women seemed to cherish in the name of "intimacy."

When I finished with Noelle I was physically and spiritually exhausted. I wanted to sleep. Noelle wanted to talk, to tickle me, to bite me.

"When was the last time you changed your sheets?"

"That was Laura's job. I never got the hang of sheets."

"They're beginning to smell really bad."

The only odor I was conscious of at the moment was the low-tide smell of Noelle's sex. I didn't feel equal to the task of dealing with bed sheets at the Laundromat. It was a big enough challenge for me to get my underwear clean. Maybe I should turn on Mrs. Pappas's beast of a fan and drive the stink of sex out of the room. The idea of having to lug the thing back downstairs to her cellar added to my general sense of total fatigue. The phone rang; I tensed and rolled over on my back.

"Aren't you going to answer it? You know it's Laura. She'll want to say she's sorry for hanging up on you. She'll tell you it's all her fault, but she won't mean it. She'll despise us forever for what she thinks we've done to her. I know her."

"Do you think you could refrain from braying like a donkey if I answer it?"

"I'll be good." But Noelle's eyes were all mischief. Yet I wanted desperately to answer the phone, to talk to my wife, to make things right again. I didn't believe Noelle's assessment of Laura's motives.

"It took you long enough to answer. Playing house with Noelle? Sorry if I interrupted."

"I just walked in the door. I went out for a pack of smokes."

"Good God. You haven't gone back. How could you, Paul?"

"It wasn't that hard."

"I suppose I'm to blame. Look at all the bad habits you've picked up in the short time you've been out of my sight."

"I don't consider seven weeks a short time."

"Please tell me you're not seeing Noelle."

I doubted that I could convince anybody, let alone my wife, that Noelle's arrival in my apartment at the precise moment she called was pure coincidence. "I'm not seeing Noelle. She's nothing to me. You'll have to take my word for it. She came by tonight out of the blue. I wasn't expecting her.

"I want to believe you, Paul, I really do."

"Come home and I'll prove it to you."

"No, Paul. You come here. You won't regret it. I promise you."

"This is beginning to feel like *déjà vu.*"

"I've thought about this for a long time, Paul. I'm convinced now more than ever that we have to get away from Garrison if it's the last thing we do. As far away as we can."

"Okay, let's go to Australia, or Hong Kong, or Shanghai. Why does it have to be San Francisco?"

"Are you trying to be cute?"

"Sid took me back."

"Have you no pride? Did you actually go back there with that awful man, those awful men?"

"Easy for you to say. What was I supposed to do, live on unemployment and the buck an hour I earn part time at Archie's? And where you were coming from made the decision a cinch. He gave me a half a buck an hour raise. I'm knocking down two-twenty-four an hour, and there's plenty of overtime."

"I know you want more than that, Paul. At least I thought you did."

"Yeah, two-fifty an hour would be nice."

"Be flip all you want, but you're going to have to face facts sooner or later. There is no future for you in Garrison, Paul. There certainly isn't a future for *us* in that place."

"So I've been told." Noelle poked her head into the kitchen and mouthed *goodbye,* and *call me.* My hand went instinctively over the mouthpiece.

"How are my babies?"

"They're fine. Honcho is forbidden to leave the apartment." I didn't have the gumption to tell her about J. Alfred. She'd find a way to lay the blame on me, blame I was capable of taking on.

"That isn't natural for an animal, Paul, but I understand your concern."

"Not natural? Cats are domesticated. They're bred to be happy indoors or out."

"That's such nonsense. Let's not argue. All right?"

"That's fine with me. How's the job scene?"

"I've got what I think is a good lead on a position with a product design firm. I go for my interview tomorrow. I feel good about this one, Paul."

"Great. Good luck with the interview."

"If I get this job everything else will fall into place. As soon as I find a decent place for us to live you can come out, and …"

"And what do you suppose I'll do with myself out there? You don't paint such a rosy picture of the employment opportunities where you are. They don't sound any more promising than they do here. At least for a guy like me, who can't do diddly. I repeat, what do think I'll do?"

"Go to school is what you'll do."

"And you expect to earn enough on your own to support us in that city? Be real, Laura."

"I've got enough in my trust to tide us over until we get on our feet."

"I don't know, Laura. You know how I feel about this. I don't cotton to the idea of being kept."

"You and your male pride. You infuriate me. Times are changing, Paul. This isn't your father's world, or my father's world anymore."

"Now you're sounding like Devlin."

"He sees the trend; he's just got its meaning twisted. Can't you see, from now on marriage has to be totally collaborative."

"I thought that was always the case."

"Traditional roles have to change if any of us expects to survive marriage."

"Is Tommy's Joynt still on Market Street? And what about the Blackhawk? I think it was on the corner of Turk and Hyde. Those places still around?" I spent a couple of days in San Francisco en route to Fort Ord for discharge in '61. I remembered those two places and a nightclub called the Hungry I, or some such, where I saw the comedian Dick Gregory perform.

"I don't know about the Blackhawk, but the delicatessen is still doing business. Paul, you're going to love living here."

I had every reason to believe my wife. At the same time, I experienced the strong realization that I loved Garrison, New Hampshire, too. It was the place where I was born and reared and had lived for all but two years of my life. I didn't share this epiphany with my wife. She said she would call Thursday to tell me how the job interview had gone, and begged me to stay away from Noelle. Noelle's sexual essence, still powerful in my bedroom, would make promises like that hard to keep. I promised anyway.

TWENTY-TWO

"You must feel better now that you're back to work, Paul." Mrs. Pappas had on her uniform: black dress, cameo brooch, and kitchen apron with the floral pattern. She was sweeping the walkway, something she did every day of the week, except Sunday, in clement weather. She had been scrupulous in not asking about my wife since I had revealed to her the rift between us.

"Yes, much better. Now I can manage to pay you the rent and afford to eat, too."

Mrs. Pappas laughed and waved her hand at me in an old-country gesture I had never seen from Americans. "You'll never go hungry as long as I'm around to cook for you, young man."

"How's Charlie? He doesn't come around anymore looking for Laura. I suppose it's for the best."

"He still misses her. I told him to stop pestering you. He's got to learn."

"You didn't have to do that, Mrs. Pappas. He's no bother. It breaks my heart to see his face fall when I tell him she's not here. By the way, I talked to Laura yesterday. We may be on the mend."

"That would be wonderful, Paul. I miss her so. Charlie would be so happy to see her again."

I didn't have the heart to tell Mrs. Pappas the conditions of our "mended" relationship. And who knew how long our latest truce would last?

"She misses both of you a lot too. Why don't I bring your fan downstairs."

"There's no hurry to do that, Paul. The way the weather has been this summer you might need it again."

I was frankly not unhappy to put off lugging the beast back down to Mrs. Pappas's dungeon of a cellar. I bid her goodbye and headed upstairs for something to eat before my shift at Archie's.

* * *

"I won't say I told you so, Paul," Doc said, "but didn't I tell you so? Anyway, I think it's great. Now try not to act like a horse's ass and blow it again. Get on a plane and get yourself to San Francisco."

"There are still a few things to get settled." I told Doc about Laura's job interview, which had taken place today according to her. It hadn't occurred to me to ask her why she should wait until Thursday to call and let me know how it went.

Archie came into the back room bearing a fresh carton of milk for Doc. Whitey sat in the wooden chair against the wall; he was already on the nod. He held on to the neck of his beer bottle with one hand, securing the base of it between his knees. He had on his denim work outfit, as if he were still on the job at the Navy Yard instead of still among the ranks of the laid off. Ray Duffy had left earlier to join his girlfriend for supper at her place. "Gonna get into the tall grass tonight," he'd said, cryptically.

Doc informed Archie of my reconciliation with Laura. "Better start looking around for new help, big-balls. You won't have Paul to exploit much longer."

"Is that a fact?" Archie said, chewing his unlighted cigar stub. His expression conveyed skepticism.

"It looks that way, Arch. Who knows what tomorrow will bring?" I said.

Doc poured a dollop of vodka into his milk and raised the cup to his lips. "To a new beginning." Archie didn't join in Doc's toast to my hopeful future. Whitey's chin fell to his chest.

"I better get him up and pointed toward home," Archie said. Whitey lived on Kirkland Avenue, which ran perpendicular to Washington Street. It was no more than a five-minute walk, even when Whitey got so drunk he had to steer a crooked course.

"Put him in my car," Doc said. "I'll drop him off. I've got to shower, shave, and change. I'll be back in forty-five minutes or an hour." Doc and Archie had dates with their bimbos tonight. It dawned on me that I hadn't seen the Black Dahlia in the store for a long time, maybe a month. I said as much to Archie as he put a hand on Whitey's shoulder and shook him gently.

"Don't say that cunt's name out loud when I'm around. Give me a dose of the clap. That's the last I see of her. Moved out of her apartment owing two months' rent."

"Jesus." I recalled her invitation to "call me sometime." I had even toyed with the idea of taking her up on it. The clap. I thought I had seen the last of all diseases venereal when I left Korea

"Three shots of peni in his fat ass took care of that. And you can be sure Betty was grateful for the holiday from big-balls' overtures," Doc said.

"On the rag all that week anyway. Wont no matter. Come on, Whitey, up and at 'em."

Doc shook his head and winked at me. He finished off his cocktail. "I'm on my way. Let's go, Whitey. Time to get home to the wife."

Whitey lifted his heavy eyelids and flashed a drunk's grin. At that moment Whitey looked a tad senile to me. It felt like something heavy had lodged in my stomach.

"Take it easy, old timer," Archie said to Whitey as Doc steered him out of the room by the elbow.

* * *

It was a slow night in the store for a Wednesday. I kept a paperback copy of *The Wapshot Scandal* under the counter for nights like this. Laura was a big fan of Cheever, but I couldn't claim any enthusiasm for his writing from what I had seen so far in this novel even if I recognized the brilliance of his prose. I had long ago despaired of ever being able to match my wife's aesthetic sensibilities for literature and art.

"You might try reading beyond the first ten pages before passing judgment," she had said to me after I gave up on *Lord Jim*. I had always been an avid reader, but the kind of books I used to think were masterpieces Laura looked down her nose at. *Hawaii* I had read while I was in the Army, and *The Carpetbaggers*. Both of these books had impressed me greatly. Laura was incredulous. "That isn't literature," she sighed. "Have you ever heard the expression *potboiler*?"

Now, I made every effort to avoid "potboilers" even if I enjoyed the high art of the Cheevers, Faulkners, Conrads, and Wolfes less than the Micheners and Robbins. You might say that Laura spoiled the enjoyment of reading fiction for me, although I confess to being drawn to writers like Hemingway and Fitzgerald, and lately Mailer. Laura's fervent wish was for me to major in English when I enrolled in college full time. When that might be seemed more uncertain than ever these days.

"The village stood on three leafy hills north of the city," I read on page 47, "and was handsome and comfortable, and seemed to have eliminated, through adroit social pressure, the thorny side of human nature." I closed *The Wapshot Scandal* and was conscious of a sigh escaping my chest. "Adroit social pressure." The phrase had a resonance about it; its precise meaning in the context of the novel would no doubt be revealed in pages to come. My concentration was poor, however, and I had no desire at the moment to continue reading. Adroit pressure was what my wife seemed to be consciously exerting on me. To eliminate the "thorny" side of my nature? Until she took it upon herself to leave me, I doubt she was aware that my nature had a thorny side. My antics with Noelle, in the meantime, surely gave her a glimpse into it. Yet she professed to forgive me, to offer me another chance at redemption. Some voice deep inside me warned against so simple an outcome. There would be a price to pay, of that I was certain.

I walked to the back of the store with no particular mission. On impulse, I reached in the cooler and pulled out a bottle of beer. I popped the cap with Archie's church key and took a long swallow. It was no use. I would never acquire a taste for beer. I took the bottle down cellar and emptied it on the dirt floor to mingle with the piss of human and feline. When I came back upstairs three Kappa Sig brothers were crouched in front of the beer cooler pulling out several cases of Budweiser from the bottom shelf.

"Getting an early start this week?" I asked.

"Homecoming weekend," one brother said, as if I should have known as much. Weekends of such social importance always began on a Wednesday, I had learned. Kappa "swig" had the reputation as the hardest drinking house on campus. Many of the brothers looked like career students; some of them looked my age, or older.

"Right. So, who are we clashing with on the gridiron this weekend?" I asked only to make small talk. I had no interest in football.

"U. Conn."

"They're tough, aren't they?"

"Suppose so. Who cares?" The brothers looked at each other and laughed. They had no stake in any football game. Their sport was all night drinking and the conquest of inebriated co-eds.

The three of them carted away six cases of beer. Thirty bucks in Archie's cash register in less than ten minutes. He would be pleased. In all the months I'd worked for Archie I still had no idea what kind of profit margin he operated on. I had a feeling that the bulk of his income came not from his profits on beer and groceries but from his illegal gambling activities. Then, on the other hand, he could not have been burdened with high overhead, not in this dilapidated building with the furnished three-room apartment above the store that hadn't been occupied in two years. I don't think even Archie would be surprised if tomorrow the city condemned the building and ordered it torn down. Hey, Mr. Cheever, you want to see the "thorny" side of human nature, come on down to the corner of Washington and Green.

TWENTY-THREE

"How did you make out yesterday?" I asked my wife.

"I think the interview went well. I won't hear anything for a few days, probably not until the middle of the week."

"What kind of money are we talking about?"

"There was no mention of salary at this point. They called it a preliminary screening interview. If they're interested, I'll be called back for a follow-up. That's when the issue of salary will come up. How are you doing, Paul?"

"I'm all right. Plenty of work at Sid's for a change. It's nice not having to wonder what dark vengeance Chessy is sending in my direction. Laroche and Brother James' constant prattle is hard to take, but I got enough to do I can shut them out most of the time."

"You won't have to put up with any of them much longer, Paul. I feel good about this job."

"J. Alfred's dead, Laura. I came home a little over a week ago and found him on the bottom of his cage. Laura?"

"I heard you, Paul. I'm so sad."

"Me too. I buried him out back, by a hemlock."

"Had he not been feeling well?"

"He looked all right to me. It took me completely by surprise."

"I'm not surprised, Paul."

"What do you mean by that?"

"What do you think I mean?"

"Are you telling me I'm to blame for his death?"

"You are just so … unobservant."

"I'm telling you, he was fine. He was eating, and drinking his water …"

"How often did you clean his cage?"

"More often than you have in the last three months."

"That's not fair."

"Is that so?"

"Listen to us, Paul. What's done is done. Is Honcho all right?"

"How would I know? I'm not very observant, remember?"

"Stop being childish."

"Honcho is fine. I told you, I don't allow him outside privileges anymore."

"I'm so sad."

"I know. What can I say?"

"I wish you were here with me. I miss you so, Paul."

"I miss you, too."

"It won't be for much longer, darling."

"I hope so."

"Give my love to Mrs. Pappas and Charlie. And Devlin and Maggie. Tell them I miss them."

"I will."

"Goodbye, darling."

My wife's phone call, her insinuation of my dereliction in the care of J. Alfred Prufrock, put me in a black mood. I had been willing to assume the guilt at the time of his death. Now that Laura had put it squarely on my shoulders I felt curiously righteous. Was this the way it would be with us when we resumed our life together? I felt my marriage taking on the weight of a curse. I shouldn't be thinking these kinds of thoughts. Then I found myself dialing Noelle's number. William answered and I hung up.

A half hour later Noelle knocked on my door.

"Why did you hang up?" Noelle asked me, winding her arms around my neck.

"How did you know it was me? William answered."

"He knew it was you. He said 'Noelle, your boyfriend called.'"

"How could he have known it was me? I hung up as soon as I heard his voice."

"He's got kind of a sixth sense about these things. Of course, he could have been guessing."

"It's uncanny."

"Kiss me, Paul."

"Come inside. I don't want Mrs. Pappas getting an eyeful." I had often wondered what my landlady would make of my conduct with Noelle. I had no wish to find out. If I could hear Charlie's nocturnal wailings from downstairs, surely Mrs. Pappas could have heard Noelle's rapturous squeals from my bedroom. In the living room, I kissed Noelle obediently. She removed her shoes, planted her feet on mine, and endeavored to walk me into the bedroom. I resisted. She stepped away from me and gave me a look, head cocked to one side.

"You look amused. What is it?" I asked her.

"Oh, I don't know. Sometimes you can be so … dishonest." She sat down on the love seat and tucked her legs underneath her, showing me plenty of bare thigh and lavender panties under a black mini-skirt.

"Dishonest?"

"I don't suppose you have anything to drink in the house."

"No. What do you mean, dishonest?"

"Why are you seeing me, Paul?"

I turned away from Noelle's unblinking scrutiny. "I'm attracted to you, why do you think?"

"Think about it. Do you really believe I enjoy being used by you to get to Laura? Just because I put up with William doesn't mean I have no pride." I turned to Noelle and saw tears start up in her nearsighted eyes.

"This has nothing to do with Laura. I'm physically attracted to you, Noelle, but I'm in love with my wife, not you. What's dishonest about that?"

"Have you told Laura this?"

"Oh, sure. That's just what she'd want to hear."

"How noble of you to tell her only what she wants to hear."

"I made the biggest mistake of my life telling her about us in the first place. Call it dishonest if you want to, but I'm not about to compound the damage I've done already. Call me what you want."

"Just forget it, Paul. Forget everything I said. Let's just go to bed."

"What about your pride?"

Noelle got up and slid onto my lap; she took my face between her hands. "Haven't you heard? Pride goeth before the fall."

"I don't want Mrs. Pappas to hear us. She'd be very upset with me if she found out I was cheating on Laura. She might even toss me out."

"You're not serious."

"She could. She thinks the world of Laura."

"It's not as though we haven't done it before. Wouldn't she have said something to you about it by now?"

"Why push my luck?"

Noelle rearranged herself in the straddle position on my lap. "Well, why don't we just do it like this. Quietly."

* * *

I lay in bed, unable to find sleep, wishing I had been born without a conscience, like William, or like Archie and Doc. I was helpless under Noelle's spell. It was only a matter of time before I'd spill my guts to Laura again, if Noelle didn't get to her first out of pure spite or gleeful malice.

Charlie had knocked on the door while we were at the height of our passion on the uncomfortable chair. Charlie, who hadn't been at my door in I don't know how many days, had to choose this moment to come calling. Mrs. Pappas had taken me at my word about not being bothered by his visits. Noelle found it amusing at first, then became vexed when I could no longer perform, as we waited out Charlie's monotonous knocking, which had to have gone on for five minutes before he gave up and clomped down the stairs.

Noelle had been stimulated by the thought of Charlie taking it in his head to push open the door to find us coupled on the living room chair. Having nothing at stake, Noelle could afford to indulge her whimsy.

"What would Charlie have made of us?" she had wondered. "Do you suppose he gets horny like normal teenagers? How awful it must be for people like him. Paul, we should find Charlie a little mongoloid girl and get him laid. What do you think?" I didn't think it was funny, and I told her so. She put a hickey on my neck. I asked her to leave. She stuffed her lavender panties with Thursday stitched on them in her handbag and pretended to stalk off in a huff. But she stopped at the door and shot me a sly smile over her shoulder. "I'll be seeing you ... after you get over yourself."

Yes, I was as helpless as an infant. I hoped desperately that Laura would get this product design job, and I could soon be on my way to join her. That hope soured in an instant, and I was left where I was before, where I had been ever since she'd been gone. Nowhere.

TWENTY-FOUR

The guys at Caplan's Auto Supply had nicknamed Ingemar "Iggy" Swenson "Mr. Clean" after the TV ad's baldheaded mascot for the household cleaner. Indeed, Iggy's head was as smooth as a billiard ball, which accentuated his huge ears, ears that sprouted from the sides of his head like jug handles. Iggy was powerfully built. I'd seen him lugging entire automobile engines into the machine shop with his bare hands. Iggy had worked for Sid for eight years, and in all those eight years — every day, six days a week — he had brought his brown bag lunch of tuna salad sandwiches on white bread.

Even Tommy Laroche, who had his share of eccentricities, had trouble with Iggy's diet.

"Jesus, Iggy. Don't you ever get sick of tuna?"

"I love tuna. I never get tired of it," Iggy would say.

"Ever have it for supper?"

"Sylvie makes a nice tuna wiggle on Wednesdays."

Tommy would shake his head in disbelief and pound away at his ten-key calculator. Every day for eight years! I wondered if this routine was unique to his employment at Caplan's or had it gone on at the place or places he'd worked before? It seemed like too personal a question for someone like me to put to him. I didn't know the man except to say hello to.

Now that I had taken over Chessy's old job, I got to sit at his desk with my back to the door. The gasoline vapors from the machine shop, always present in my office, seemed all at once to increase in intensity. I turned around to find Iggy Swenson standing in the doorway, calloused thumbs hooked onto his belt buckle, long fingers splayed out on the front of his jeans. Iggy seldom had occasion to stop by the office, so I was surprised to see him there framed in the doorway, a tentative smile on his broad face.

"Hey, Iggy," I said, swiveling around in my chair, "what can I do you for?"

"Just stopped by to let you know we're all glad to have you back on the job." Iggy shifted his weight from one foot to the other; he looked slightly ill at ease. "That's about it."

"Well, thanks a lot, Iggy. I appreciate it." The fact that I'd been ten days back on the job didn't seem to matter where Iggy Swenson, Mr. Clean, was concerned. I was touched by his words, but I didn't know quite what else to say to this big, taciturn mechanic with the metal belt buckle fashioned in the head of a long-horned steer, such as the kind found in the southwest. Was that where Iggy was from? His accent was as New Hampshire as Saturday night franks and beans. Before I could ask him about his belt buckle he smiled, waved, and disappeared into the machine shop.

For some reason I could not articulate, Iggy Swenson's simple gesture filled me with melancholy. I spent a good part of the morning staring out the window across the street at Spiro's Sweet Shoppe instead of writing orders, checking inventory, and updating jobber contracts the way Tommy Laroche had taught me to do. By lunchtime I was tempted to punch out early, go home and sleep, even if I was less physically fatigued than spiritually wrung out. Besides, I was supposed to work tonight at Archie's, a responsibility, especially on Fridays, that was becoming a chore. Then, I couldn't afford to lose a whole afternoon's pay. Neither could I bring myself to beg off from my shift at Archie's.

I punched out for lunch and found myself, without thinking, ordering up a toasted tuna salad roll at Spriro's. Spiro, who had lost a lot of the hair on his head since I was a high school kid, was a heavy-set man in his early forties with a perpetual five-o'clock shadow, and a perpetually dirty apron draped across his ample middle. Spiro had never married. He gave me a long look.

"You never order tuna. What's the deal?"

"I don't know. Why? Your tuna tainted?"

"No. It's just that you don't strike me as a tuna type. Listen, eat all the tuna you want. Want fries with that?"

Spiro's tuna salad was dry and tasteless. I wondered if Iggy Swenson's wife made good tuna sandwiches for him. Or perhaps it was his mother who made the sandwiches, or his sister. I wasn't sure he was married. Maybe he made his own sandwiches.

After lunch I made it a point to ask Tommy Laroche.

"Of course he's married. Ain't everybody?" Then I remembered Iggy referring to someone named Sylvie, who prepared him tuna wiggle on Wednesdays. Sylvie could be a sister, or an aunt. "Why the sudden interest in Iggy Swenson?" Tommy wanted to know.

"Just curious." But even I was aware that this was taking on the features of an obsessive curiosity.

"Lives out on Stage Road. Got two boys in junior high. Wife works at Miller Shoe. Anything else you want to know?"

"Where'd he work before he came here?"

"Had his own place up in Melvin Village. Couldn't make a go of it."

"Too bad. Iggy's good people."

"The best. Sid would be up shit creek without Iggy."

"You think he shaves his head every day, or does he have that hereditary condition, what's it called?"

"You mean baldness?"

"There's a scientific name for it. Apacia, apecia, or something like that."

"I wouldn't know about that. Why don't you ask him?"

"I couldn't do that."

"Well, then forget about it."

* * *

"*Alopecia*," Doc said, in answer to my question. "*Alopecia areata*, to be exact. You're not worried about that, are you, you with that head of hair?" I told Doc I wasn't concerned about myself. I described Iggy Swenson to him. "How do you know he doesn't shave it himself? Maybe he likes it that way. Like Yul Brynner," Doc said.

"So how do we know Yul Brynner shaves his head? Maybe he's a congenital cue ball himself."

"Jesus, Paul. Who the fuck cares? What's with you?"

"I wish I knew."

"What's the matter with Paulie," Archie said, pausing to remove cigar detritus from his tongue, "is it's been too long since he had his horn scraped." I knew better than to disabuse Archie of his assumptions about my sex life. As if I hadn't taken enough of their good-natured abuse, first over my wife's disappearance, and then about the shit slinging incident.

"What about the myth that baldheaded guys are more virulent than their hirsute brethren?" I asked Doc.

"If you mean *virile*, then I guess you'd have to take big-balls as a case in point. He's got all his hair, right?"

"You know what I meant. Everybody misspeaks now and then, don't they?" My face was hot. I didn't like getting caught in a verbal gaffe.

"All I'm saying is that you should learn to use words properly if you fancy yourself a wordsmith."

"Paul," Archie said, coming to my rescue, "you doin' anything tomorrow night?"

"I'd have to check my social calendar." I assumed Archie wanted me to work Duane's shift Saturday night.

"Good. Come on over to the house. I got some new skin flicks from Canada. We can play some friendly poker, too, you want. Whitey and Ray'll be there, and a couple guys from the neighborhood you ain't met."

"Sure."

"I'll pick you up here at six-thirty."

TWENTY-FIVE

Archie lived in a development with the genteel sounding name of Riverside Terrace. It consisted of prefabricated ranch-style, and split-level houses. There was no sign of a river in the warren of short streets that meandered through the development. Without a house number, one would have been hard put to distinguish Archie's house from the rest of the dwellings on his street.

Archie led me into his house through the kitchen door. Betty was at the stove dressed in tight fitting slacks and a sleeveless blouse, looking harried as usual, even from the rear. Several of their kids lolled in kitchen chairs at the table, scribbling in coloring books amidst a clutter of plastic drink cups, bowls with the remains of Franco-American spaghetti, and paper napkins. The baby that perpetually discharged dense snot from its nostrils was tethered to a highchair. The tray was covered with the spaghetti he had emptied from his bowl. He was, of course, bawling loudly, his little sauce-covered face screwed up as if he suffered excruciating pain, his open maw full of half chewed food. Archie reached for Betty's ample rear end and gave it a squeeze, looking over his shoulder at me for approval. Betty swatted his hand away without taking her eyes off the pot she was attending to on the front burner.

"C'mon." Archie motioned toward a door off the kitchen. It led down a short flight of carpeted stairs bearing food and drink stains, to the basement, also carpeted wall-to-wall.

"You fuckers drank up all my booze yet?" Archie said to the foursome at the bar.

Archie's "playroom" had all the essential features of a cathouse except, of course, the "cats." Ray, Whitey, and two men I presumed to be Archie's neighbors occupied four of the six barstools. The room was illuminated in a dim red light suffused with cigar and cigarette smoke. The source of the red light came from two enormous lamps bearing fluted canvas shades with tassels. The bases were sculptured naked women with oversized breasts and grotesquely swollen labia. Where, I wondered, on planet earth had Archie ever found such … monstrosities?

A mirror occupied the entire wall in back of the bar and reflected his stock of liquor bottles arranged on a two-tiered shelf. The front of the bar was lit up like a jukebox.

Archie introduced his neighbors as Al and Bud. No last names.

"Bud's been tryin' to get into my wife's drawers since he moved to the neighborhood."

"Whadya mean tryin'?" replied Bud, a fat guy with a crew cut like Archie's, and no neck. Al laughed heartily at Bud's assertion that Betty's drawers had, indeed, been gotten into. Whitey was still *compos,* but he wouldn't be for long, as he pounded double shots of whiskey with beer chasers. Ray, on the other hand, looked torched already. Neighbor Al, who continued to guffaw over Bud's comment, had the kind of face that seemed perpetually on the verge of smiling, and I had the impression it would not take much to send him into out-of-control laughter. Al was as thin as Bud was fat; he had unruly gray hair, and big ears with detached lobes.

"What're you drinkin', Paulie?" Archie asked me, heading behind the bar, a fresh stogie in his jaws. The front edge of the L-shaped bar was padded, as were the seats and backs of the six stools.

"You got beer?"

"Of course. Want a shot with that?"

"I don't think so."

"How do, Paul," Ray said, raising his glass.

"How you doing, young fellow?" Whitey said, in his brief interval before total inebriation.

"You boys ready for some good movies?" Archie said, rubbing his hands together as if he were preparing to sit down to a good meal. He had his 8mm projector set up on a card table, and aimed at the far wall on which he had hung a white bed sheet. "After you see these flicks I may have to lock Betty in the bedroom to protect her from you horny bastards." The men slid off their bar stools and found places on the sofa or in the easy chairs, getting comfortable in anticipation of an evening of prurient entertainment.

Archie turned on the projector and doused the lamps. Now, the only light in the room flickered off the bed sheet as several frames of blank footage preceded the opening credits; a hand-lettered white card held by a pair of male hands flashed on the screen/bed sheet: *The TV Repairman.*

It was clear to me from the beginning that this Canadian pornographic filmmaker was operating on a low budget.

In the first scene, the repairman is knocking on the door. He is a tall man in his early thirties. He has a bad complexion, and his long hair is generously pomaded; he has on a windbreaker and a pair of chinos that are too short for him. He carries his tool kit in his hand. A voluptuous black woman, dressed in skin tight T-shirt and leotards, answers the door with a seductive smile on her heavily made up face. Her fingernails look to be four inches long.

The next scene is in the living room where the ailing TV set is the backdrop. It seems that the black woman is servicing the repairman before the repairman gets to service the TV. It is a most awkward position she assumes, bending from the waist to attack the repairman from the side. He stands there, passively, tool kit in hand, while his customer goes to work on him.

"And on skin flute, Aunt Jemima," Archie chimes in.

There is a quick segue to the living room floor where our hero and heroine have shed their clothes and lay coupled, buck naked, in front of the still unattended TV set, a Motorola, I think, with perhaps a twelve-inch screen. There is no dialogue, no sound track whatsoever. What we are treated to for the rest of the film is mostly close-ups of their genitalia from different camera angles. Even the boys grow restless after several minutes of this relentless, clinical, and passionless copulation. Their initial boisterous encouragement yields to an almost catatonic silence. Al, finally, has had enough.

"Hey, Arch, this is kinda fucking boring. You know what I mean?" Whitey's chin had already started to bounce off his chest.

"Quiet. It's almost over," Archie said.

The film ends rather abruptly with the repairman standing over his customer as he ejaculates on her chest while she lies there looking bored.

Archie rewound the film and fit another reel on the projector.

"This one better be good," Bud warned Archie.

"This one'll have you beatin' off. I guarantee it."

There are three characters in the next film: two sallow, slightly overweight white women in their late thirties or early forties, and one unbelievably well endowed black man. There is no effort to supply a plot. The film opens right in the middle of their business.

"How come spades are all hung like mules?" Bud mused.

"Goddamned if I know," neighbor Al replied. "Maybe it makes up for 'em being stupid, I don't know."

The characters act out their *ménage `a trois* like robots, with the same lack of erotic interest we witnessed in the first movie. Archie claimed this flick had got him hornier than a "bear." "You guys might have to excuse me while I go upstairs and tear off a piece."

"You do that, Archie. We'll get set up for some poker," Al said. "Nobody wants to watch anymore of this shit. Where'd you say you got these, Canada? I guess it's true what they say. Them Canucks can't do nothin' but play hockey. I'd get my money back, I was you, Arch."

"You just ain't got no appreciation for good movies. Ain't that right, Ray? What do you think, Paulie? Hot stuff, huh?"

"I've never seen anything quite like it."

"See, you asshole," Archie said to Al, "Paulie's got good taste."

Archie's poker house rules forbade all wild card games, and the action was restricted to five card draw, jacks or better to open, and five and seven card stud, no checking and raising. I was the only one at the table who was not drinking. I was clear headed enough to win a few good-sized pots in the course of the evening, but way too early I was ready to go home. I was also at Archie's convenience for transportation unless I wanted to walk or hitchhike. Neither of these alternatives appealed to me.

When the evening finally came to an end, even Archie, who held his booze better than his drinking companions, had to admit that he was in no condition to drive me home. Neither was Ray. Whitey had passed out on the sofa hours ago; Bud and Al were in a stupor at the card table.

"You can find a place to curl up down here, Paulie, or I can get Betty up. She can drive you home."

"I'll just call a cab. I don't want you to bother your wife." I'd won about twelve bucks, so I could indulge myself in a taxi.

"Don't worry about her. Wait here." Archie went upstairs to wake up his wife. While Archie was upstairs I used his downstairs phone to call City Cab to come pick me up. Al and Bud stumbled up the stairs, Al laughing like a simpleton. Ray had passed out in the armchair next to his drinking buddy, Whitey, who was snoring on the sofa. I went upstairs to say goodnight to Archie. I hoped to intercept him before he got his wife out of a sound sleep. Archie was nowhere in sight. I listened for a while. No sounds came from the rooms beyond the kitchen. I closed the door quietly behind me and waited outside on the sidewalk for my cab. The air was warm for late September. Clouds had moved in since I'd been down in Archie's subterranean lair, clouds that obliterated both moon and stars. My mouth was rancid from too many cigarettes. I lit up the last one in the pack. Tomorrow I would try again to give them up.

TWENTY-SIX

When I got home last night, exhausted, I crawled into bed to discover Noelle there.

"My, aren't we out late tonight," she said, running her hand along the inside of my thigh.

"Jesus, you scared the daylights out of me. How long have you been here?"

"Oh, the tone. Aren't you glad to see me? Where have you been all night? And don't tell me you were working. I stopped by Archie's."

"You sound a lot like somebody's wife."

Noelle's hand found its way to my cock. "You haven't been busy with someone else tonight, have you?"

"He takes the fifth," I said. "You wouldn't believe what I saw tonight. I may never want to have sex again." I told Noelle about Archie's Canadian porn.

"Wouldn't it be fun to watch some together? Good ones, I mean."

"Is there such a thing as a good porn flick?"

"I'll bet the French have made some good ones. Or the Japanese. Now there's a sexy race."

"Yeah, if you like perversion."

Noelle went to work on me, slowly, arousing me out of the sexual torpor Archie's movies had put me in.

* * *

I was awakened at ten in the morning by the sound of heavy rain. Noelle was gone; her side of the bed was cool. Rain had come in through the open screen. The windowsill and floor were wet. I closed the window and mopped up the water with a dirty towel. Rain lashed the side of the house putting me in mind of the poem my French professor had asked the class to memorize and recite to her one-on-one in her office.

> *Il pleure dans mon cœur*
> *Comme il pleut sur la ville*

When it came time for me to recite Verlaine's poem to Mademoiselle Billet, she turned her back on me after the first two lines, my accent was so abominable to the ear of the smelly old harridan. I could read the language well enough; I could translate it and write it. What I couldn't do worth a damn was speak it. All that nasal twanging only caused me embarrassment.

> *Quelle est cette langueur*
> *Qui penetre mon cœur ?*

Ah, if I knew that ... I had to be at work in half an hour. I would have given anything to be able to crawl back between my malodorous sheets. Noelle had not commented on their fragrance last night. Maybe she was getting used to them, as I had. This thing with Noelle had to end before it was too late, if it wasn't too late already.

*　*　*

A cool drizzle persisted through the day. Business was slow at Archie's because of the weather. I had too much time to think, too much time to contemplate my future. I tried getting back into *The Wapshot Scandal*, to no avail.

One way to avoid contemplating your future, I reasoned, would be to make a concerted effort to summon the past. But what part of the past, and to what end? Mere escape seemed to me a fitting justification. I closed my eyes and tried to conjure a moment in time that I had, intentionally or by some psychological sleight of hand, exiled to my subconscious:

Wait, here comes Sally Youngblood, of American Indian descent. She's in my arms on the dance floor of the Crystal Ballroom, which is upstairs over a savings and loan office on the corner of Washington and Locust. After three weeks of grueling instruction in the two-step, foxtrot, and waltz, Mr. Anderson, our basketball coach and dance instructor, reluctantly declares us ready for the eighth grade social. He is responsible for training all the eighth grade boys in Garrison's schools. We're not ready. At least I'm not, and neither are the other guys on my basketball team. The girls need no instruction in dance. Dancing apparently is part of their hereditary make up.

I cling to Sally like a drowning man hangs on to his kapok, as we shuffle to the music. "Why Don't You Believe Me?" I believe is playing as I try my damndest to keep from trampling on Sally's feet. She is warm and soft in my arms. I discover to my horror that my thirteen-year-old pecker is stiff. If Sally is aware of it, she seems not to be bothered; she presses her lower body against me. For a long while I stop breathing.

Sally Youngblood goes to the Hutchins school on the west side of town. I attend the Franklin school on Main Street. Its asphalt basketball court slopes about three degrees. Boys who know who she is are cruel to Sally, calling her "squaw" and "Pocahontas"; they yell out war whoops whenever she comes into view. I have always found her exotically attractive with her long black hair, dark complexion, and oriental features. The clothes she wears look homemade. Tonight she has on what I suppose is a white dress whose material looks like it may have come from something that held flour or feed of some kind. The shoulders are puffy, which makes the dress look about a size too large for her. I frankly don't care what my classmates think of me for dancing with her. It isn't as if I have asked her to dance; we were partnered randomly by the chaperones.

The house lights have been dimmed; stage lights with colored gels play on the large mirrored globe that hangs over the middle of the dance floor. I am grateful for the low light given my condition. By unspoken agreement, Sally Youngblood and I stay on the floor for the next dance, and the one after that. In fact, we dance every dance together that night. They are all slow songs because Mr. Anderson hasn't gotten around to teaching the boys how to jitterbug. The girls, of course, know how to jitterbug and would gladly teach the boys, but the chaperones won't allow it.

The dance ends. I find myself walking Sally home. We have not spoken word one to each other all evening. I believe I am in love. What else explains the warm exultant feeling I have in my breast? I am emboldened to take Sally in my arms and kiss her in front of the rundown shack of a house she lives in on Walden Street. Sally is pliant and submissive; we kiss for a long time, and then part without so much as a word. That is the last I will ever see of Sally Youngblood.

* * *

So much for adolescent love. Why I never pursued Sally Youngblood I simply can't remember. It no doubt involved pressure from my friends. As far as I know, Sally never made it to high school. She may have dropped out of school, or her family may have moved away; I never inquired. If I allowed myself to sink into a deep enough funk, I could draw parallels between the way Sally Youngblood and my wife vanished from my life. I could not allow that to happen. Close your eyes, I told myself, try harder.

> O bruit de la pluie
> Par terre et sur les toits!
> Pour un coeur qui s'ennuie
> O le chant de la pluie!
>
> Il pleure sans raison
> Dans ce cœur qui s'ecoeure
> Qui ! nulle trahion ?
> Ce deuil est sans raison.
>
> C'est bien la pire peine
> De ne savoir pourquoi

Sans amour et sans haine
Mon cœur a tant de peine !

Even if I had inflicted a lot of pain on Mademoiselle Billet with my version of a French accent, I was able, at least, to memorize the lines, lines that were still etched in my memory. At the time, the poem struck me as impossibly corny and maudlin, probably inspired by Verlaine's fag relationship with Rimbaud. Thinking about the lines now, I felt something quite different than I had in her airless little office. Maybe it was the steady rain that did it for me. I had showed my translation to Laura. She laughed and told me I was too literal ; that I had missed the essence of Verlaine's intention in the poem. As I said, I despaired of ever measuring up to my wife's aesthetic sensibilities.

I opened the door for a look outside. Since I had come on duty the rain had increased in intensity. Archie's thermometer read forty-four degrees. There was no automobile traffic moving on Washington Street; no pedestrians in sight. It wasn't yet noon. I would never last eleven more hours like this. I closed the door against the chill.

* * *

That night I had a dream sequence that I remembered with uncommon detail upon waking. I decided to write it down and pass it by Laura to see what she made of it. To me it was an enigma.

My wife beckons to me from a darkened room off the one I am standing in amongst amorphous pastel colored candles with guttering flames. They are on the floor, on the mantle of a boarded up fireplace, on windowless windowsills. Laura is dressed in black tights; her face is white, like a geisha's face. To my distress, her hair has been shorn so that it is now no longer than my own.

"Come, Paul. Don't be afraid."

I take a step forward and hesitate, as if I am about to enter the abyss. My wife backs away, still beckoning with her forefinger. Then she melts away from my sight, like an image on a movie screen. Andrea Kincaid materializes; Andrea, her college classmate and current roommate. Andrea is dressed in black tights identical to the outfit Laura had on. She is thin and flat-chested; her hair is pure white.

"She's waiting for you, Paul. In the other room." Andrea smiles, and suddenly the right side of her face is illuminated revealing a strawberry colored birthmark the size of a half dollar, and in the shape of a toy poodle. "In the other room, Paul. Come." There is something diabolical in her smile, in her voice, in the poodle birthmark on her cheek. I try to speak. No sound issues from my throat. I am strangling, unable to call for help. Andrea fades out. Another young woman, also dressed in black, but faceless, appears. She is accompanied by a faceless man in a business suit, carrying a briefcase in his hand.

Now I am in a bus. I am the only passenger. I sit in the back, next to the toilet. The landscape through the window is tropical; the dirt road the bus travels on is narrow. Broadleafed plants brush against the sides of the bus; the canopy shuts out all but a sliver of blue, cloudless sky. Spanish moss hangs abundantly from the tops of trees; bromaleids are in bloom. I move across the aisle and look out the window at an alpine landscape. The bus lurches forward, angles downward sharply. There is deep snow in the foreground, evergreens with snow-laden limbs. I see mountains in the distance, great mountains whose summits disappear into the clouds. The bus picks up speed. I hurry to the front of the bus to plead with the driver to slow down. There is no one at the wheel.

I find myself walking on a deserted road with open fields of dead corn stalks on both sides as far as the eye can see. I see a car on the horizon heading in my direction. It slows down as it approaches me, and stops alongside where I am walking.

"Get in," an elderly man says from behind the steering wheel. He opens the door of the 1953 green Oldsmobile for me. I get in. The man drives off.

We arrive at a farmhouse next to a freshly painted red barn. The house looks down on a lush green valley. The old man gets out of the car and walks toward the farmhouse. I get out of the car and follow him into the house with a screened porch on three sides. He leads me into a parlor with a large sofa and overstuffed armchairs adorned with embroidered doilies on the arms and headrests. On the fireplace mantle are many framed photographs of three teenaged girls, triplets, dressed in cheerleader outfits. I step forward for a closer look at the photographs. I recoil when I see the triplets' faces—it is my wife's face, and each of the girls is missing her right arm!

A door opens and the three cheerleaders with my wife's face perform one-armed cartwheels into the small room. They drop to the kneeling position, side by side, left arms draped over each other's shoulders. They begin a cheer :

> Paul Embry, he's our man,
> If he can't do it, no one can.

I am outside, standing beside the '53 Olds. A fat man I recognize as Bud, Archie's neighbor, approaches from behind a large maple tree.

"Don't think for a minute I don't know how people like you look down on us legitimate used car salesmen. And you have the nerve to ask two-thousand five for this lemon?" Bud shakes his head in disgust and disappears back behind the maple.

TWENTY-SEVEN

"I never heard you talk about your dreams before, Paul."

"I was never a dreamer. This might be the first one I ever remember having."

"Don't be silly, Paul. Everyone dreams. Some people recollect them better than others."

"I still don't remember ever waking up with the recollection of a dream. I'm sorry."

"From what you've told me it sounds like you had a sequence of them."

"The bus ride doesn't fit. What do you make of it?"

"It should be obvious, Paul. I mean you don't have to be Doctor Freud to interpret its meaning. Think about it."

I had thought about it. I hadn't been able to make sense out of any of it. I wasn't about to admit as much to my wife. "Any news on the job interview?"

"I'm afraid so, darling."

"I'm sorry, babe. What's wrong with those people? If they only they knew what they were missing."

"Please don't be too disappointed, Paul. Andrea has given me two leads that look promising. I'm going after them tomorrow."

"I understand. Tell me one thing, though. Who do you think the guy was, the one without the face in the business suit and briefcase?"

"I don't know, really, unless it's Floyd, Lydia's boyfriend."

"Oh, yeah. The middle-aged accountant."

"He's not middle-aged."

"Does he have a face?"

"Accountants don't need actual faces as long as they have a head for numbers."

It didn't escape my notice that levity had crept into our conversation, maybe for the first time since she had been gone, maybe even before she left.

"I miss the hell out of you, Laura. Promise me if you don't find something soon you'll come home. We can start over."

"I'll find something, Paul. You can depend on it. Take care of yourself, darling."

I didn't share with my wife a fact I had learned at work today. I was on coffee break with old Harry Lamb and Ernie Golding in shipping. After Ernie's daily dirty joke the talk got around to the subject of pets in general, unusual pets in particular. Ernie boasted that he had once owned a coati, and that at present he had a five-foot boa living with him and his family. For exotic potential my poor cockatiel couldn't match Ernie's menagerie, but I told my story of the life and death of J. Alfred Prufrock anyway.

"Funny name for a female," Ernie had remarked.

"J. Alfred was a male," I said.

"Doesn't sound like a male from the way you describe it. Had to be a female. Males got yellow-colored heads."

"No shit? We always assumed it was a male."

"That what they told you where you got it?"

J. Alfred had come not from a pet store but from Siegel's Department Store where they kept caged birds for sale, mostly budgies and green parrots. A cockatiel was an exotic bird by Siegel's standards. Thinking back, neither of us inquired about its sex; we just assumed that it was male, an assumption based, apparently, on pure ignorance.

"Sounds like the thing may have been egg-bound. A lot of birds die of the condition, I hear," Ernie said.

"I'll be damned."

I stopped by the library after work and did a little research on cockatiels. Sure enough, Ernie Golding had it right about J. Alfred's gender. I was ambivalent about sharing the news with Laura. She was not one to take kindly to suggestions that she had made a mistake. So, even if the fact could be interpreted as vindication for me, maybe even get me off the hook for neglecting the thing, I couldn't bring myself to tell her. What would it have proved that was worth the risk of breaking the spell of conciliation between us?

After I hung up with Laura, Charlie came to the door asking for her again.

"She's visiting her mommy, Charlie," I explained to him for the umpteenth time. He had never challenged this explanation, had never done anything except cast his slanty eyes to the floor before going back down the stairs full of disappointment. Tonight Charlie surprised me when he stuck his head into my living room.

"Can I see the pretty bird?" Charlie had put on a few pounds, and he wasn't exactly svelte to begin with. The polo shirt he had on, with its horizontal stripes, did nothing to slim him down either.

"The pretty bird's gone, too." I couldn't hide the annoyance in my voice.

"Gone to see his mommy?"

"No, Charlie," I said, not able to help myself, "gone to birdie heaven. He's dead, Charlie. Do you understand what that means?"

Charlie's mouth opened; saliva escaped and ran down both sides of his chin. He said nothing. He backed away from the door, black eyes open wide, and went heavily down the stairs as fast as I had ever seen him move.

I regretted instantly the way I had talked to the boy. I moped around my apartment full of regret for maybe an hour, then on impulse went downstairs and knocked on my landlady's door.

"Come in." Mrs. Pappas, dressed in her black dress, sat in her big sofa, needlework to her left and to her right, and a piece of it in her lap. Charlie was on the floor at her feet working on his ten-piece Bozo the Clown jigsaw puzzle. He didn't look up when I came in the room. My intention of apologizing to Mrs. Pappas for the way I had treated Charlie remained just that, an intention. I seemed as incapable of uttering the appropriate words to my landlady and her son as I was when Laura called with talk of divorce. "How nice to see you, Paul. Charlie, say hello to Paul."

"Hello, Paul."

"Hi there, Charlie. Mrs. Pappas, I was on my way out. I thought I'd stop by to see how you were doing, and ask if you needed anything from Archie's."

"I can't think of anything, dear. It's so thoughtful of you to ask. How have you been?"

"I'm fine. But don't hesitate to let me know if there's anything I can do for you." Charlie was completely absorbed in his task. I detected no tension from either Charlie or his mother. Maybe I had imagined Charlie's discomfort earlier. "I guess I'll be on my way, then."

"Thank you, Paul."

I couldn't go back upstairs now that I had given Mrs. Pappas the impression that I was on my way out. What must the poor woman think of my odd behavior?

The temperature had dropped twenty degrees since the sun had set. I hadn't put on a sweater or a jacket. A long walk was out of the question, and I didn't feel up to the back room at Archie's. How subtly my claustrophobic apartment, my downtrodden neighbors, Caplan's Auto Supply, and Archie's Corner Grocery had circumscribed my life. Not to mention the dangerous and slippery slope I was on with Noelle, and the ongoing battle of the will with Laura, a battle she seemed to have won. Something told me the war was not over.

"What are you doing out here in the cold without a jacket?"

"Jesus! Don't sneak up on me like that. I've had combat training; I could hurt you." Noelle had startled me from behind.

She laughed. "Let's go upstairs out of the chill."

"No can do. Mrs. Pappas thinks I've gone out."

"So?"

"I told you before, I don't want her to know about us."

161

"I need you, Paul. Right now." Noelle wound her arms around my neck.

"Not here. Come on." I took her hand and led her down the sloping driveway to the back of the house. We got in to the back seat of my disabled Chevy, under Mrs. Pappas's porch. The interior smelled of mildew from the long humid summer.

"This is so romantic, Paul. Brings me back to high school."

"I thought you were a good girl in high school." Noelle worked her way onto my lap.

"I did my share of necking in the back seats of cars, but I told you, I never went all the way, not till I started college."

"I talked to Laura this evening. It's looking good for us, Noelle. We have to stop seeing each other. You understand?" I felt her stiffen; then she relaxed in my arms.

"What if I tell her what we've been doing? How good do you think it will look then?"

"Do you think that would make me feel kindly toward you? Or are you just vindictive?"

"I'm not vindictive, and I'm not possessive either. You must know at least that much about me. Don't worry; I won't say anything to Laura. I really don't want to possess you. All I want is what we've had together since she's been gone. No more than that. For as long as you're here. Is that unfair?"

"I doubt that my heart would be in it, Noelle."

"I'm not interested in your heart," she said, deftly unzipping my fly.

* * *

I lay in bed wondering how many marriages had gone in the toilet because of a found out lie. For a while it seemed to me that in Laura's hierarchy lying was a greater liability to a marriage than mere infidelity. Infidelity, of course, was a lie in its own right. And why excoriate me for confessing my "indiscretion" with Noelle? I could argue that Laura's position placed morality on the same plane as illusion. Cheat on me all you want, just don't let me find out about it; and God forbid you should tell me yourself. It amounts to rubbing my nose in it, which is no more than another act of moral cowardice. Deception was the principle that ruled Archie's and Doc's marriages. There was no pretense of love; Doc even went so far as to publicly despise his wife. As for Archie, I really believed that he had a degree of affection for Betty and for his family. Not enough, apparently, to prevent him from consorting with his Lorettas, his Black Dahlias. Archie could be written off as a lower life form, but what to do about Doc Robinson with his Harvard Medical School pedigree?

This was the kind of dead end reasoning that gave me a colossal headache. For all this agonized introspection I knew no more about myself or what it was I wanted than I did before Laura ditched me.

TWENTY-EIGHT

Oscar Michaud, the Lakes Region sales representative and an avowed Kennedy hater, was in a rant to the countermen when I came out front to collect sales slips.

"The bastard should be impeached," he said, in his loud, high-pitched voice. "His behavior amounts to treason."

I was no close follower of the daily news, but anything as momentous as treasonous acts by the President of the United States would not have escaped my notice. Michaud droned on about Kennedy's shortcomings as a president and as a human being. His hatred of the man was obsessive.

"Michaud, you don't know what the fuck you're talking about," Gil Freese said, turning to wink at me. Freese was no Kennedy supporter himself, but he enjoyed getting a rise out of Oscar Michaud, who could get nearly as physically agitated as old Harry Lamb. "Where do you get your information, off the shithouse wall?"

"Certain people in Texas know the truth."

"Texas? Well, there you go. Everybody knows all they got in Texas is steers and queers."

Michaud shook his head in disgust and dismissed Gil Freese with a wave of his hand. But it had shut Oscar Michaud up for the time being, and for that I was grateful. I was getting weary of listening to the opinionated salesmen and countermen run off at the mouth about politics. I was as uninformed as they were about political matters. The difference was that I had enough sense to keep my mouth shut when I didn't know what I was talking about.

Later, in my office, when Gil Freese came in to check a part number, I asked him what he made of Michaud's charges of treason against Kennedy.

"Beats the crap out of me. You know Oscar. Wouldn't put it past the son-of-a-bitch, though."

"Michaud?"

"No. Kennedy."

"You can't be serious. Everybody knows Michaud's a crackpot, a John Bircher."

"Why not?" Tommy Laroche piped in. "The guy's capable of anything crooked. Right, Brother James?"

"Don't get me started on Kennedy," Brother James said. Now I regretted bringing the subject up with Freese. I took my coffee break early, and headed across the street to Spiro's to get away from the Kennedy flogging by these ignoramuses. I drank a cup of coffee, ate two honey-dipped doughnuts, smoked three cigarettes, and tried to put them out of my mind.

Spiro's ancient mother sat behind the cash register at the end of the counter. She came in two or three days a week for an hour or two to work her son's cash register, to keep her hand, as it were, in the business. Until three months ago she shared the duty with her husband. George Panopolous was no more, and Mrs. P. looked like she was on her last legs as well. Greeks, French Canadians, and Jews made up the bulk of Garrison's ethnic mix, with a few Lebanese, East Indians, Italians, and Chinese scattered about. The Greeks ran the restaurants, soda fountains, and barbershops; the Jews owned the factories the French Canadians toiled in; the Jews owned all the "respectable" businesses as well: the clothing and jewelry stores, and the hardware store on Center Street. Laura's father owned the other hardware store in town; his place had never counted Jews among its patrons.

Garrison, New Hampshire, was officially a city because of its incorporated municipality, I imagined. Its population was in the neighborhood of twelve or fifteen thousand, and had a city manager instead of a mayor. It had no conspicuous virtues, none that could account for my tenacious loyalty to the place. There was nothing here that set it apart from other small cities in the state of the same ilk. There were no really good restaurants in town (as provincial as Laura believed I was, even I could tell the difference between a good restaurant and a place like The Cantina). There was nowhere to go to listen to good music, view fine art or drama. Garrison's defenders pointed to the fact that it was less than an hour from Boston, fifteen minutes to the university, a half hour to the beaches, no more than an hour to the ski slopes, and far enough away from "coloreds" and other purveyors of crime and social deviance that its citizens felt safe and sublimely indifferent to the problems faced by the larger cities on the Massachusetts border to the south.

As I said, I had lived here all my life save for the short time I spent in the Army. I knew all about its shortcomings, and would frankly be content to remain here for the rest of my life. My wife had other plans; she was determined to uproot me, to lure me to the West Coast, to the big city. I have always been put off by large cities, especially American large cities. I remember the first time my parents took me to Boston by train. I was five years old. How terrified I had been of North Station with its great steel diesel engines, steam billowing from beneath the cars, the crowded noisy platforms, the Negro porters with their impassive faces, pushing around wagons piled high with luggage.

In the city I was frightened by the noise, the smells, the large buildings, the streets clogged with automobile traffic, the sidewalks filled with people wedged too close together, and in too much of a hurry. It was my first glimpse of chaos. My crying had angered my father; when I clung to my mother for dear life my father had given me a look I have never forgotten, a look I saw again, this time on my wife's face the day I had come home to find Perry Potter in my kitchen.

A few months later I had another experience that helped form my opinion of big cities:

My cousin Roy Jr. was also five years old, but he was enrolled in kindergarten. For this reason, I was intensely jealous of him. Roy Sr., his father, my uncle, was a cub reporter for the *Boston Herald*. His wife, Lucinda, had gone mad after bearing her third child, a girl she named Janice. My mother was furious that Lucinda had given her daughter the same name my mother had given my sister. They lived on the first floor of a triple-decker apartment house in a densely populated neighborhood in Brighton, Massachusetts. My mother had brought me along for a visit with her brother and his family. Later, when I was older, my mother explained that her brother had implored her to come down to the city to look after Lucinda and the children, as he feared she might do something "dreadful" to them or to herself.

I am, of course, sketchy on the details of what happened the day my mother grudgingly allowed me to accompany my cousin to his kindergarten class, which was only a short walk from their apartment house. I was instructed to walk Roy Jr. to his school and to return immediately without "dawdling."

I said goodbye to my cousin as he joined his little kindergarten companions on the dirt playground with the swing set and jungle gym. I watched for a while as he played with the other kids before being summoned inside a one-story building with a flat roof by a young woman. I remember thinking it odd that a woman who worked with kindergarten kids would have a cigarette dangling from her lips as she herded her charges inside.

After the last kid disappeared into the building, I started to walk back in the direction I had come with my cousin. Soon, however, I began to have doubts about which one of the many triple-deckers belonged to my uncle and his family because, to my eye, they looked identical. Then the street took a turn that I didn't remember it taking when I walked with my cousin to his school. Nothing on the street, nor on the streets that branched off the one I was on, looked remotely familiar. I felt something inside my stomach that must have been fear. And on these streets with so many buildings the sidewalk was eerily deserted, and hardly any automobiles passed by. In a few minutes I found myself on a wide thoroughfare with plenty of automobiles, pedestrians, and tall buildings. It was the kind of scene that had sent me into a panic on my first visit to the city some months before. I began to cry; people stopped to stare at me. They stared, but no one spoke to me, no one asked me my name or where I lived.

The next thing I remember is a police car pulling up to the curb, and two uniformed officers getting out to accost me. They talked to me in quiet voices. One of them asked me what street I lived on. I had no idea what the name of the street was that my uncle and his family lived on. I had heard Uncle Roy use the word "Brighton" once; perhaps thinking that this was the name of the street, I repeated it to the officers. They laughed and put me in the back seat of the police car. They didn't appear worried, and it was perhaps their casual lack of concern that had a calming effect on me. They said they would take me to the station house and wait for someone to claim me. Just as we were pulling away from the curb, the driver caught sight of my mother in the rear view mirror, waving her arms. As my mother told the story later, she had spotted the top of my head in the rear window of the police car and began to yell and wave her arms. And that was the end of it. Over the years, my mother and my Uncle Roy seemed to enjoy telling the story to my relatives. My cousin never missed an opportunity to tell the story on me to his friends. I was glad when they put Lucinda in the mental hospital, and moved out to the San Fernando Valley in California.

It was not as though I lacked ambition; I wanted a college education, a good job, a comfortable life. I had no desire, like many of my co-workers, to work for Sid Caplan all my life. And I wanted to be married to Laura, despite everything that had happened between us these past weeks. That was the rub, wasn't it? She could not, or would not, understand what it was that held me here. I liked to think that I was at least capable of understanding what made her so dead set against the place. Her parents were the chief reason. From the time she was a little girl they had striven to control every facet of her life. They picked out her clothes (even when she was a teenager), disapproved of her choice of friends, and decided where she would go to college (she had been accepted at Radcliffe with a generous financial aid package; they had refused to let her attend). They would have had no compunction in choosing a husband for her if she hadn't finally rebelled. The thought had crossed my mind more than once that she had married me more out of defiance of her parents than love for me. The only way I would ever know for sure would be to hear it from her. She'd had plenty of chances to use it as wedge against me since we had known each other, but she had never gone near it. In our present fragile state of being I lived in a kind of anxious limbo, half expecting the truth to come out over the phone from California.

* * *

"I hear that friggin' song one more friggin' time I'm driving over to WTSN and yanking it off the turntable. Jesus, it's all they play!" Tommy Laroche whined.

"What friggin' song?" I asked him, though I could not have been less interested.

"Louie friggin' Louie. That's all they play, I swear to God."

"You just don't appreciate good music," Brother James said, deadpan.

"You can't even understand the words. I read somewhere they were dirty. Who could tell? I'm telling you, it's all they play on that station."

"So listen to a Boston station," Brother James counseled.

"I can't listen to that classical shit, either. Why can't you find a station around here plays good songs, hit parade type songs? Like "Shrimp Boats," or "On Top of Old Smokey," songs like that. All this rock and roll crap gives me a headache. Hey, I bowled a one-nineteen last night," Tommy said, through with his diatribe against radio stations.

"Sure, in your dreams," Brother James said.

"I'm not shittin' you. I was unconscious."

"You're so full of shit your eyes are turning brown. You never bowled over ninety-five in your miserable life."

"Ask Stu Newman. He was there. I was making impossible spares; seven-ten splits, you name it."

"Yeah, right. You lie and Newman swears to it. I'll believe it when I see you bowl a hundred with my own eyes."

If rock and roll music gave Tommy Laroche a headache, his dialogues with Brother James gave me one. I told Sid I had stomach troubles and punched out early. What was troubling me was in my head, not my stomach.

On my way home I spotted Charlie surrounded by three urchins just past Archie's store. One of them was trying to get the paper bag Charlie was carrying away from him. The other two were jabbing at him with their fingers. My favorite urchin, the shit-slinger and leader of the pack, was not with them today. Then they had Charlie on the ground. The bag flew out of his hands, its contents spilling out. A carton of milk exploded on the pavement.

"Get up, re-tard," I heard one of them say before he kicked Charlie in the side. Another one gave the two-pound bag of sugar a kick, busting it open. I had taken off on the run, but they spotted me and fled before I could reach them. Charlie writhed on the sidewalk making sounds like a dog run over by a car. There was a red welt on his cheek, and foamy saliva had gathered in the corners of his mouth. His body began to convulse.

169

"Take it easy there, Charlie. Settle down." He was wild-eyed. I grabbed him under the arms and tried to hoist him up. I could manage his dead weight only to the sitting position. I caught a whiff of his peculiar odor, no doubt exacerbated by his fear. I shivered. "Come on, Charlie. Give me a hand. I can't get you up if you don't help." Charlie continued to wail. Cars slowed down; people stared. No one stopped to lend a hand. I kneeled down and held Charlie in my arms. He drooled on my favorite tan jacket.

"It's all right, Charlie. Don't cry. Everything's all right now." He cried harder. I tried rocking him in my arms. "You're a big boy, Charlie. Big boys don't cry. You wouldn't want Laura to see her big boy cry, would you?"

"Laura? Laura?" Charlie said, a bubble of snot inflating in his nostril.

"That's right. Now come on. Show Paul what a big boy you are. I'll help you get up." All of Charlie's weight seemed concentrated in his shoulders. I got him on his knees, straddled him from behind, and holding him under the arms, pulled as hard as I could. This time, Charlie helped. "Hurray! Way to go, Charlie!" Charlie snorted out a laugh.

"We going to see Laura now?" Charlie brushed off the blue parka he had on despite the fact that the temperature was in the mid-sixties. His hand movements were clumsy, uncoordinated, like a baby's. His jacket was torn under the arm; down spilled out and floated to the sidewalk. Except for his bruised cheek he seemed unharmed.

"All right, Charlie, what do you say we go tell your mommy about your adventure?" I picked up what was left of the bag of sugar. Charlie started to sob.

"Bad boys. Bad boys," he said over and over as I held on to his arm and walked him the short distance home.

"Yes, Charlie. Very bad boys."

Mrs. Pappas was waiting on the sidewalk in front of the house, hysterical.

"My baby! What have they done to my baby? Oh, mommy shouldn't have sent you out all alone."

"He's all right, Mrs. Pappas. Just a little scared."

She was all over Charlie, hugging, kissing, crying. This got Charlie crying again. They stood there on the sidewalk in each other's embrace, like reunited lovers.

I called the police from Mrs. Pappas's apartment. I told them what had happened in broad daylight, gave them a description of the three urchins (as if they didn't know by now their identities intimately) and got in a few licks about the streets not being safe for kids under thirteen, and old people, what with these guttersnipes running loose day and night. People deserved better protection from their police force.

"Thank you so much, Paul. I should never have let him go to the store alone, but I was feeling so ill. I wrote him a note for Archie's …"

"It's not your fault the streets aren't safe, Mrs. Pappas. Maybe the cops will do something this time." And maybe not, I thought.

TWENTY-NINE

"That's the end of them, Paul," Devlin said in a queer voice as the Dodgers from Los Angeles finished off the mighty New York Yankees in four games. I had to agree with Devlin, the Yankees had a look of utter defeat about them as they walked off the field looking weary and dejected as their pinstripes disappeared into the dugout. Devlin made it sound like the end of a cherished way of life. I was more concerned by the fact that Laura had not called in a few days.

"Cheer up, Dave. There's always next year. That's what Sox fans always say."

"No. That's the end of them." Devlin took down his shot and stared into the empty glass.

"Forget it; concentrate on the Celtics. What do you think their chances are of winning six in a row?"

Devlin was in no mood to make light of the Yankees' humiliating defeat.

"Fucking Dodgers. Fucking Koufax."

* * *

I had just turned the burner on under a pan of Dinty Moore beef stew when I heard Charlie's knock on the living room door. I wasn't really in the mood for Charlie so soon after the street scene, but he knew I was in, and he wouldn't go away until I answered the door.

"Is Laura here?

"No, Charlie. She's still visiting her mommy. She won't be back for a long, long time. I'll tell her you were asking for her when I talk to her on the telephone. All right?"

"Can I see the pretty bird?"

"He's sleeping. Maybe tomorrow you can see him.'"

"All right." Charlie turned and went heavily back down the stairs.

I had to wonder how Charlie could keep in his memory the fact that there was a bird in the apartment, yet forget that I told him it had died. He was probably incapable of grasping the concept of death. His fixation on Laura had persisted, unabated, for nearly two months. How would I ever be able to explain to the kid what that was all about? It was obvious that his mother had not explained anything to him about Laura and me.

I smelled something burning. I ran to the kitchen to find smoke, but no flames, rising from the saucepan. I scraped the charred stew into a garbage bag, ran water in the pan and left it in the sink. I wasn't really hungry anyway.

I put on some Chopin by Rubinstein and opened up *The Naked and the Dead*. Honcho climbed into my lap and began to purr. I stroked his pelt and tried to concentrate on Mailer. But I hadn't been able to concentrate on anything since Laura had been gone. Laura's failure to call left me with a cold foreboding. My worst fear was that she had called Noelle, and Noelle, despite her promise to keep her mouth shut about us, had spilled it all to my wife.

Then Noelle was knocking on my door and coming into the room without waiting to be invited, which annoyed the hell out of me.

"What are you listening to? It's nice." She scooped Honcho from my lap and began to stroke his side. "You were off somewhere inside yourself the other night, in the back seat."

"So what? You got what you wanted."

"Don't be cross with me, Paul. What's wrong?"

"I tried to explain. You weren't listening." Noelle sat down on the sofa with Honcho squirming in her arms. "I believe he wants you to let him go." She released the cat; he bolted for the kitchen.

"You'll regret it, Paul." Noelle brushed cat hair off the front of her slacks with her open palm.

"Regret what?"

"Going back to her. She'll break your heart. She's using you, Paul. Can't you see that? Look what she's done to you already."

"What concern is it of yours?"

"I could make you happy, Paul. I could do a better job than she has. You have to know that inside."

"I thought you said you had no interest in my heart."

Noelle got up from the sofa and stood in front of me. She started to unbutton her blouse. "I say a lot of things I don't mean."

"Cut it out." I got up and walked to the kitchen. Honcho waited patiently by his food bowl. Noelle followed me. She opened the refrigerator.

"You don't even have any beer?"

"Afraid not. Hand me the cat food while you're in there, will you?" Her blouse was unbuttoned to just below her bra. I heard Devlin's screen door open. He came out on the landing, hawking phlegm. I didn't want him to see Noelle in my kitchen.

"Why don't you go in the other room. I'll be in after I feed Honcho." I meant the living room. Noelle assumed I meant the bedroom. She was out of her clothes and into my bed by the time I finished putting down food for my cat. She sat up in bed, naked, brushing her long hair with my hairbrush.

"You're a beautiful girl, Noelle. You've found out what a pushover I am, and you're playing it for all it's worth." I sat down at the foot of the bed. Noelle had a coy smile for me.

"You don't do anything you don't want to do. You still have your free will."

"Sometimes I doubt it. Sometimes I feel like a robot, and you're working my controls."

Noelle giggled. "All right, then get out of those clothes," she said, in her robot voice, "and get into bed. Noelle commands you. Come to Noelle." She beckoned to me with both hands and slid down low in the bed.

"I'm going out for a pack of smokes. I'd just as soon not find you here when I get back. Understand?" Noelle smiled and put her thumb in her mouth like a little girl, and struck a sex kitten pose. "I mean it." I turned and left the apartment.

I killed some time in Archie's back room talking to Whitey, and Ray Duffy, wondering what my reaction ought to be if I found Noelle still in my bed when I returned.

"You working a full day on Saturday, Paul?" Ray asked me.

"I suppose so. Why?"

"Me and Whitey are going over to the Greeks for the October Harvest blowout. We thought you might like to come along. We'll be heading over around noon."

"Yeah. I'd like that. I'll punch out early and meet you guys here."

"Hope it's a little cooler on Saturday. Whoever heard of it hitting ninety degrees in October?" Whitey shook his head in disbelief too. He couldn't ever remember a warmer October, and Whitey had been around for a spell.

I was hyperconscious of the clock on Archie's desk. I wanted to be gone at least a half hour to give Noelle a chance to get bored and leave, in case she was too stubborn to go just because I had asked her to.

"As long as the nights are cool enough for sleeping," I said. I could talk weather with the best of them. When sufficient time had passed, I bid Ray and Whitey farewell and walked slowly back to my apartment. On the way I discovered that in my groin I wanted to find Noelle waiting for me, naked in my bed.

There was a note for me from Noelle on the kitchen table:

Call me when you come to your senses.
You know you want me.
Don't deny it.

THIRTY

The October Harvest Fest, I was not surprised to see, was an all male event. The Greek pavilion was the site of this annual event as well as a couple of Greek picnics during the year. It was a nice spot, set back from the road on high ground with a lovely view of Great Bay.

On the short drive from Archie's, Whitey had fallen asleep in the back seat of Ray's car. They had got a bit of a head start at Archie's; Ray's face was flushed, his pale blue eyes watery. He drove the winding road at a maddening twenty miles an hour. I pressed my feet hard into the floorboard, and held on to the armrest as Ray drifted into the oncoming lane and back several times on the trip. I considered myself lucky to arrive in the parking lot alive.

The pavilion was open on three sides, connected to the main building where the Greek community met and held their dances, game nights, and benefit concerts. Three fifty-gallon oil drums cut in half lengthwise served as barbecue cookers. The grates were full of sizzling half chickens. Long folding tables covered with white cloth and laden with bowls of potato salad, coleslaw, baked beans, condiments, paper plates, napkins, and plastic utensils were set up next to the barbecue drums. Three kegs of beer had been tapped; men already had the kegs surrounded, paper cups in hand. A fat man in a billed cap sold tickets at five dollars apiece at a card table. Ray and Whitey paid up and made a beeline for one of the kegs. I looked over the food table, my belly growling from hunger.

"Chicken'll be up in ten minutes," a thin man dressed in jeans and white T-shirt said to me. He wielded a set of tongs and was busy turning chicken halves over as flames from burning fat leaped from the coals.

"Smells almost good enough to eat," I said, picking up a paper plate and loading up on potato salad, crescent rolls, baked beans, and coleslaw. When my chicken was ready, I looked for a place to sit down and have at it when William was at my elbow.

"This must be my lucky day," William said.

"What's luck got to do with it?" I was, to say the least, not pleased to run into William, especially as I was about to sit down to a good meal, a meal that William the gourmet cook would no doubt disparage.

"Luck that my car would break down at this particular place, and that I'd find you here."

"I wouldn't have thought brand new cars would break down so easily." I heard the ice in my voice, and hoped that William heard it too.

"You know how many miles I put on that baby week in, week out? I've got to ask you a favor, Paul. A big favor."

"You can ask, but I doubt I can be any help with your car. Just because I work for an auto parts company doesn't mean I know anything about what goes under the hood of an actual auto." I sat down at a picnic table; William sat across from me. He looked sharp in a blue blazer and maroon ascot. I caught a glimpse of Whitey and Ray over William's shoulder, jawing with some men around the keg. I picked the chicken up in my hands and bit into it. Blood oozed from where I had bitten, instantly taking the edge off my appetite. William noticed the uncooked chicken and made a face.

"Looks like the chef may have been too long at the keg. Take it back, Paul. You don't want to get sick."

"Don't worry. I'm not about to eat this."

"Listen, I really do need a favor," William looked over his shoulder. "I was on my way to Portsmouth to see a client when my car gave up."

"This is kind of an odd way to get to Portsmouth."

"I wanted some scenery. Anyway, I got this important client I'm supposed to meet at two o'clock. Can you give me a lift? I'll pay you, of course."

"I didn't drive here, William. Remember, my car's not running. I came over with some guys."

"Well, I guess I'd forgotten about your car. Who'd you come with? You think they could help me out?"

"I don't know. I wouldn't feel comfortable asking, you know?"

"Come on, Paul. This is important to me. I'm kind of desperate, if you want to know the truth."

I looked at William's handsome, clean-shaven face. He did look a little on the desperate side. "Wait here. I'll see what I can do."

Standing close by the keg, Ray Duffy was in no mood to give up an afternoon of beer drinking to drive some stranger to Portsmouth. He reached in his pocket, swaying back and forth, and tossed his car keys at me without a word.

"You sure, Ray?" I said, fingering the keys, excited at the prospect of finally getting behind the wheel of Ray's sweet Caddy. Ray waved me off and turned to the spigot for a refill.

"I really appreciate this," William said, as I steered out of the parking lot onto the winding back road to Portsmouth, mindful of the last time I was behind the wheel of a borrowed car. "Let's put the top down. There won't be many more days like this, Paul. Let's take advantage of it." It was indeed a fine early autumn day, maybe in the low sixties, but I had no intention of taking liberties with Ray's baby, and putting the top down I considered taking liberties.

"Ray told me the switch is on the bum. It'll go down, but he can't get it back up except by hand. I don't want to screw it up."

"Too bad." William looked over his shoulder through the rear window. In the space of two or three miles, I noticed he did this several times.

"We being followed?" I said. William laughed, but it sounded to me like a nervous laugh. I glanced in the rear view mirror just before the Route 4 intersection, and was surprised to see a State Police car behind me. I felt, instinctively, in my back pocket for my wallet. I had been known to leave home without it, and if the cops stopped me and I couldn't produce a driver's license ... that would be just one more aggravation I didn't need.

"Now we got the law on our tail," I said. William swung around in his seat.

"Jesus. Step on it, Paul. We can't be stopped."

"You're kidding." I turned to William, but his attention was out the back window.

"No, I'm not kidding. Trust me, we don't want to be stopped."

"What's the deal, William?" I saw the cruiser's roof light go on. "Don't look now, pal, but it looks like we're going to have to stop whether you want to or not. You better tell me what's going on, William." I turned off onto the shoulder before the intersection and stopped the car. The cruiser, light rotating, pulled in behind me.

"This is wrong, Paul. You shouldn't have stopped. Christ, I should have known better than to trust you to ..."

Two very tall and muscular troopers in tight fitting uniforms got slowly out of their car. They moved toward Ray Duffy's '59 Cadillac convertible, one on the driver's side, the other on the passenger side. William sat rigidly, his head moving back and forth, his eyes fixed on the windshield. I stuck my head out the window as the trooper approached.

"What's the trouble, officer?" Peripherally, I saw the other trooper on William's side.

"You mind stepping out of the vehicle?" the trooper asked me. His partner requested that William do the same. I had not had much experience with traffic stops, but this seemed like anything but routine. "May I see your driver's license?" The trooper stepped back to give me room to get out of the car. I reached for my wallet. The other trooper said something to William I couldn't hear. I handed the big trooper my license, my hands trembling.

"Registration's probably in the glove compartment," I said. "This belongs to a friend. He let me borrow it to ..."

"We know all that," the trooper said. He sounded bored. His eyes darted over my license. "Don't bother with the registration. Who's your passenger?"

179

"My passenger? William St. John. He's a friend … I mean he and his wife …"

"Where are you two headed?" He handed my license back to me. I wanted to see what was going on with William and the other officer, but something told me not to look in that direction.

"I was taking him to Portsmouth to see a client. His car broke down back at the pavilion. He asked me to take him. He's got a two o'clock appointment, I think. William?" I turned toward the passenger side of the car. William was spread out, his hands on top of the car. The trooper was patting him down.

"Listen," my trooper said to me, "we're going to have to take William here in for questioning. We don't have any business with you, so you can be on your way."

The next thing I saw as I got back behind the wheel was William St. John, gourmet cook and libertine, being escorted to the police cruiser with his hands cuffed behind his back. I felt a smile forming on my lips, in spite of myself.

THIRTY-ONE

"Paul, I'm so sorry he had to involve you. He is such a ... user," Noelle said.

"Don't be sorry for me. I'm not the one facing prosecution for bunco. Why did you do that to your hair?"

"I felt like being a blonde for a while. You like it?"

"Makes you look like a street walker."

"You're full of compliments lately."

"Can't you see? I'm trying to break this thing off with you."

"Have you talked to Laura?"

"She's about to land a job. Then I'll go out to join her. I don't need any more guilt than I've got already. I'm sorry if I led you to believe that there could be anything between us, Noelle. Truly sorry."

She laughed harshly. "No you're not." Her myopic eyes took on a flinty hardness, and I had never heard such bitterness in her voice. "You're no more sorry for what you've done to me than William is, so don't put on the virtuous act for my benefit. It sounds tinny coming from you. I have a good mind to call Laura and set her straight about her little saint."

"You've got her number?" Noelle didn't answer. "You told me once you weren't the vindictive type. What could you possibly gain by doing such a thing?"

"Revenge. Revenge against you, and better yet, revenge against her. Laura and her sanctimony," Noelle hissed.

"I gave you credit for more character." Noelle produced another harsh laugh. "Whatever made you think that there could be anything between us beyond what we had? You led me to believe that your interest in me was purely physical. Now you're laying this revenge crap on me."

"You're like every man I have ever known."

"Laura's no man. Why have you got such a hate on for her? You used to be best friends."

"I have always despised her. Nobody was ever good enough for her, with her high standards. Look what she's done to you."

"Noelle, I wish you would leave now. Do what you feel you have to do, but just get out of my sight before I do something I'll regret."

"Don't listen to me, Paul. I don't mean any of this. I'm just so miserably unhappy. I suppose I fantasized about us. I knew it would never come to anything, that we would never have a life together, but ... I could never do anything to hurt you, as much as I hate Laura. Don't worry, Paul. If it doesn't work out for you and Laura it won't be because of anything I say. Believe that."

"All right, Noelle. But I still think you had better go now."

"Goodbye, Paul. And good luck."

* * *

Noelle had succeeded in thoroughly shaking me up. I lay down on the bed next to my cat.

"Did you get an earful of that? Do you believe she'll keep her mouth shut? I'm not sure I do. Of course, I'll have to tell your mother myself what really happened. Everything ought to be out in the open. That's the way I always want our marriage to be. I can't live a lie. It's just that I don't want her to hear it from Noelle. Did you ever think of your mother as sanctimonious? I confess, there were moments when I thought she might be walking a thin line on that one. I'd rather deal with a little sanctimony once in awhile than vengeance, if you want to know the truth. Are you getting any of this?"

* * *

I awoke from what must have been a troubling dream because I felt anxious and out of sorts. I had no recollection of its content. Laura claimed that dreams are inevitable even if they can't be remembered. I tried to go back to sleep, but I could only shift from one uncomfortable position to another, and by three o'clock I was fully awake. In the short time we had actually lived together, (and according to her, all of her life) Laura had been prone to bouts of insomnia. She would have none of fighting it out in bed; she would get up immediately, make a cup of coffee and read, or work crossword puzzles. I seldom experienced sleeplessness. On the rare occasions that I did, I would remain stubbornly in bed, determined not to give in to insomnia, not to sacrifice any more of my precious sleep than I had to. This morning it was no use. I gave up trying, got dressed in the cold bedroom, and went into the equally cold living room. I turned on the TV knowing that at this hour I would get only test patterns. I sat and stared, trancelike, at the snowy screen for several minutes, feeling dread creep into my insides, the way the cold had penetrated the apartment. October had been all warm days and cold nights. My calculations told me that I hadn't heard from my wife in nine days, too many days for me not to think that something had gone wrong. I had tried, unsuccessfully, to pry Lydia's unlisted telephone number from the San Francisco operators. That meant I was, for all practical purposes, incommunicado with Laura.

* * *

"I've been out of my mind."

"I know, Paul. I'm so sorry. It's been just awful. I'm so discouraged."

"Don't be. It's the same story everywhere, I hear. I thought you'd changed your mind, if you want to know what I thought. It's been ten days, and I thought ..."

"I'm ready to come back. That's how desperate I am, Paul. Paul? Did you hear me?"

"Yes." I never expected to hear such an admission from her, and after all these weeks here it was. And here I was, hesitant, ambivalent.

"Well, isn't that what you've wanted all along?"

"I don't think I ever wanted you to come back here because you were desperate, Laura." And since my involvement with Noelle had gotten so complex in my wife's absence, the idea of them being in each other's proximity again gave me pause.

"You surprise me, Paul. I never expected to hear these words from you."

"I guess I could say the same thing about you. I suppose we're all capable of change, given enough time."

"It means a lot to me to hear you say it, Paul."

"I only want you to be happy, Laura. That's all I ever wanted."

My wife began to cry. "I don't know what to say. I can't bear to be away from you a minute longer, but I just don't know when, or if, anything will break for me."

"Something will turn up. You'll see."

THIRTY-TWO

I nearly lost my breath when I opened my pay envelope and saw the check for one hundred-twelve dollars and sixty-six cents. It was only the largest paycheck I'd ever received in my life. At this rate I would make more than my old friend Jack Scanlon. The fact that I had to bust my rear end fifty-eight hours a week to earn this amount did nothing to dampen my momentary euphoria. Add to that the twenty or so hours I put in at Archie's Corner Store and I could make a case for my being overworked. As my father was fond of reminding me with annoying regularity, when I worked for him at the bakery after school and during summer vacations, I was no slave to the work ethic. I liked the pay well enough. I could think of no one who wouldn't be considered a slacker if they compared themselves to my father, a true work junky. What hard work had got for him was an early grave. I had to rule out heredity because his own father was still hale at seventy-five, and his mother, my grandmother, was seventy-two herself, and still drove her Ford convertible around Sarasota, Florida. No, it was definitely the work that did my father in. As Jack Scanlon, who was as averse to work as I was, was fond of saying: "Work is the curse of the drinking class," a play on the words of Marx, or one of that crowd.

If I had any sense I'd beg off a few hours at Archie's. Even if I could lose Friday nights, it would go a long way toward making my life more bearable. After everything Archie had done for me in my hour of need, for which I had repaid him by smashing up his convertible, I could not bring myself to ask him for the favor. Now that I was flush, I could afford to eat out Saturday night, maybe someplace with good seafood. I didn't relish dining alone, and I couldn't think of anyone who would go out with me. Noelle came to mind, but I would have to be demented to open that book again. A good used car is what I needed. I had been grounded long enough. If I had reliable transportation, I could drive out to the West Coast, save myself the anxiety of air travel. I could get some tranquilizers for Honcho (maybe even some for myself) and have a traveling companion. That's what I should do. Tomorrow I would search the ads in the *Record*.

Earlier, Gil Freese had come in the office with a big grin to invite me on another Sunday afternoon golf outing. The temperature was supposed to hit seventy, if the weatherman was to be believed, he'd said. I was quick to remind him about our last experience on the golf links.

"I'm surprised you have any clubs left in your bag," I said to him.

"I got clubs up the ass. Listen, every golfer has a bad round now and then. You gotta keep going back."

I stuck to my promise never to cast a shadow on a golf course again as long as I lived.

"Jesus, Embry, you need to get out more. You need to have some fun once in a while." Gil Freese had it right about my needing to have fun. It was just that I had a hard time associating fun with the game of golf.

"Ask me to kick at bowling balls in my bare feet, but don't ask me to play golf."

"You'll change your mind, Embry."

If there was little chance that I'd change my mind about subjecting myself to another humiliating experience on the golf course, there was no such certainty where my marriage was concerned. Here I was, making some financial progress in my new position at Sid's, while my wife was spinning her wheels in San Francisco. I knew that the issue wasn't all, or even a little bit, about economics, but it galled me that my wife had taken it on herself to set this crisis in motion. Now I found myself wanting her to strike out, to end up begging to come back to me in this place she claimed to despise. It would be simpler if Noelle had not entered the equation. I reconsidered asking her out to dinner Saturday night. If we could work out a truce, an understanding—if she could give me the assurance that she wouldn't spill the beans to Laura—then I would be in a better bargaining position.

* * *

"I'm sorry for the way I treated you yesterday, Noelle. You don't deserve it."

"Oh, I probably do. I've been such a clinging vine, such a limpet. It's no wonder you want to be rid of me."

"Speaking of shellfish, how would you like to go out to dinner Saturday night? We could eat some seafood at Hannon's." I had spoken without considering what a bad idea it would be for me to be seen in a public place with Noelle. If Laura did end up back in Garrison, it would take about eleven seconds for the news to get to her that I was dining out with her best friend, lately become my sexual consort. "On second thought, Hannon's might be a bad idea."

"I understand. We could go out to the Dragon Seed. I haven't had Chinese food in ages."

"There's a small matter of transportation."

"You can drive William's car. He jumped bail and took a bus to Florida to be with his mother. Of course, that's probably the first place they'll look for him."

"William's Corvair?" That appealed to me on a couple of levels. "I'd like that. What time shall I come for you?"

"That depends."

"On what?"

"You know what."

"I was hoping we could just have a meal and maybe talk over a few things, like what we'll do if Laura takes it in her head to come back."

"I don't think there's much chance of that happening, but don't worry, Paul. Didn't you believe me when I promised not to tell on you?"

"We sound a lot like school children."

"Well, do you believe me?"

"Sure."

"Then come over early. You have nothing to worry about except yourself."

"Myself?"

"Yes, your penchant for confession."

"I believe I've learned my lesson."

"Good. Come at five."

THIRTY-THREE

At two-twenty in the morning I was awakened by the sound of my pounding heart. I thought immediately of my father's heart condition and the hereditary implications. I hadn't had a physical since I mustered out of the Army. The truth was, I had little confidence in the medical profession, and Doc Robinson's antics didn't do much to allay that feeling. Nevertheless, I found myself dialing his office number during my coffee break that morning. He agreed to see me during my lunch hour.

* * *

"No, Doc. I actually heard it. I was lying on my side and it woke me up. It was loud, like a tympani." Doc had a listen with his stethoscope.

"There's nothing wrong with your ticker, Paul. Your contractions are strong, your rate nice and slow, like an athlete." The only physical exercise I was getting lately involved sexual gymnastics with Noelle. I was relieved to hear Doc's words, however, even if I wasn't sure I could trust his diagnosis. "You should plan on having a complete physical every now and then, given your family history."

"I realize that. The truth is, I'm not crazy about getting pricked and probed."

"Who is? It's one of those unpleasant facts of life. Get used to it."

It felt strange to talk to Doc in this fashion, here in his office which was in the old Belmont Elementary School building, lately converted to office spaces for doctors and lawyers. He looked very professional, sitting there behind his desk with his white smock, stethoscope slung around his neck.

"What's the damage?" I said, reaching in my pocket, wondering if he would charge me the going rate for office visits.

"Save it for your reunion with your wife. When are you planning to join her?"

"Hard to say. It depends on whether she can land a job. As soon as she does, I'm gone. She's not having much luck."

"Yeah, it's tough everywhere. Too bad she's not here. I got two tickets to the opera in Boston I'm trying to unload. Gounod's *Faust*. I bet Laura would enjoy it."

"Where'd you get opera tickets?"

"The wife's a member. I can't make that date. She won't go by herself, and none of her snotty friends can make it."

"Why don't you try Archie? I'll bet he and Loretta would enjoy an evening at the opera."

Doc laughed. "I'm trying to picture Archie and Loretta in a balcony seat with opera glasses."

"I can't even picture myself at one."

"If you plan on taking up residence in a place as culturally sophisticated as San Francisco, you had better learn to picture yourself at the opera. And the symphony, and the ballet while you're at it."

"My grandmother used to say 'You can't make a silk purse out of a sow's ear.'"

"Your wife can pull it off if anyone can."

"You think very highly of her, don't you?"

"You're a lucky young man. I hope you realize that. Now don't fuck up again. You banging anybody in your wife's absence?"

"Hell no."

"Don't get defensive. There's nothing to be ashamed of. You're a male, aren't you? Getting laid is a male imperative."

But I was enough of a Puritan to avoid admitting, even to Doc, that I was cheating on my wife in a big way. If he was as high as he claimed he was on Laura, who was to say he wouldn't judge me?

Saturday, before I took Noelle out to dinner at the Chinese restaurant in Kittery in her husband's Corvair convertible, we made love three times, once on the living room floor, on William's favorite newspaper reading spot, for old time's sake. When we returned from the restaurant, we did it standing up, fully clothed in the doorway to the bedroom. Then we ate leftovers out of the cardboard containers before having another go at it, this time while dancing naked to a Sinatra album. No, it was going to take more than mere promises for me to get Noelle St. John out of my system. The drunks had their AA, but what did I have? There ought to be an organization for people like Noelle and me—sex fiends anonymous had a nice sound to it.

THIRTY-FOUR

A week ago a killing frost had leveled both beds of the touch-me-nots Mrs. Pappas had planted on both sides of the front walkway. The maples in back of the house, and all along the west end of Washington Street, had reached peak autumn colors. What followed were several days of Indian summer with daytime temperatures in the eighties. I couldn't remember a warmer October in my lifetime. Neither could Devlin, but who could say how reliable his rye-soaked memory was?

"No, my boy. This has got to be the warmest October on record."

"I can't remember one this warm," I added to our banal weather talk. Then I made the mistake of telling Devlin about my plans to join my wife in California.

"For what it's worth, my boy, I think you're making the biggest mistake of your life."

"You could be right, Dave. I've got to give it a roll, though. You understand?"

"I'm afraid I don't understand." Devlin's speech was starting to turn to mush, as his speech was wont to do after the fourth or fifth jigger of whiskey.

"I want to get back with Laura. What's so hard to understand?"

"Nothing's so simple as it appears. Everything has a price. You get what I mean?"

"Sure, but ..."

"But nothing. You go out there you better be prepared to part with your soul."

"My soul?"

"You heard me." Devlin pulled himself up by the handrail and, a little wonky on his feet, went inside to fetch his bottle. I was annoyed at Devlin, even if I knew his opinion was informed by whiskey, for going on about my soul, the drunken old hypocrite. Devlin never made it back outside. I heard the argument with Maggie start up in the living room. I went inside to look for something to eat. I found nothing except cat food in my cupboard. I had a sudden yen for one of The Cantina's fifty-cent meatball sandwiches.

* * *

I suppose I shouldn't have been surprised to find George Stacy drinking a glass of beer at the bar. It was more unusual that I had not run into him before today.

"Why don't we get a booth?" I said, not wanting to eat my sandwich at the bar because I had a thing about having people observe my eating technique.

"How have you been, Paul? Jack filled me in on your problems, you know, with your wife."

I brought George up to date on the state of my marriage. "What are you up to, George? You going to school?"

George had matriculated at U.N.H. last year, but had to drop out for financial reasons. At present, he worked as a stockroom clerk at Northeast Aviation, and had enrolled for the fall semester in a political science course at the university extension. His wife, Elaine, worked for a finance company. She had a bachelor's degree in history, but she had no desire to teach.

"It's been a long time, Paul. Funny how easy it is for friends to get out of touch."

"Do you see Jack? How's his new job in Boston?"

"We were down to see him last weekend, as a matter of fact. The job's all right, but the way he and Katie are with each other... I don't think we'll be visiting them again anytime soon. Not if my wife has anything to say about it."

"The way he described his marriage to me, I'm not surprised. Poor bastard." Glenda came around to take my order. "You going to eat something, George?"

"Not when I'm drinking."

"Jesus. You and Scanlon are truly birds of a feather."

George Stacy had considerably less hair on his head than when I saw him last. Despite Doc's assurances that *alopecia* was not in my immediate future, heredity was not on my side in the hair department. My father was showing a lot of forehead by the time he reached forty. If George Stacy had lost a little off the top, his facial hair was still abundant. George had always been able to cast a five o'clock shadow by noon.

I finished my meatball sandwich while George swilled beer after beer. I ordered up another sandwich; George's beer glass needed refilling.

"It's getting to the point where I don't know anybody in town anymore, except for the guys I work with," I said. "All of the old crowd seems to have disappeared."

"Anybody with any sense has got the hell out. I guess that leaves just you and me." George laughed. "If I manage to get a degree before I turn senile you can bet your ass I'm going to put some distance between myself and Garrison. Elaine can't wait to get out of here either."

"The Garrison exodus." I remembered the Leon Uris novel, *Exodus*. I read it when I was stationed in Inchon, thinking it was a damned good book before Laura disabused me of that judgment.

"But you're right. None of the old gang is on the scene. There were some real characters around when we were in high school, weren't there, Paul?" George smiled and shook his head.

"I sometimes wonder what became of some of the girls we panted after. Where did they all go?"

"Married. Most of them, I imagine." George finished off his beer and signaled Glenda for a refill. "Won't you join me in a glass or two, Paul? We've got some catching up to do."

"What the hell. But don't let me overdo it." I told George about getting blotto with Jack Scanlon, and paying for it all next day.

"I'll keep an eye on you. A lot happened around here the years you and Jack were away. I was around long enough to see some pretty weird stuff."

"Tell me about it. Laura clued me in on a few people but she never traveled in our circles."

George leaned against the backrest, and made figure eights on the table with his beer glass; he looked pensive, as if he were deliberately organizing his thoughts for chronicling the events that occurred while Jack Scanlon and I were serving in the Far East.

"Here's one," George said, a grin forming on his lips. "You remember Marcia Bridges, right?"

I remembered Marcia Bridges. I remembered her father too. Malcolm Bridges owned a chain of movie theaters in the state; the Colonial in Garrison was one of them. He lived in a big house on Grove Street, big enough by Garrison's standards to be considered palatial. He was one of the few decent members of the Garrison Country Club that I encountered in my years there as a caddy. We hit it off so well, in fact, that he hired me on as his personal caddy. He would take me along whenever he played other courses around the state; he even took me to Massachusetts with him a few times during the season.

Marcia, his daughter, was in our high school class. She was fairly nondescript with short brown hair, and brown eyes. She was about five foot three, and while she didn't have a bad figure, neither was it the kind of figure that made guys take notice. At the same time, all the boys agreed that there wasn't anyone who could match Marcia Bridges for sex appeal. When she looked at a boy, he knew he was under sexual scrutiny. She was too much for the boys her own age; the older guys could barely handle her. When the word got around that she put out, it didn't take long for Marcia to get a reputation as a slut. She didn't seem to mind that her female classmates shunned her. On the contrary, Marcia wore her reputation with a kind of pride, and showed nothing but disdain for those girls whose cream cheese morality and provincial values she found contemptible, hypocritical.

Not long after the beginning of her senior year, Marcia dropped out of school. The official word was that her father was fed up with her rebellious ways, and had her sent off to boarding school. I knew Mr. Bridges pretty well, but I didn't see it as my place to ask after his daughter. Later on, rumors started going around that she had gotten pregnant, and her father had sent her away somewhere to have the baby. That was the last news I had of the fate of Marcia Bridges.

"Didn't she get knocked up, or something, senior year?"

"That was the story around town," George said, "but it wasn't the whole story. That came out a couple years later. It seems that our friend was messing around with the guys from the base, the flyboys. Seems she had a preference for, shall we say, *swarthy* types." George swallowed some beer and continued. "She got pregnant all right, and I guess her old man had come to accept the fact, but when she brought home a pickaninny the guy went completely ape shit. Kicked her and her dusky whelp out of his big house. Nobody saw hide nor hair of her for a year or so. Then, out of the blue, she turns up back in town. And it looks like she's back living at home, but there's no sign of a kid, of any color."

"This was when? '59?"

"Yeah. Must have been not too long after you went overseas. You surprised the crap out of me when you joined the Army. I would have bet the store that you were college bound. I think Jack regretted not going to school, though he won't admit it, even today. By the way, he's taking courses at Boston State."

"There were some things my father and I didn't see eye to eye on at the time. I thought it would be better if I put some distance between us. Then he had to go and croak on me just when I believed we had things worked out."

"Yeah. That's a bitch, Paul. I'm sorry. I meant to send you a note, condolences, whatever, but I'm no good with grief."

Too bad about you not being good with grief, I thought. How do you think I felt? I said no such thing to George Stacy, however. Why stir up the pot?

"So Marcia's back home, and all is well with dad?"

"Not exactly."

The Cantina was starting to fill up with the college crowd. Somebody pumped coins in the jukebox, and the room was soon enveloped in loud music and boisterous conversation. I leaned in to hear George better.

"Go on, George. So things weren't all sweetness and light between them ..."

"Miss Marcia tried, the best way she knew how, to give her old man a coronary. She started dating this spade from the base. She'd show up on his arm at the Colonial, or Marcia would make sure she was seen swapping spit with the dude in the lounge of the Emerson Hotel by people who'd report back to her dad. She flaunted this guy around just to piss off her father.

"Remember Ahmed Hassan, used to run the Army-Navy store on Fourth Street? He was black enough to be considered a Negro in Garrison even though he was middle-eastern, some kind of Arab. There was a story—and I don't know if it's true or not, but I hope it's true—that old man Bridges, who liked to cruise through the theater after the cameras started to roll to check the number of patrons against ticket sales, walked up the aisle of the balcony and spotted his daughter blowing this camel driver. That's when Marcia exited for the second time. No one has seen her since."

I didn't say so to George, but my sympathies were with Mr. Bridges, the kindly golfer who used to tip well, who never failed to buy me a cold drink after every nine holes of golf. So what if his bag weighed a ton and seven-eighths? As for Marcia, it was one thing to be sexy and rebellious, quite another to use your sex as a weapon of vengeance against your family. But what did I know about what really went on between Marcia Bridges and her dad? I wondered where the mother was in this drama.

"Tell me another story, George, before we won't be able to hear anything but that freaking jukebox. What in hell is that music?"

"Get with it, pal. That's The Beatles from England. They're all the rage."

"Do you know what became of Neil Sullivan?"

George's eyes opened wide. "Why, did you see him last week too?"

"I haven't seen Neil Sullivan since high school. Why last week?"

"Because last week is when he paid us a visit. Sully and his older brother Jerry. It's just funny you should bring his name up now."

George picked up his glass and waved it at Glenda when he caught her eye. Glenda, whose face, according to Jack Scanlon, inspired George Stacy to want to drive nails through it. "Two more Knicks over here, darling. Please."

"Not for me, George."

"Oh, hush up."

"Your friend will have to finish the one he's got in front of him before I can serve him another," Glenda said, and her word was law in The Cantina.

"Drink up, Paul. Take a look around. This may be the last chance we get at Glenda."

"Don't worry about your service, mister. I can take care of the house."

"So why do I think Neil Sullivan and his older brother perpetrated evil deeds upon your household?"

"Elaine's just now starting to talk to me again. After tonight, who knows?" George laughed himself into a fit of coughing. "So, we're getting ready for bed. It's almost midnight. I see a set of headlights coming up the driveway, then a couple of car doors slam. I don't think anything of this—just the neighbors coming home. Then I hear 'Stacy. Stacy, where the fuck are you? Come on out and play, Stacy.' I recognize Sully's voice right away. So does Elaine. She tells me not to answer the door if he figures out what apartment we're in. Remember, she's still getting over two weeks of Jack Scanlon as our houseguest. She tells me she's not in the mood for an animal like Sully. But Sully's not one to give up. He keeps yelling my name, so it's either let him in or have the neighbors sic the cops on me, or worse, have the landlord all over my ass. So against Elaine's wishes, I let them in the house. They got two shopping bags full of quart bottles of beer. You know Sully's brother Jerry?"

"Never met him. All I know of him was that he was in the Army, serving in the Middle East."

"Well, Sully's what, six-five, six-six? Jerry's got two or three inches on him, and about ninety more pounds. My living room is tiny, and with those two in the room, it's claustrophobic. All I can see are legs. They drink their beer out of these quart bottles that look like stubbies in their hands.

"They hang around, drinking and talking loud till four-thirty in the morning. Elaine is coming to a boil. Finally, she gets up and stomps off into the bedroom, and makes a point of giving the door a good slam. Sully and his brother had ignored her completely, and her dramatic exit didn't faze them in the least. It was as if she were invisible. So Sully has to reminisce about every fucking thing we ever did together in high school. Jerry sits back and takes it all in, drinking his quarts of beer like soft drinks.

"Sully's on his way to the West Coast; he was accepted at Pomona, can you believe that?"

"Is Pomona something special?"

"You bet your ass it is. He's talking about getting back into the track and field thing, you know?"

"To compete? At his age? I doubt he'd be eligible. But what do I know?"

"He looks in shape, which is saying something given the way he lives. He could throw the discus a mile, in high school."

"Yes. I recall he had a fairly unorthodox training regimen. What was it, one six pack, or two before a meet?"

"Says he's going to major in history, go after his doctorate. Jerry's a senior at Middlebury. He's a French major. Wants to go to work for the U. N. He can put the beer away, I tell you."

"Maybe that will give him a leg up with the U. N. Who else have you got the low down on, George? Come on, out with it."

By now, George Stacy was well oiled. Consequently, he didn't need a lot of prodding to share what he knew about the fate of our old friends and classmates.

Two things stood out for me as George recited his litany of the destinies of the people we knew who had fled Garrison: the number of them who had chosen the West Coast, especially Southern California, as their destination, and the number of them who had succumbed to some degree of alcohol addiction. The most disturbing, and most heartbreaking for George and me, was Jimmy Bickford's story.

Jimmy's family had moved to Garrison in the summer of 1954. They lived two blocks from me on the same street. Jimmy hit it off with our crowd—the non- jocks—right off the bat. He became particularly tight with George and Jack. As it turned out, Jimmy was impressed with their drinking habits, and brought a good-sized habit of his own to the mix. He was all charm and good looks, too. He was an instant hit with the girls, a fact that might have created tension among his male friends except for the fact that part of Jimmy's genuine charm was that it was just that, genuine. It was a charm he seemed not to be self-conscious of, or willing to exploit for mere social gain.

Senior year, he got a job as usher at the Colonial. Ushers were required to wear uniforms, like doormen, and it was Jimmy's maroon usher's outfit with gold braid on the sleeves that gave his friends the opportunity to give him good-natured grief. Still, he willingly risked losing his job by opening the back door of the theater so his friends could sneak in without paying. That could have been why Mr. Bridges adopted the practice of checking out patrons against ticket sales. It couldn't have been Jimmy who was the source of the story about Mr. Bridges catching his daughter giving head to Ahmed in the balcony because Jimmy would have been long gone by 1959. George wasn't sure who it was that wore the usher's uniform at the time, but surely that's where the story must have come from.

During one Sunday afternoon matinee—and the Sunday matinees were not well attended—Jimmy let three of us in through the back door in the usual fashion. I was with George Stacy and Neil Sullivan. Neil had brought along a dozen bottles of beer in a paper bag to drink during the show. *Fear Strikes Out*, the story of Boston Red Sox centerfielder Jimmy Piersall, starring Anthony Perkins (recently of *Psycho* fame), was playing.

George and Neil had already drunk a lot of beer by the time we arrived at the Colonial. We skulked up to the empty balcony and took our seats. George and Neil popped their beers and drank them off. In a little while they had become drunk enough to dispose of what few inhibitions they had to begin with. They started commenting in loud voices on the action taking place on the screen. Neil mimicked Perkins' rendition of Piersall's crackup; as Perkins began to crawl up the screen in the ball park, Neil Sullivan screamed, "I gotta get back, I gotta get back, I gotta get back to the womb!" Then he rolled empty beer bottles down the carpeted aisle; they bumped down the steps and came to rest with a thunk against the half-wall that separated the balcony from the main floor. What few patrons there were in the house kept their eyes fixed straight ahead, not wanting to deal with the madman in the balcony. This brought Jimmy to the balcony on the run.

"Are you out of your fucking mind, Sully? You trying to get me fired?" Neil handed Jimmy a bottle of beer. Jimmy looked around furtively, chugged half the bottle, and wiped his mouth with his gold embroidered sleeve.

"Bridges isn't around today," Neil said. "Don't sweat it."

"Yeah, but old Tommy's down in the office and he'll blow the whistle on me if he finds out I let you guys in. So cool it, will you?"

On the screen, they were hauling Anthony Perkins off to the funny farm. I had seen Jimmy Piersall play at Fenway when I was playing Garrison Park League ball. Once a season the city hired buses to bring kids to Fenway Park for a Sunday afternoon game. Piersall seemed to enjoy jawing with the crowd out in the centerfield bleachers, the fifty-cent seats. He had a reputation for playing shallow no matter who was up at the plate, and wowed crowds by chasing down long fly balls that, had he played his position properly, would have come to him without his having to take more than a step or two in any direction. This, and the fact that relief pitchers in the bullpen would smoke cigarettes and drink beer during the game, disillusioned the hell out of me as a kid.

Jimmy Bickford kept his usher's job, but that Sunday marked the last time he ever left the back door open for his friends.

After a memorable graduation party in which Jimmy, George, Jack, and Neil managed to get themselves arrested for underage drinking in public, we all went our separate ways. Jimmy's family headed west for California, and Jimmy went with them. I got only one letter from him while I was in the Army. It was from other friends that I got reports about Jimmy's escalating drinking problem, exacerbated by what must have been a way of life in Southern California. It was in early June of this year when George heard from Jimmy's mother that they had found her son's body in a motel room on Laurel Canyon Boulevard. He was a John Doe for three days. The coroner reported that Jimmy had died of alcohol "poisoning." All Jimmy had in the room by way of luggage was a cardboard suitcase packed with pint bottles of cheap vodka.

As George told it, you could go to certain places in Garrison even today and witness the lives of a half dozen or so of our former classmates in the process of going down the alcoholic toilet. You could find them in places like Marty's Lunch, The Honeybee Café, The Bar Café, The Railroad Café, or the The Social Club.

Larry Stickney had dropped out of school the day he turned sixteen. He took a job at Miller Shoe to make enough to pay for his adolescent drinking habit. By the time he turned twenty-one he had held and lost four more low-skilled jobs, put on about fifty extra pounds with booze calories, and drank so often and so much that he couldn't even hold a job anymore. Today, at the age of twenty-three, unemployed and in poor health, Larry was the first customer in the door of the Honeybee Café when it opened, and the last one to be shooed out at midnight when it closed.

Steve Pope, whose itinerant house painter father was one of Garrison's leading drunkards, followed dutifully in his old man's footsteps by staying drunk every day of the week, and dividing his time between the Bar Café and the County Farm where he did regular thirty day stretches for drunk and disorderly, vagrancy, or failure to pay his debts. Steve was twenty-four.

And Lilly Fowler, if not the prettiest girl in my sixth grade class, was the best kisser, as I found out one night at a spin-the-bottle party at Sally Moreau's house. She had also dropped out of school upon turning sixteen, and at present spent her evenings in the back booths of The Social Club giving hand jobs to old men in return for drinks. Lilly was twenty-five. George said she looked forty.

And there were the drinker warriors, Bobby Perrera and Marvin Crutcher, who were the scourge of all the beer joints in Garrison, picking fights on whim, causing bodily harm and property damage. One night, Crutcher and his adversary's dispute spilled out into the street where Crutcher threw the guy through the plate glass window of Harriet's Apparel Shop on lower Center Street. That act earned Crutcher a six-month stint in the County Farm, a light sentence considering the fact that the guy he'd tossed through the window had required about two hundred stitches. A couple of more inches here or there, and Marvin Crutcher would have been doing a life sentence in Concord.

Bobby Perrera's specialty was sucker punching unwary targets in bars. His most talked about punch took place in The Railroad Café where he started at one end of the bar, and went to the other end on the run where he unloaded a haymaker to the side of the jaw of an unsuspecting drinker perched on the end barstool.

"I've got enough material here for a doctoral dissertation," George said. "The Effect of Alcohol on the Social Fabric of an American Small City. How's that for a title, Paul?"

"Yeah, Garrison's a case study all right. You may be on to something, George. Christ, that's just awful about Jimmy. He was such a great guy. How could Jimmy have let himself get so far gone?"

George was starting to look slightly "far gone" himself, except that his speech was okay, and his reasoning power didn't seem impaired. His face was flushed, however, and his eyes were shining brightly.

"I don't know. I used to think intelligence had something to do with it, but you take guys like Jimmy and Larry Stickney, and that theory doesn't stand up. Both of those guys had good heads. Maybe it's education, I don't know."

"Is Larry dead, too?"

"I don't think so. Why?"

"You said both guys *had* good heads."

"No, I don't think Larry's dead. All you'd have to do is go around The Honeybee and see for yourself."

George wondered if education had anything to do with out-of-control alcoholism. It would be hard to make that case for Doc Robinson, who seemed on the road to his own brand of self-destruction even with a Harvard Medical School education under his belt. Maybe it was the kind of education that mattered. As George and I analyzed Garrison, New Hampshire's casualties of booze, among whom I could not rule out my friend George Stacy, I never felt luckier in my life, and lately I hadn't been feeling exactly lucky.

"There must be some success stories. I can't believe all of us bit it."

"Shall we exclude present company? I don't like to think you and I, or Jack has 'bit' it, Paul. Not yet anyway."

"What about the Drew Allens, the Arthur Hendrys, the Elizabeth Merchants? They aren't down and out in Garrison's beer halls, or dying alone in cheap motel rooms, are they?"

"Come on, Paul. Those people weren't really us. You know what I'm talking about? What do you say we have another glass?"

"I thought you said you were going to keep an eye on me. I've had my limit."

"I can't believe it. You haven't changed a bit, Paul." George didn't sound as though he admired the fact that I hadn't changed my drinking ways. "You're probably right. I should have been home two hours ago. Elaine's going to let me have it with both barrels."

"Tell her you bumped into an old school chum. She'll understand."

"Sure she will. I could take you home as my shield, but I wouldn't subject a friend to such a fate. When will I see you again, Paul?"

"Hard to say. I could be on my way to California any day now. Which reminds me, I've got to look around for new wheels."

George and I parted company in the street in front of The Cantina. I marveled at how steady on his feet George was after all the beer he'd put away in the last two hours, and I wondered if I would ever see George Stacy again.

THIRTY-FIVE

"Floyd is becoming absolutely insufferable. I don't know how much longer I can put up with him. I can't bear to be in the same room with him."

"What do you expect from an accountant? What is it, exactly, that he does to get under your skin?"

"I've never met a more opinionated, self-satisfied, egotistical ... Nobody has anything useful to say on any subject, in his view. And he is so condescending to Lydia. To everyone, for that matter." My wife made a guttural sound that was meant to convey her vexation. Her description of Lydia's Floyd could aptly describe William, but I was smart enough by now not to bring up the comparison. Talk of William would invariably lead to Noelle. I didn't feel mentally nimble enough to deal with that subject at the moment.

"You used to be able to turn idiots like that inside out. What makes this guy so tough?"

"You'd have to meet him. He's relentless."

"I'm hoping I'll get the chance soon. How goes the hunt?" My wife's sigh was palpable.

"Paul, I'm ready to give it up and come back. I mean it."

Ironically, it was beginning to sound like I would have my wife back in Garrison after all, which is what I wanted from the beginning. Now I would definitely have to find a way to deal with Noelle.

"I'm making pretty good dough now, honey. If you could get your old job back we might be able to get somewhere."

"You know it will kill me to go back there, don't you, Paul?"

"Do your parents know where you are, Laura?"

"You're joking."

"What about your sister?"

"I haven't talked to anybody in my family in I don't know how long. I'll bet they haven't called your number, either."

"No. And now that you mention it, I haven't heard anything from my side, either. For all we know, everybody could be dead. Aren't we a pair?" I tried a laugh, but it came out clenched.

"So, now you're having second thoughts about the extended family? I don't care if I never see any of them again. I'll be so humiliated if I have to come back."

"How's your money holding out?"

"I've got enough for a couple of months. I can't be away from you that long, Paul. I miss you so."

"Why don't I just come out there? Take my chances. I could do that, Laura."

"No, darling. That would be too risky. We couldn't stay with Lydia, and there isn't enough money to get a place of our own, not without a job."

"We seem to be in a bind. Maybe if we had talked about this before …"

"Please, let's not go over all that again. We've been all over that, Paul."

"Tell me about it." Just because we had been over the subject before didn't change the facts. It was my wife's impetuous act that had put us in the bind we were in. I simply wanted to make it clear to her that I hadn't forgotten.

"I'm so desperate, Paul, that I'm going for an interview at a department store tomorrow morning, a very fancy department store. There's an opening in sales. Ugh." Laura felt the same way about salesmanship as she did about waitress work. "It shouldn't take them long to size me up as unsuitable for the position."

"It shouldn't be hard to give them that impression if you put your mind to it."

"I'd love to. I'm sure it won't pay enough to even tempt me. But I'm so desperate."

"I can just picture you behind the cosmetics counter, spritzing perfume on the wrists of San Francisco dowagers."

"Oh, thank you."

"You're welcome. Why don't you throw caution to the wind and let me have Lydia's number so I can call you once in a while?"

"Floyd would have a fit."

"Can you think of a better reason to give it to me?"

"You're right. If he answers, just hang up. Okay? The best time to call is around five. He doesn't get home until six or later. Don't try to call on weekends."

* * *

I searched the Want Ads in the paper for a lead on a used car, but I didn't see anything in my price range. And as I thought more about it, I finally came to the conclusion that it made no sense to spend, say, five bills on a used car only to drive it across the country. In the city I'd have no need of a car. It might actually be a liability. Still, I missed having wheels. It was un-American. And I couldn't get Noelle out of my mind. Our Saturday night sex marathon was still burned in my memory. There was just no possible way I could deal with both Noelle and my wife in the same geographical space. I had no business doing what I did with Noelle Saturday night, male imperative or not. If I weren't careful I could become the architect of my own sexual prison.

Part of me regretted not joining Gil Freese on the golf links Sunday afternoon. It might have acted as a kind of purge for my transgressions of the night before. Today, Gil Freese had come into my office high from the ninety-seven he'd carded Sunday afternoon, the first two-digit score of his golfing career.

"You should have been there, Embry," he'd said. "I was making putts like you wouldn't believe. Now that I've broken that cherry it's only a matter of time before I break ninety."

I couldn't let his euphoria go unchecked. "Yeah. In another ten years would be my guess. Of course, we have only your word for this breakthrough, right, Gil?"

"Fuck you. Stu Newman was with me. Ask him."

"Ah, Stu Newman again. He has a knack for being present when guys like you and Laroche have these days. Unbelievable. What, do you guys pay Newman for this service? Remind me to take him around Frenchie's with me sometime. He could have me running off a hundred balls."

"You want proof? I got the scorecard in my truck. You want me to get the fucking scorecard, Embry?"

"You call a scorecard proof? Don't make me laugh." It had always amused me how the golf crowd put so much trust in what they considered the "honor" of the game, which included honesty in score keeping. I knew better, from my experience as a caddy.

"Why don't you just fuck yourself, okay, Embry?" Gil Freese said with a good-natured laugh.

Oh, how simple life could be if women weren't in the picture. I should seriously consider celibacy. What a mess I was making of my life. No wonder men took to drink. I had no such refuge.

To add to my latest burden of guilt, I had not paid Mrs. Pappas a visit since Charlie's run in with the urchins. And lately I had ignored Charlie's knocks on my door as well. I had to work at Archie's tonight, a duty I was not eager to discharge. Tuesday nights were generally quiet; maybe I could make some progress in *The Wapshot Scandal*.

* * *

The atmosphere in the back room was one of concentrated gloom. Archie's face sagged; Whitey, beer bottle in hand, leaned against the door jamb and stared at the floor; Ray Duffy sat in the straight-backed chair, forearms on his knees, contemplating the label on his bottle. Doc's absence in the recliner was conspicuous.

"Who the hell died?" I asked, trying to be funny.

"It's Doc," Archie replied.

"Doc's dead?"

"No, no. But he might wish he was."

"What's going on?"

"Colleen's accusing Doc of raping her. If that ain't enough, one of his patients is bringing a malpractice suit against him."

"Christ! Who's Colleen?"

"The nurse he been banging for the last six months. She gets a hair acrost her ass because she don't think Doc's been paying enough attention to her lately. Then this candy striper catches Doc nailing her in an empty hospital bed and reports them. Colleen probably thinks she's defending her reputation."

"What about the malpractice thing?"

"I don't know for sure. Some fucker claims he got infected after Doc pulled out his appendix. Claims Doc was drunk during the operation. How could anybody know that when he's knocked out with ether?"

"Face it, Arch, it wouldn't have been the first time he went inside under the influence."

"So what? Doc knows what he's doing."

Neither Whitey nor Ray had anything to add.

"What's he going to do?" I asked.

"Don't know. He's coming by later. He's seeing a few people."

"I imagine one of these people must be a lawyer."

"Yeah, Freddy Garabedian."

"Ah, the shyster."

"It's what you need these days." Archie unwrapped a fresh cigar, inserted in whole in his mouth to wet it down before firing up.

If Doc planned to come by later, I hoped that at least one of these guys would be on hand to deal with him. I found myself rather unsympathetic to Doc's thorny dilemma; the rape was one thing—the woman's word against his—but to operate on a patient, drunk? To be honest, I was surprised he hadn't been taken to task long before this. As much as I liked and admired Doctor Tom Robinson, I could not countenance his "professional" conduct, at least in the operating room. It was horrific enough to have to go under the knife, without having to be sliced open by a scalpel-wielding drunk. No, I didn't want the burden of having to lift Doc's spirits.

I was behind the counter when Doc came in the store a half hour later. He walked right past me without so much as a hello. He wasn't wearing his trouble well: his big shoulders sagged under his blue serge jacket; his face was gray, and his mouth turned down at the corners. I said nothing to him as he headed for the back room to huddle with his drinking companions who were still back there holding their silent vigil. A few minutes later, Archie and Doc solemnly left the store. I went down back to see what was up with Whitey and Ray.

"Where are Doc and Archie off to?" I asked them.

"On their way to Loretta's place to have some drinks and talk things over. There's a chance Colleen might show up," Ray said.

"Colleen? That sounds promising, right?" Whitey nodded.

"Doc thinks she'll probably drop the charge if he sweet talks her enough, gives her a present. He's more worried about the malpractice suit. When Garabedian gets through with him he'll be eligible for welfare." Ray smiled ruefully.

"Jesus, what if he loses his license? I'm sorry, you guys, but hasn't Doc taken a lot of chances?"

Whitey and Ray looked at me, uncomprehending. In their eyes Doc could do no wrong. I heard the door open out front. I was grateful for an excuse to avoid further conversation with these guys. While I rang up a couple of beer sales, Whitey and Ray filed out of the store. Neither one of them said goodbye to me.

* * *

Sid Caplan discouraged his employees from making or receiving personal phone calls in his place of business.

"You want to make a personal call," he had said, "make it on your coffee break. Use Spiro's pay phone." He had no advice for guys who might need to be contacted by their people at home in case of an emergency.

So I was taken by surprise when Sid stuck his head in my office to announce that my wife was on the line, and I could take the call in his office. It was two o'clock; eleven in the morning on the West Coast.

"I am going to get so much shit from Sid for this call, Laura. Couldn't it have waited till I got off work?"

"No, it couldn't. Oh, Paul, I am so excited."

What had my wife in such an excited state that she couldn't hold onto the news for another four hours was the fact that she had been offered the sales job at the fancy department store. I had to understand, she told me, that this was not your Woolworth, not your five-and-ten-cent store. They wanted her to spend six-months in retail sales in the lingerie department, mainly to acquaint herself with their line. Then, they assured her, she would be promoted to buyer, which commanded a handsome salary and benefits, not to mention frequent travel opportunities. Laura had impressed management with her keen mind, her independent spirit—her "creativity." How all of these virtues, which I truly believed she possessed, had manifested themselves in a forty-five minute interview, I didn't ask. My wife sounded as high off the ground as Gil Freese had after breaking one hundred on the golf course last Sunday.

For my part, after I replaced the receiver of Sid's office phone in its cradle, I felt awash in a mixture of elation and dread. During the nearly three months I had been estranged from Laura my life had taken on a new stasis, one I was getting accustomed to. Now it looked like this was soon to come to an end. I would need to discover a new way to achieve equilibrium. This could account for the dread. So could the fact that I'd have to face the prospect of seeing my wife again after all the time apart. Where the elation came from I couldn't be sure. Of course I wanted to see Laura, to have her back, to get to some kind of normal state of being with her. It would be like starting from scratch; we'd have to get reacquainted. Would we be compatible in our new setting, or would the time we were apart have changed us in ways that made compatibility impossible? These thoughts caromed in my brain for the rest of the day, making concentration on work impossible.

Sid had said to me, when I finished talking with my wife, that he hoped everything was all right. He sounded almost sincere. I felt I owed Sid at least two weeks' notice, even if I knew he was capable of letting me go on the spot, of accusing me of turning on him after all he had done for me. A letter of reference from Sid would make me feel better about searching for work in California, but such a letter was no guarantee from a guy like him. I had already prepared Archie for my departure. That left Mrs. Pappas and Charlie ... and Noelle.

I dialed Lydia's number as soon as I got home from work. I was relieved when Laura answered.

"You're higher than a kite, aren't you? When do you start?"

"Monday. I am high, Paul, and you should be too. Do you know what this means?"

"I do. How soon can we start the ball rolling? We've got to talk about details."

"I'm going over the listings in the paper right now. I can't be sure how long it will take to find something that will suit us, darling, but it shouldn't be awfully long."

"Is it safe to assume that Andrea and her boyfriend are no longer part of the plan? Please tell me they're not."

"Of course not. That was just a worst case situation."

"Good. I still can't get over the fact that you're so giddy over landing a job as a sales lady. I thought that was the kind of work that made you want to puke."

"You weren't listening. I'll only have to do sales for six months. Then I'll have my own office, get to travel all over the country to shows, maybe even get to go abroad. I'm so excited."

"I'm not really looking forward to breaking the news to Mrs. Pappas. Charlie will be crushed. And there's Sid to deal with. He's capable of canning me on the spot. I'd like to get as much pay out of him as I can. Devlin's dead set against me going out there."

"You shouldn't do anything until you hear from me. I want to make sure we have a decent apartment and I'm settled in the job. Then you can do what you have to do knowing that everything is taken care of out here. All right, darling?"

"I guess so."

"What is it, Paul?"

"Nothing. It's just that this is all so ... sudden. You know what I mean?"

"It will have been worth it. Trust me, Paul. This will have been all for the best."

"I'm sure. Listen, what's today, November fourth? When would you estimate we could start rolling?"

"My guess would be no more than three weeks. I won't let it be any longer, Paul. I promise."

* * *

I took three deep breaths before knocking on Noelle's door. She answered the door wearing a white chef's apron.

"Now that's one article of clothing I never dreamed I'd see you wearing."

"It's William's. Now that he's gone I've had to fend for myself in the kitchen. How nice to see you. Come in the kitchen. I'm feeding Teddy his supper."

"I can't stay long. I've come to tell you something, and it's not going to be easy for me to tell it. Can we go in the living room?" I didn't want a witness (not even an uncomprehending one, like little Teddy) to what I intended to say to Noelle. She stopped, and glanced over her shoulder at me. She untied her strings and shrugged out of the apron. I thought I saw something dark pass over her face.

"All right, Paul. Go on in while I see to Teddy."

I sat down on the sofa and waited for Noelle, conscious of that patch of living room floor where we had last made love, feeling wretched and cowardly.

"I don't have to ask what it is that's so difficult for you to say to me," Noelle said, standing directly in front of me.

"Why don't you sit down, Noelle?"

"I don't need to sit down. So which is it? Are you going, or is she coming?"

I looked up at her face. Her eyes had that flinty hardness I had seen in them the time we quarreled. "What else did you expect, Noelle? You knew the score. Why make it harder than it is?"

"You haven't answered my question."

"In a few weeks; four or five weeks. I'll be the one leaving."

"That long? Why tell me now? There's still plenty of time for us." Noelle sat down beside me and put her hand on my leg.

"That's just it. There's not really any time at all for us. I can't let there be. It's got to end now, and it has to be cold turkey, like giving up cigarettes."

"Oh, Paul, you're such a romantic!" Noelle rose from the sofa and stood in profile, a hand on her hip. "You are such a poet."

"I'm sorry, Noelle. You must know how fond I am of you, but this is the way it has got to be."

"I want you to leave now, Paul."

"I ..."

"Please don't say another word. Just get up and go away. Now."

I got up and started to say something, but thought better of it. "Goodbye, Noelle," I mumbled, and walked meekly out of her life.

THIRTY-SIX

Now that I was starting to get a feel for the job, I was less in awe of Chessy Chessman and the mystique he had created for himself as somehow indispensable to the smooth operation of Sid's business. In truth, it was routine work, work of the mind-numbing kind. I was already bored with it, and happy to have the end of it in sight. The rush I'd experienced when I opened last week's pay envelope had passed. Even if it was more money than I had ever made in my life, I knew it was really peanuts. I was half tempted to announce to Sid right now that I was on my way out. To do such a thing would no doubt guarantee that something would go wrong at Laura's end, and I'd be up the creek once again. But I was antsy for things to happen, eager to get on the move.

Laura's first day on her new job had gone well. She had always, she said, loved looking through fashion magazines, and had more of a sense of what was chic in lingerie than she had given herself credit for. This had always seemed like a personality anomaly to me. So she didn't even mind that much having to deal with the public. It helped that the San Franciscan "public" was nothing like the rabble she would have encountered in such a job in Garrison.

* * *

I went to work at Archie's to find Doc in repose on the Naugahyde recliner, his legs splayed out. He was dozing, a paper cup in his hand balanced precariously on his middle. I eyed the cup, thinking I should take it out of Doc's hand before its contents ended up on Doc. His eyes opened as I approached him.

"Sorry, Doc. I didn't mean to wake you."

"I wasn't asleep. Just resting the eyes. How are you, Paul?"

"More important, how are you?"

"Hah. Looks like it's my turn in the barrel." Doc laughed harshly. "And a barrel is what I'll be wearing when that prick Garabedian gets done with me."

"Can't you find someone else?"

"Sure, but nobody as unscrupulous as Freddy. What matters now is winning."

"I see what you mean. By the way, it looks like I'll be joining Laura in a few weeks." I realized the moment I finished speaking that this was not the best time to be trumpeting my good fortune.

"Good for you," Doc said without enthusiasm.

"I wish there was something I could do for you, Doc. You've always been there for me."

"Thanks, kid, but you needn't worry about me. I can take care of myself." Doc shot his cuff and looked at his watch. "I've got to sit down with Freddy in half an hour. Tell big-balls I'll be back here at seven, okay? And my wife is apt to call, looking for me. You haven't seen me, right?"

"Sure. How's she taking all this?"

Doc had another sardonic laugh ready. "She's delighted, of course. She doesn't give two shits that Colleen's busting my balls, but the idea of her cash cow drying up doesn't sit well with her. I got a hunch she's consulting lawyers of her own."

"Ray told me he thought Colleen might be ready to back down."

"Maybe. With a woman you never know for sure. You don't need me to tell you. Last night she seemed ready. Tonight ..." Doc shrugged his shoulders and hauled himself out of the recliner.

"Good luck, Doc."

"Yeah." Doc brushed away the wrinkles off the front of his shirt and jacket, shook out his pant leg, and headed for the front of the store. I meant it when I told him I wished there was something I could do for him. He had lost the spring in his step, and for the first time since I'd known him, Doc looked like an old man.

I closed the store at ten o'clock, feeling restless. I couldn't go to sleep this early, and there was nothing on TV that would interest me. Was it Tuesday night that Frenchie told me there was a lot of action? I decided to check it out.

* * *

There was action, indeed, at Frenchie's. All six tables were in operation, and all the straight-backed high chairs against the far wall were occupied with spectators. Even the three illegal pinball machines were in use.

Sherm Hubbard, in his trademark moth eaten maroon sweater, was at table one. He hadn't changed much since my high school days. Sherm hadn't hooked himself a fish tonight. Instead, he had Bailey Layton for an opponent. They were clashing in a one hundred twenty-five pointer. I looked up at the wire and saw that it was a close match. Sherm and Bailey were well matched even if their styles were as different as two styles could be. Bailey Layton gave the first impression of a natty dresser in his gray suit that, to the untrained eye, looked well tailored. Close up, and in better light than you could find in Frenchie's, Bailey's suit was grease stained, the cuffs of the sleeves and collar frayed, the elbows

212

threadbare. Bailey Layton looked about Devlin's age. Sherm could have been forty-five, or he could have been sixty-five, or any age in between.

A game of three-six-nine was in progress on table two. I recognized Mike Rousseau, a big, curly-headed building subcontractor—one of Garrison's better sticks—and Phil Cane, the local prodigal son, currently enrolled in some third-string private college in Manchester or Nashua, I forgot. Phil Cane drove an MG sports car, and was a sharp dresser. Tonight he had on a camel hair topcoat, and wore a white silk scarf draped over his neck with studied casualness. He kept the coat on when he played, and the scarf would collect on the felt when he bent over for a shot. He was a consistent loser, but he didn't seem to care, as he flung bills on the table as if they were Monopoly notes. The other two players I didn't recognize, so they were probably not locals. It looked like high school kids took up the rest of the tables. The law said you had to be eighteen to play pool in the state; I doubted if any of these kids was older than sixteen.

The only light in the room came from the shaded lamps that hung by long cords from the ceiling over each table. I stood in the shadows and watched for a while. I itched to get in on the three-six-nine game, but five was a crowd.

Sherm Hubbard and Bailey Layton were a pleasure to watch. Layton was a spectacular shot maker and a better position player than Sherm. He had a queer stance, crouched like a cat, knees bent deeply. He had an unorthodox bridge, with his fingers in the vertical position, their tips on the felt. Sherm's strong suit was his safety game. He would never run more than four or five balls in succession, unlike Bailey Layton who could consistently run thirty balls, but when Sherm didn't have a sure chance at a ball he'd leave his opponent with no shot at all.

Bailey walked around the table like a dancer, in his high-top sneakers, studying the shot that Sherm had left him, which wasn't much. He was kissed against the six-ball at an angle that didn't permit a combination for the eleven, which was poised in front of the corner pocket. Even I could see that his best option was to bring the cue ball off the far rail to make the eleven. It was a fairly routine shot for a player of Bailey Layton's skill. But if he was a skillful player, Bailey was also a showoff. He liked to play for the crowd. He brought his cue stick up to a nearly vertical position over the cue ball, took a few practice strokes, and then made a sharp downward stroke off center. The cue ball skidded away toward the far rail for eight or ten inches before sharply reversing direction to sink the eleven in the corner. The spectators loved the masse shot and Bailey knew it.

"East wind got ahold of that one," Sherm said, unfazed.

It was likely that this game would go down to the wire, but I was growing restless again, and left abruptly. I walked to the corner of Orchard and Center, stopped a moment in indecision, and finally turned left on Center Street.

Garrison had not changed that much in the time I was away overseas. Ten o'clock had always been a sort of witching hour in Garrison, when everything in the world above ground came to a stop. It was different in the underworld, the world of beer joints, social clubs, poolrooms (of which there were three), and a couple of diners that remained open until 2:00 a.m. The drinking establishments were required by law to close up at midnight. Then the hardcore drinkers would migrate to the Monarch, or Stoney's Diner to get enough food in their bellies to nullify a full evening of steady drinking. My friends and I, on a busy Friday night at the Monarch Diner, had been known to beat it out the door without paying the check after wolfing down a couple of hamburger plates each.

I walked uptown past Calhoun's Bakery, Harriet's Apparel Shop (whose plate glass window had received the body of Mel Crutcher's victim), McCall's Jewelers, and at the bridge, Hannon's Fish Shack. Hannon's was closed at this hour, but the odor of fried food filled the air, mingling with the stench issuing from the Cocheco River as it coursed under the Center Street Bridge. I stopped on the bridge, put my forearms up on the railing, and looked down into the murky water eddying below. The Cocheco River's waters were pristine until they reached Garrison's city limits from the northwest. The river received its first insult from the Nossif Tannery on Orchard Street in the form of untreated waste. It then flowed under the Center Street Bridge, and over a small dam before getting hit again, once from Miller Shoe's effluent, then less than a hundred feet later, by pipes spewing forth crud from Northeast Aviation in the stockroom of which toiled my friend George Stacy. It was dealt its final blow by Caledonia Electronics on the south side of Washington Street. From there, now thoroughly polluted, it slogged its way to the Atlantic, first merging with the relatively untainted Piscataqua River.

It was the Cocheco River, thanks to Garrison's industry, that had given rise to the expression so well known to the citizens of Portsmouth and Garrison, "Portsmouth by the sea, Garrison by the smell." I had heard that plans were afoot in Concord, and in Garrison city hall, to clean up the river in an attempt to restore it to some form of recreational use.

I continued toward the upper square. Across the street, Mack's hot dog wagon was parked in the alley between Montgomery Ward, Devlin and Maggie's employer, and Sandy's Donut Shop. There was one customer at Mack's window, one solitary car parked on the east side of the street in front of Mack's wagon. When school was in session, Mack rolled his wagon up to the side entrance of Garrison High School and peddled his fifteen-cent dogs (two for a quarter) and soft drinks at lunchtime. Most Garrison High boys knew they could purchase condoms from Mack along with their dogs, that is, if they had the nerve to ask for condoms. I never understood the mystique that surrounded the buying of rubbers from Mack—why the purchase was always so furtive, with the goods being passed from Mack's palm to the customer's as if it were marijuana being bought and sold, not prophylactics. It even got to the point where code words were necessary in the transaction. "Two dogs with the works; make sure the skins are on." I was sure that some of my friends spent good money on condoms even if they couldn't have gotten laid if their life depended on it, just to give the impression that they were getting it. For old times' sake, I crossed the street and had Mack fix me one dog with the works.

I stayed on the east side of Center Street and walked north. Storefronts stopped at a traffic island that separated Center from Main Street. I paused to finish off my dog; the smell of onions from my fingers filled my nostrils.

While I had no reason to doubt George Stacy's account of the self-destructive tendencies of people like Steve Pope, Larry Stickney, and Lilly Fowler, I felt obliged to see it for myself. George had listed the Bar Café, The Social Club, and the Honeybee Café as their regular haunts, but I had forgotten who haunted which place. Across the traffic island, on upper Main, was the Bar Café. The Honeybee was on Fourth, two streets up from where I stood. The Social Club was way up on the south end of Center Street, farther than I cared to walk at the moment. I settled on the Honeybee.

As far as I knew, food had never been prepared and served at the Honeybee Café. What passed for solid food I could see on the bar from my vantage point in the doorway of Lord's Snack Bar, with its oblique view through the front window of the bar: gallon containers of ham hocks and pickled eggs, Slim Jims wrapped in cellophane, and a huge plastic beer glass full of dime packages of beer nuts. I had never set foot inside the Honeybee, and I had no intention of going in now, even if it was difficult to see much detail through the dirty window. The light in the room was dim, made dimmer by all the cigarette smoke.

The bar ran straight down the left side of the room for about a dozen stools before veering left for three stools that faced the front of the place. Across the street, the Colonial Theater's marquee advertised *The Ugly American*. Lord's flanked the Honeybee on the right; the Army/Navy store, (where the "swarthy" Ahmed Hassan, Marcia Bridges' consort, once worked, but worked no more), was on the left.

I had a better view of the booths that ran along the right side of the room than I did of the bar itself. When my eyes became accustomed to the light inside, I began to make out faces. Some I recognized. A surge of country music suddenly blared from the jukebox. The old Greek who owned the place was working the taps tonight. There were half a dozen customers at the long end of the bar, one solitary drinker in the short section facing the street. A man and a woman sitting on the same side of the table occupied the booth closest to the door. I recognized Kenny "Killer" Kilcullen in his black leather jacket (which he wore in all seasons) billing and cooing with some old Harpy with orange hair. Killer had long black hair slicked down with hair oil. He wore his sideburns long. Killer was a veteran brawler, and when he smiled there were a few spaces where teeth should have been. He looked thoroughly drunk tonight, as he would have to be to get so cozy with the wild-haired beast he was cuddled up to. Killer was by now in his early thirties; the woman he was with had to be fifty.

The only other woman in the room was Nadine "the troll" Kroll, as she was known. Nadine was a dwarf, a well-known habitué of Garrison's beer joints, who cheerfully gave blowjobs to anyone willing to fork over two dollars. Perched on the bar stool, Nadine looked like a child that had aged prematurely. The guy next to her I didn't recognize; he looked like a man in his sixties (Nadine liked old men), and he had on a brown double-breasted suit jacket over a pair of bibbed overalls. I searched the room for a sign of Steve Pope, or Larry Stickney, not sure I would recognize them if they had been, as George had said, going after their dissipation with such a vengeance.

Then a guy sitting near the end of the bar leaned over and said something to the heavyset guy who sat at the short end of the bar facing the street. They got up from their stools and walked to the back of the bar where the shuffleboard was, against the wall. It was when he got up that I recognized Larry Stickney. A bloated and aging Larry Stickney, but Larry Stickney, no doubt about it. I turned away, taken aback at the sight of him. As a teenager, Larry had been athletic, and powerfully built; he hadn't been a bad student either. He made the varsity track team freshman year, running the hundred-yard dash in ten seconds flat. But, as George had said, he gave up his formal education the day he turned sixteen. His older brother had been killed in Korea, on Pork Chop Hill, the day before he turned eighteen. Larry didn't follow in his brother's footsteps and join the Army since there was no war on, and if there were no war what would have been the point? Larry reasoned. I asked myself that question more than once during my own tour in Korea, not that I was eager for a war to break out.

I was beginning to have second thoughts about checking out the Bar Café after what I had seen of Larry Stickney. What would Steve Pope have in store? I walked around the back of the building next to the railroad station parking lot. On the other side of the building was a little room no bigger than a hole in the wall, at present called Natalie's Novelties. It had been, over the years, among other things, a barbershop, a shoeshine parlor, and a fish-and-chips joint. The entrance to the upstairs poolroom was next door to Natalie's Novelties, and finally Marty's Lunch, another beer parlor that offered nothing in the way of lunches. Beyond the parking lot, facing Fifth Street, sat the Railroad Café, two actual railroad passenger cars from the early part of the century joined end to end. The Railroad Café sold six ounce glasses of flat beer for a nickel. Only old geezers and the truly down-and-out did their drinking there.

Now that passenger train service to Boston had stopped, the railroad station was deserted. I could get Devlin's gorge to rise just by saying the name McGinnis, the man Devlin placed sole blame on for bringing the Boston and Maine Railroad to financial ruin.

The lights were on upstairs in the poolroom. I wondered who owned the place now that old Sam David had passed on. Sam was a little old Syrian with bright eyes, yellowish skin, and a kind heart. He was one of my favorite grownups when I was a high school punk aspiring to be a pool shark. When there wasn't any action on any of the three tables with their oversized pockets and dead rails, I used to play eight ball with Sam. Whenever he had a winning shot on the eight he'd always say to me,

"How's your heart, Paul? Go dago dago like Bruno Hauptmann?" I had no idea at the time who Bruno Hauptmann was, and I didn't want to appear ignorant by asking.

The other poolroom in Garrison was on Fourth Street, attached to the bowling alley above Page's Furniture Store. There were three tables that were in better condition than the ones in Sam's place, but the room was a draw for the leather-jacket types who were trying their best to be like James Dean, and who were always looking for trouble. Next to the bowling alley was a paint store, and next to that, Cohen's Delicatessen where Jack Scanlon worked from the time he was in sixth grade until he graduated from high school. The last building on the south side of Fourth Street was the Emerson Hotel where, in the lounge, Marcia Bridges reputedly carried on in public with a black airman from the base for the sole purpose of humiliating her father.

I walked behind the Railroad Café onto Fifth Street, crossed Center and turned down Main in the direction of the Bar Café. I had to see these things for myself, come what may.

It was Harley Pope, not his son Steve, that I spotted through the filthy glass door. Harley was dressed in his paint-splattered work clothes. He was the only customer in the bar tonight. His son Steve, with whom, according to George Stacy, Harley often drank, could have been on one of his County Farm vacations. I had a view of Harley's left sunken cheek, and his hawk-like nose in profile. It was Harley Pope's habit to work only long enough to finance a two-week or, occasionally, a whole month bender. When the money ran out, he would go back to work, and there seemed always to be work for house painters in Garrison and surrounding towns. Every house painter that I had ever known was a drunk, but not as big a drunk as Harley Pope. He was also the best house painter in town.

I continued south down Main Street. A little ways past the Bar Café was a private club called the A & H. I never understood why such places advertised as "private" when all anyone had to do to get in was push a buzzer. The bartender would release the door latch no matter whose finger was on the buzzer. What the letters A & H stood for I never knew; maybe "Alcohol and Hallucination." Beyond the A & H club in the next building was the Greek coffee house where Garrison's old Greeks gathered to play cards, drink strong coffee, and reminisce about the old country.

My old school, the Franklin School, with the sloping asphalt playground, was directly across the street from the coffee house. In addition to grades six through eight, which were located on the second floor, the building had served as a vocational school for high school kids on that track, and a school of cosmetology, all on the ground floor. At present, the building was empty. I crossed the street and put my fingers through the chain-link fence and tried to conjure images of us as kids at play on the basketball court, with baskets nailed to crude, wooden backboards made by the vocational school students. The lack of twine on the rims caused us to spend as much time arguing over disputed baskets as we did actually playing the game.

The girls would huddle near the back of the building during recess and watch the boys play ball. Sometimes they would work on impromptu cheers to use when we'd play our league games in the high school gym. They never got organized into an actual squad with uniforms or anything; they'd just show up for games in various random combinations and yell out cheers from the bleachers. I used to hold hands with Theresa Townsend in the Arcadia Theater during Saturday afternoon matinees. Theresa was as precocious and sexually aggressive as I was shy and passive. Theresa soon grew tired of trying to get a rise out of me and sought out faster male company among the vocational school boys. I could almost smell those institutional cooking odors from the Franklin School cafeteria.

Main Street merged into and became Washington Street as, in turn, Washington became Main from the opposite direction. On the corner was Northeast Aviation, and across the street the looming four-story presence of Caledonia Electronics. I walked up the sidewalk and over the Washington Street Bridge under which the Cocheco River once again rushed from the momentum it had gained from the dam above, and while the Cocheco headed for the Piscataqua River in Maine, I headed for home, my heart a bit heavy in my chest.

THIRTY-SEVEN

"I love my new job, Paul."

"That's great, baby, just great. Hey, do you remember Steve Pope? Larry Stickney?"

"Not really. Why? I'm learning so much about the lingerie line, Paul. It's not at all the way I imagined. I can't believe how we are so capable of closing our minds to possibilities."

"Yeah, I hear you. Let me tell you about the walk I took the other night ..."

"It's good that you're walking, darling. You don't get nearly enough exercise. Wait until you get to San Francisco, if you want to walk."

"Yeah, I remember those hills. This was a different kind of walk, Laura."

"You'll love Meg, my supervisor. She is by far the hippest woman I have ever met. Remember you were asking about the Blackhawk? She goes there at least once a week. She caught the MJQ last Friday night. Can you believe it, Paul? We're going to have such a life!"

"I'll bet we are. When do you think we can get started on it?"

"Well, if you're bound and determined to give Sid two weeks' notice, which, by the way, I don't believe for a minute that you're morally bound to do, given the way he's treated you, I'd say two weeks."

I glanced at the calendar on the wall by the phone.

"So, the twenty-first?"

"Yes, the twenty-first. I can't believe it. It's just as I imagined it would be. I'll send along a letter in a week or two, with details for packing and shipping our stuff, and instructions on how to make travel arrangements, and all the little things that you're too busy to bother with."

"So, it looks like this is really going to happen. If you want to know the truth, it feels very weird."

"I know what you mean. It's going to be all right, Paul. You've got to know that."

"Yeah, I know."

* * *

On Thursday, the twenty-first of November, I girded my loins and asked to talk to Sid in private. All the night before I had rehearsed my speech. When it came time to deliver it to Sid's face, I found myself standing mute in front of his desk.

"I know what you're going to say, Embry. I knew it a long time ago. Don't worry, I understand. Didn't I tell you I was out of line, what I said about you bettering yourself?"

"Thanks, Sid. I don't know what to say. It's my wife, really ..."

"I figured."

"I can work till December 5th. Would that be all right with you?"

"Yes, that'll be okay. I wish you all the luck, Embry; you know how I mean?"

"Yes, Sid, I think I finally do know how you mean."

* * *

"Hey, you guys," Gil Freese said from the doorway of my office just before lunch on Friday. "You hear the news about Kennedy? He's been shot. In Dallas or Houston or someplace, in Texas."

"You know something, Gil," I said, "that's not freaking funny." I assumed Freese was trying to be funny because he was grinning, as he always did, when he was trying to be a wise guy.

"That's right, Freese," Tommy Laroche added. "He may be a shithead but he's still the president. You're going too far this time."

"I'm telling you, Red Hansen from Garrison City Ford's out front. He heard it on the radio on his way over here. I shit you not. Go on out front and ask him yourself, you don't believe me."

Twenty minutes later, Gil Freese was back. This time he wasn't grinning. "Kennedy's dead. I can't fucking believe it. Took a couple shots to the head." Freese had a look of genuine dismay on his pink face.

"How can that be?" I got out of my chair and headed for the front of the store for confirmation. The countermen and several customers sitting on metal stools were talking in loud, animated voices. Someone had produced a radio. I heard the announcer say, "The President of the United States is dead by an assassin's bullet or bullets." Sid, at his usual perch at the end of the counter, an unlighted cigarette in his lips, massaged his forehead with his thumb and forefinger.

"I can't believe this," I said to him. Sid shrugged his shoulders. "Are you going to close early?"

"Close early?" Sid looked at me and blinked. "What for? What will closing early do for the man now? Besides, business is business."

"I know you got no use for Kennedy, but wouldn't closing the store show respect for the office, for the institution?"

"Don't preach to me, Embry. Punch out early you're so concerned about respect for the office. The store closes at six, like always."

Palmer, the head counterman, agreed with me that Sid ought to close the store, let the men go home to their families, even if none of them had any particular fondness for Kennedy. It was a national tragedy. Sid held his ground. It was all right with him if anyone wanted to punch out early to be with his family. That would be their business. But he wasn't about to send everybody home early with pay. There were his customers to think about. The men grumbled, but no one, not even I, punched out early.

I left the store and went out into a fine, warm drizzle, which added to the gloom that seemed to have descended on Garrison, as it no doubt had all over the nation, like a heavy blanket. Spiro's Sweet Shoppe, which normally stayed open until eleven o'clock on Friday nights when school was in session, was dark. The street and sidewalks on Washington Street were deserted.

I headed for home, walking slowly, my mind numb. At the store, our talk had ceased after Sid had declared that he would not close early, dead president or no dead president. I was surprised to see lights on in Archie's. I tried the door; it was open. I went inside. No one was at the counter, and there were no customers in the store. I heard laughter and voices from the back room.

"Hey, Paulie," Archie said. "What, the Jew make you guys work today?" Doc was slumped in the recliner, looking morose, holding onto his paper cup for dear life. Whether he was morose over the death of Kennedy, or was feeling the increasing weight of his own personal problems, I couldn't know. Ray and Whitey sat in straight-back chairs. Archie swiveled back and forth in the chair in front of his ever-cluttered desk. By the looks of them, they had used the assassination as a reason (as if they needed one) for serious drinking.

"Yeah, he did," I said, "and it looks like you're open for business, too."

"Nah, I'm not open. Just ain't gotten around to locking the door. Nobody's out anyway. World's going to hell in a hand basket. Get yourself a beer. That's what we been doing since we heard the news. Thank the good lord for drink." Archie raised his beer bottle in a toast to "the good lord."

I did as I was told and got a beer from the cooler. I spent a few minutes sharing platitudes with my sodden companions. Archie said it was a damn shame; and Doc lamented the passing of Kennedy: He who was so young and gifted, who had given the country hope, a refreshing new sense of purpose and style. What would become of Camelot now that LBJ was at the con instead of JFK? I wondered how this kind of talk would play at Caplan's Auto Supply. I left after one beer, and walked the short distance to my apartment in the steady drizzle, feeling something that I could only compare to a void. There was a letter in my mailbox, a rare event except at the end of the month when the bills turned up. It was too dark in the vestibule for me to make out the handwriting. In the light of my living room I recognized Laura's ornate script. The letter was postmarked November 18, San Francisco, California. There was a Hyde Street return address; I thought I understood that Lydia's place was on Haight. These would be my instructions for cutting all ties to Garrison that she had promised to send along.

I dialed Lydia's number. There was no answer. I tried again a half hour later with the same result. For the next hour and a half I dialed her number at ten-minute intervals. I tried my wife's number at work; there was no answer there either. It would be only five-thirty where she was. They would have gotten news of the assassination earlier than we had on the East Coast. It made sense that she would not be at work. I would have been surprised if the whole city of San Francisco hadn't shut down to mourn their dead president. So where was my wife, shameless in her adoration of John Fitzgerald Kennedy, doing her mourning? I continued to try and reach her at Lydia's number until one o'clock in the morning, then gave up and fell into bed, too exhausted to fall asleep. My phone rang at two-thirty.

"I was at a vigil. Meg invited the whole department to her home in Burlingame. Paul, I'm so upset. How are you feeling?"

"Better, now that I'm talking to you. I'm telling you, none of this seems real to me."

"It isn't real. It's ghastly. Did my letter get there yet, darling?"

"Yeah. Looks like I've got a lot to do. This thing's not going to make it any easier."

"I assume by now you've given Sid your notice. What about Mrs. Pappas? That should be the hardest thing, Paul. Poor Charlie."

"Sid was a prince, even if the jerk refused to let us quit early today, yesterday, whatever. I planned on breaking the news to Mrs. Pappas this weekend. I need to work up the nerve."

"I'm so upset." My wife began to cry softly. "I have to go now, Paul."

"I noticed a Hyde Street return address, Laura. Does that mean what I think it means?"

"I wanted it to be a surprise. I was careless. But I'll be here at Lydia's for one more week. I'm not telling you any more, but I think you'll be pleased, darling. Very pleased. Goodnight, sweetheart."

* * *

I just didn't have the stomach to go into work on Saturday. I called in sick and spent part of the day with Devlin in front of the TV watching all the post-mortem commentary. Devlin drank boilermakers, and offered up his assassination theories, one of which involved Fidel Castro. Devlin said he'd bet a week's pay that the shooter, this Lee Harvey Oswald guy, was on Castro's payroll. Castro had Kennedy bumped off as revenge for the Bay of Pigs. As if all the embarrassment and bad press were not payback enough for that fiasco, I countered.

"To hell with Fidel," Devlin said. He poured a shot of rye into his beer and drank it down. Devlin had not strayed far from his armchair in front of the TV since news of the killing broke yesterday. Maggie was disgusted with his morbid preoccupation with the events in Dallas. She refused to be part of it. "Did you see Walter Cronkite break down and cry like a baby on the news last night, Paul?"

"You know my TV, Dave. I couldn't have seen it if I wanted to."

"Yeah. Cried just like a baby. All them TV people are such Kennedy ass kissers."

Lee Harvey Oswald appeared on the screen. A clutch of reporters fired questions at him; flashbulbs went off and made him squint and turn his head away from the cameras. It was impossible to glean anything coherent from the reporters' questions or Oswald's answers. Chaos prevailed. Devlin had tried to fill me in on what happened yesterday:

Apparently this Oswald character had used a bolt-action rifle with a scope to take out the president from a window on the sixth floor of a book depository overlooking the street where the motorcade passed. A cop went into the building to investigate after a witness reported seeing a man in the window with what looked like a rifle. The cops found boxes stacked by the window that looked like they had been arranged to support and aim a weapon. They also found three spent cartridge casings. Then they discovered the rifle, partially concealed, on the same floor. While this was going on, according to Devlin, this Oswald guy had been challenged by a Dallas cop some distance from where Kennedy had been shot. Oswald shot the poor bastard, the cop, with a pistol, then beat it down the street and ducked into a movie theater without paying. The cashier called the police and they came and nabbed him in the theater, after a tussle, and charged him with murdering the cop. Then it came out that he fit the description of a guy who worked at the book depository and who'd gone missing, the guy the cops suspected of pulling the trigger on Kennedy. All this took place only about forty-five minutes after Kennedy got hit.

"That didn't take long," I said. "Anybody else in on it?"

"Who the hell knows? Don't make sense one guy could pull off a thing like that without help. I'm telling you, Castro's behind it."

This seemed implausible to me, for no particular reason, but I wasn't about to challenge Devlin, not when he was pouring boilermakers down his neck. Devlin got out of his chair and staggered to the kitchen to fetch his bottle of rye.

"Dave," I said to Devlin as he fell back into his chair, clutching his whiskey bottle by the neck. "I'm bound for California. I'll be leaving around the fifth of December."

"I'll believe it when I see it," Devlin snorted. "You're not cut out for big city life, my boy. I've tried to tell you that, how many times? Right here is where you belong." Devlin pointed a bony finger at the floor. "Jesus Christ! President Lyndon Baines Johnson. And we thought Kennedy was bad."

I wasn't thrilled about Johnson either. Next to Kennedy he seemed like one more crass politician, and a southern one at that.

"What if I promise to take good care of my soul?"

"I still say you're making the biggest mistake of your life. Why can't you make your wife come to her senses? She should be back here with you where she belongs. Wasn't she born and raised here? Had a good job at the bank. You two can make a good life for yourselves here in Garrison, for Christ's sake."

A good life, I thought. Like you and Maggie? "There are more opportunities to make a good life out there, Dave. She's been right all along."

"You got any idea how much it costs to live in a big city? Of course you don't. You're a babe in the woods when it comes to practical matters. California's not the Promised Land your wife makes it out to be, my boy. Listen to me."

"I believe I've had enough TV for one day, Dave. It's starting to get to me. Besides, I didn't sleep much last night. I think I'll go in and lie down for a while. Catch you later."

* * *

I had promised Mrs. Pappas that I'd spend some time with her and Charlie on Sunday. Yesterday, I had discovered her crying in front of her TV. Such a terrible thing, she had said. Like most of us, she could express only disbelief and profound sorrow.

Sunday morning I woke up with a bad case of heartburn. I had experienced this with greater frequency since Laura had been gone. I mixed myself an Arm & Hammer cocktail before heading downstairs to join Mrs. Pappas and Charlie.

"I still can't believe it, Paul. He was so young and bright. And such a pretty wife, poor dear."

"No, it doesn't make any sense." Why did everything I had uttered this weekend sound so inane? "The world doesn't make any sense."

"What kind of a world is it going to be for my poor boy when he grows up? What will become of him?" Once again, I wasn't sure how to react to this sentiment. Did Mrs. Pappas really believe that Charlie would grow up to take his place in the world, regardless of its condition? Did she really even expect him to "grow up"? I wasn't sure what the life expectancy was for mongoloids, but I had a feeling that it wasn't long. The weekend was having its bizarre effect on everybody. For a moment I envied what I imagined might be the constancy of Charlie's inner world.

On TV, they were preparing to telecast the transfer of Lee Harvey Oswald from the Dallas jail to another location. I'd had my fill of television for one weekend. I needed a pack of smokes; Mrs. Pappas was out of milk. I would need to screw up my courage on my trip to the store and back to tell her about my plans to join Laura in California. I fingered my wife's letter in my back pocket.

When I returned from the store, Mrs. Pappas was clutching the brooch at her throat. She looked like she was in a state of shock.

"He's been shot! Shot and killed right on TV!"

"Who, Mrs. Pappas? What's happened?"

"Harvey Lee Oswald. A man came right up and pointed a gun and shot him in the stomach. Right on TV!"

"Are you sure, Mrs. Pappas? How could something like that happen?"

A reporter was talking shrilly into a microphone. People were milling around in what looked like a narrow tunnel or corridor. There was too much noise, too much confusion, to hear clearly what the reporter was saying. I couldn't believe Mrs. Pappas was correct about Oswald being shot, but it was clear that something dramatic had happened. I switched the channel just as a rerun of the shooting was playing; there was the figure of man (a man later identified as Jack Ruby) with a felt hat and hunched shoulders, and Oswald's face twisted in pain. Seeing it again, Mrs. Pappas became hysterical, which upset Charlie who began his wolf howl. I punched off the TV. The absence of the flickering light, the noise, the chaos, was temporarily becalming. Charlie and his mother looked at me as if they were waiting for me to explain why I had turned off the set.

"We've all had enough of that," I said.

"Is Laura home?" Charlie practically moaned the question. "I want to see Laura." Mrs. Pappas began her pitch about Laura's mommy. This time Charlie wasn't satisfied. "Laura," he cried.

"Just a minute, Charlie," I said, reaching in my back pocket for my wife's letter. "I must have forgot. There's a letter here for you. From Laura."

"Letter?" he said, uncomprehending.

"Yes, from Laura to Charlie. Tell him, Mrs. Pappas." She looked confused but played along.

"Laura has written you a letter, sweetheart. Isn't that nice?"

"Laura!" Charlie clapped his hands like a seal, a broad smile spreading over his broad face.

I waved the envelope. "I'll read it to you. All right, Charlie?" Charlie gurgled with pleasure. I pulled the letter out of the envelope and unfolded it slowly for dramatic effect.

"Dear Charlie," I began, and took a deep breath of air to help me through my improvisation. "Please forgive Laura for not writing sooner, but she has been awfully busy. Her mommy is very sick. You are not to worry, though, because Laura is taking good care of her, just as your mommy is taking good care of you. Laura misses you, darling, and thinks about you all the time. Does Charlie remember the song Laura taught him to play on his organ?"

"Yes, yes," Charlie squealed.

"And does Charlie remember the hymn Laura taught him to sing?"

"Yes, yes, yes," he yelled, clapping his hands and jumping up and down in his seat on the sofa.

"Maybe you'll ask Paul and your mommy to sing it with you later. Laura's mommy needs her now. Remember, Laura loves you, and is always thinking of you. Be a good boy and take care of your mommy. Hugs, kisses, and a mountain of love. Laura."

"Isn't that a lovely letter, darling?" Mrs. Pappas said, stroking Charlie's back. Charlie wiggled off the sofa and got to his feet. He took his mother's hand and helped her up. Then he took hold of my hand and led us in the first verse of "Onward Christian Soldiers". I stuck the letter back in my pocket and sang in a voice as off-key as Charlie's, but, as Jack Kennedy was fond of saying, with vigor.

* * *

Honcho was asleep on the bed below my wife's pillow. I lay down beside him. He began to purr at once. "Believe me, it wasn't easy having to tell Mrs. Pappas that I'd be moving out in a couple of weeks to join your mother. She acted happy that we were getting back together finally, but I could tell she was disappointed. She would have preferred we got back together here, for Charlie's sake. I hope she'll be all right. I feel so damned guilty for leaving them like this." Honcho twitched an ear, oblivious to my blather.

"I wish J. Alfred were alive. It would be nice to have the four of us back together again. I know you weren't really interested in making a meal out of old J. Alfred. Were you? Don't sweat flying across country.

I'll get some stuff for you from the vet. I could maybe use something myself. I'll check with Doc. I'm not crazy about flying, if you want to know the truth.

"Your mother said I'd be very pleased with the place she's found for us. Wouldn't it be great if we had a view of the Bay, or the Golden Gate Bridge? Anything will be better than this dump. I won't miss this dungeon for six seconds. I'll bet you won't either. You'll thank me for teaching you how to be a stay-at-home cat. It's no picnic outdoors in the city, believe me."

As if he'd had enough of my nonsense, Honcho stood up, arched his back, made a few passes at his chest with his tongue, and jumped down from the bed.

THIRTY-EIGHT

In the days that remained before I was to leave Garrison, I would need to fetch boxes from the liquor store to pack what meager portable belongings were in the apartment, and send them on their way to California by Railway Express. The crappy furniture and the Zenith TV could go to the dump for all I cared. The rest of our so-called "affairs" were minimal considering we had no checking or savings accounts at the bank, and all the utility bills were up to date. Laura had taken it upon herself to book a flight for me on TWA out of Logan on Thursday, December 5th. I was obliged to work for Sid until the thirtieth. That would give me four days to do not much of anything except wait, and maybe say my goodbyes to the people who might be interested enough to want to say goodbye to me.

As much as my loins ached for Noelle, I was resolute in my determination to give her the widest possible arc. Of course, if she got it in her head to come calling on me there wasn't a thing I could do about that. I hadn't talked to her since the day she ordered me out of her house, so I assumed she felt that whatever it was that burned between us had gone out. She had apparently kept her promise not to blow the whistle on me to Laura. For that, I was grateful to her.

At Caplan's Auto Supply, after the ghastly weekend of television coverage of the assassination, followed by Kennedy's funeral and burial, it was as if nothing much had happened. Tommy Laroche and Brother James engaged in their usual fatuous repartee; Sid lipped his unlighted Chesterfields on his stool at the end of the counter; Ernie Golding had a new dirty joke to tell; Iggy Swenson, "Mr. Clean," brought another tuna salad on white bread for lunch; and old Harry Lamb wheezed his way through another day. The only reference to Kennedy was in the form of an unpleasant assertion by Oscar Michaud that it had come out in Dallas, on the very day of the killing, in pamphlet form, proof positive of the president's treasonous acts, just as Michaud had said all along. To everyone's credit, nobody rose to Michaud's bait, and he was left to fulminate and gloat by himself.

* * *

Tuesday was my night to work at Archie's. I had agreed to stay on through Sunday, December 1st. I sensed that Eddie Flanagan had something more he wanted to say to me after he acknowledged that he had heard I was leaving soon. Poor Eddie gulped down a mouthful of Orange Crush, and moved his lips, but no sound came out of his mouth. I could see in his eyes that he had something on his mind that wouldn't translate into words for him.

"So, Eddie, you getting much?" Eddie blushed and shrugged his shoulders. "You think I'm doing the right thing, Eddie, striking out for California?"

"At least it's war... war... warm there."

"Yeah, except in summer. I remember needing an overcoat in August last time I was there."

Eddie looked skeptical. "I... I... I... don't believe it. California?"

"Sure. Maybe not in Southern California, in Los Angeles, or San Diego, but up north it can get pretty damned cold." Eddie reacted as if this was brand new information to him.

"I thought it was warm all over."

"Does that mean you think I'm making a mistake?" Eddie rolled his head back and forth as if he were working out a kink in his neck. His hair had grown long since I'd last seen him, and it didn't look like it had seen any shampoo for a while. "You still working for Duke?" Eddie nodded in the affirmative. I could see Eddie's future: he would take over his cousin's window washing business in about twenty-five years. He shifted his weight from one foot to the other, his eyes darting around the room. I must have made him uncomfortable with my questions.

"Have another tonic, Eddie. On me."

"Sure." Eddie pulled another Orange Crush from the cooler.

"A lot of people think I'm doing the wrong thing, going out there. I used to think so too."

"May... may... maybe some people don't want you to go ..."

"Maybe," I said, oddly touched by Eddie's words. "But you know the old saying, Eddie: Out of sight, out of mind." Eddie chugged his soft drink and took the empty down back to save me the trip.

"Gotta go now," he said with a half-smile, and pushed through the door.

* * *

I was chatting with Mrs. Laughlin, a rabid Celtics fan, about the team's chances for a sixth straight championship, when Doc came through the door followed by Freddy Garabedian, who came in the store occasionally to buy cigars. Garabedian was short with a dark complexion; he was loud and vulgar. He interrupted our conversation to demand a pack of El Productos; Doc headed straight for the back room. Mrs. Laughlin continued to extol the virtues of Bill Russell and Bob Cousy, as I got Garabedian his cigars.

Garabedian shook his head as he unwrapped the package. "You people, all the time talking sports. Why don't you try reading a good book once in a while?" Garabedian directed his remark at Mrs. Laughlin, whom I doubted he knew. She regarded him with shock at first; then her look changed to amusement as the lawyer inserted a cigar in his mouth.

"And perhaps the gentleman could recommend a good book," she said in her haughtiest voice.

"Yeah. *Gone with the Wind*. It's a classic." Garabedian winked at Mrs. Laughlin and headed for the back of the store, I assumed to join Doc.

Mrs. Laughlin looked at me as if to say, what manner of creature was that?

"That's Freddy Garabedian, the lawyer," I said. Mrs. Laughlin arched one eyebrow to signify that she was aware of his reputation.

"What business does he have with Doctor Robinson? I shouldn't think they would be meeting socially." Mrs. Laughlin pulled the lapels of her fur coat tighter around her as if the thought of anyone having social intercourse with one as unsavory as Garabedian gave her a chill.

"I don't know what their business is. He comes in the store once in a while, but I've never seen him with Doc." I didn't think it was my place to gossip with Mrs. Laughlin about the real reason Doc was in Garabedian's company. The fact that Doc had brought him in store at all puzzled me. I wouldn't have thought, under the circumstances, Doc would want to be seen in public with any lawyer, let alone Garabedian.

Archie came in a few minutes later, and hurried to the back room without saying a word to me. Now, my curiosity was really stoked. Less than five minutes later, Archie came down the aisle followed by Garabedian. They left and got into Archie's car and drove off. I wandered to the rear of the store and peeked through the back room door.

Doc was stretched out in the recliner, brooding into his vodka milk cocktail. I had learned from Archie that the malpractice suit against him was about to go into motion. Once again, I felt awkward in his presence. The grief that was upon him now practically hung like a pall over his head and seemed to spread like a vapor in every direction until the whole room was full of it.

"Hi, Doc. How's it going?"

Doc put on a wan smile. "Don't ask."

"Sorry, Doc." I started to leave.

"Don't be sorry, Paul. There's nothing for you to be sorry about. I made my own bed. So, when's the big day?"

"The 5th. Plane ticket's in the mail. Speaking of flying, weren't you telling me a while back about a new drug they've come up with?

Supposed to calm you down when you're about to do something stupid that makes you feel anxious. Like flying twenty, thirty thousand feet above the planet in a machine put together by the lowest bidder. I remember you mentioning something about it."

"Yeah," Doc chuckled. "It's called Valium. I got some samples in my office. I'll fix you up. With one of those babies in your system the pilot could announce that the ship was corkscrewing toward the earth at five-hundred miles an hour and all you'd want to do is smile, or yawn."

"That one's for me."

"I've got to meet with you-know-who in his office in an hour. I'd like to be good and drunk by then." Doc took down the contents of his paper cup, and studied the inside of it. "Archie was correct in recognizing the palliative effect of alcohol, even if the Lord can't be given the credit."

I was surprised that Doc could take such a view; with his knowledge of medicine he must know the health risks for people who drank like there was no tomorrow. People like himself and Archie, Ray and Whitey, Devlin and Maggie.

Doc opened up Archie's bottom drawer and pulled out the vodka bottle. There were about three fingers left in it. He poured himself half of that and, without bothering to add milk, brought the cup to his lips. He drank off the vodka in a single swallow, and struggled out of the recliner. He had on a long blue cashmere overcoat and a white silk scarf, like the one Paul Cane, the prodigal son, always wore. On his head, Doc had replaced his summertime Panama hat with a gray fedora.

"If big-balls comes back, tell him to meet me at the Moose Club at eight o'clock, all right, Paul?"

"Sure. Take it easy, Doc. Good luck."

Doc patted my shoulder and walked up the aisle to the door as if he were walking the last mile.

When I thought about the brief meeting with the three of them, Archie, Garabedian, and Doc, I wondered if it was possible that Garabedian intended to use Archie as a character witness in Doc's defense. If that was his plan, Garabedian would have to be not only a sleazy lawyer to bring it off, but a magician as well. It felt strange knowing that I wouldn't be around to see how it all came out. I seriously doubted that there would be any correspondence between these people and me once I was out of their lives. Yes, it was a strange feeling indeed.

* * *

Devlin and Maggie had invited me for a farewell meal on the Monday before I was due to leave. Mrs. Pappas and Charlie planned to have me down on Wednesday, on the eve of the day of my departure. George Stacy had given me Jack Scanlon's telephone number in Watertown, Massachusetts, when we were together in The Cantina. On two occasions I had been on the verge of calling Jack, but each time I had hesitated, not knowing why, and in the end I never dialed his number. I experienced the same hesitation in making contact with George, to give him the news of my decision to join my wife in California, and he lived right in town, a fifteen-minute walk from my apartment. Now, I had the receiver off the hook, my finger poised to dial Noelle's number. I hesitated, then replaced the receiver in its cradle.

* * *

It was unseasonably warm on Saturday, the 30th of November, my last day at Caplan's Auto Supply. About mid-morning, Sid had made a special stop in my office to bid me goodbye and to wish me luck, in his awkward, eyes-averted way. My fellow workers were either uncomfortable or inept in their gestures of farewell to me. Or perhaps they were simply indifferent. In any case, my last day was marked by a conspicuous lack of ceremony. And to my own surprise, I felt disappointed, even a little hurt. So, I punched my time card for the last time, and walked unceremoniously out the front door as if it were the end of any other day. Directly across the street, in front of Spiro's Sweet Shoppe, I spotted Noelle pushing little Teddy in his stroller on this warm afternoon in late November. Noelle wore a light sweater over her dress. Her hair was back to its natural color.

"I see you came to your senses and decided that blondes don't have any more fun than brunettes," I said, crossing the street and coming up to her.

"I wouldn't want to do anything to displease you," she said, looking past my shoulder, up Washington Street. Teddy's eyes were closed, and his little mouth was open. Drool spilled down his chin.

"How about this weather."

"I'm surprised you're still in Garrison. I would have thought you'd be gone by now." Noelle kept her eyes away from mine.

"Five more days. How have you been? Any news from William?"

"He left his mother's house about twenty-four hours before the Federal Marshal paid him a visit. Grace thinks he's headed west." Noelle turned to me with an ironic smile. "Maybe you'll get lucky; maybe he'll pay you and Laura a visit. He was always fond of Laura."

"Wouldn't that be swell ... Noelle ..."

"Please don't say anything, Paul. You made yourself very clear the last time we spoke. Have a good trip. Goodbye." Noelle pushed off, up

Washington Street in the direction of her apartment. I was going in the same direction, but I didn't try to walk with her. Instead, I went into Spiro's for a pack of cigarettes. When I came out, Noelle was nowhere in sight.

* * *

Then the day came for me to leave, and before I knew it I was airborne, crammed into a window seat on TWA flight 1095 non-stop to San Francisco, a tablet of Valium coursing through my bloodstream, which in no time at all, produced exactly the effect Doc said it would. Somewhere in the cargo bay, Honcho, under the influence of a tranquilizer of his own, languished in his new pet carrier.

EPILOGUE

My wife had been correct in predicting that I would be very pleased with the place she had found for us to live. It was an airy five-room apartment on the second floor of a three-story building on the west side of Hyde Street, with a good view of Fisherman's Pier and the harbor. The ceilings were high, the windows large, and the rooms commodious. I was struck by the contrast between the bathroom in Mrs. Pappas's apartment with the long one in our new place, with its floor of black and white tiles, its large, claw-footed tub, the deep porcelain sink with oversized faucets. I could see myself spending a lot of time in this room.

We lived comfortably, and I believe happily, in this agreeable apartment, in a neighborhood marked by the civility of its residents. It wasn't until 1970 that I finally earned enough credits from San Francisco State, attending sporadically, to qualify for a B.S. degree in biology. We lived through the "summer of love," the legions of hippies headquartered in Haight-Ashbury, followed by the Kent State massacre and the whole Vietnam war debacle; we endured the rise of polyester (which had no measurable impact on the lingerie trade, according to my wife). Laura was promoted to head buyer in less than six months, just as the company had said she would. In fact, her job proved to be a lucrative one, and in a very short time we found ourselves fairly well off. Well off enough that I felt no pressure to take just any job after receiving my degree. I took some graduate credits in marine ecology and landed a job with the State of California as an environmental biologist, where I am employed to this day. By the early nineteen seventies Laura had made enough contacts through her position as head buyer, and with the financial backing of some rich San Franciscans, to open her own boutique on Turk Street. It wasn't long before she parlayed her little store into a string of stores down the coast to the Monterey Peninsula. In 1971 we moved to a "bungalow" in Pacific Grove, where we live at present.

Once we became entrenched in Pacific Grove, the circle of friends we had made in our San Francisco days began to shrink, slowly at first, until we realized one day that we saw virtually nobody socially any more. That seemed to be all right with Laura who was kept busy sixteen hours a day looking after her shops. I suppose I didn't miss the social scene either; frankly it was beginning to wear me down. In 1990, I quit smoking again, and took up golf in earnest, remembering my promise to Gil Freese after our Glen Lea fiasco in 1963.

In our San Francisco days, under Laura's patient tutelage, I learned to eat meat without switching the fork from the left hand to the right; I learned the correct pronunciation of Nabokov's name—four syllables instead of three—that Anna Karenina's last name had its accent on the second syllable, Thoreau's on the first. Laura finally got me to appreciate the art of John Cheever.

As for children, there were none. Laura's aversion to children (which I suspected was rooted in her physical aversion to childbirth) along with the temporal demands of her chosen profession, all but ruled out the possibility of rearing a family. I suppose I was of the same mind where children were concerned. My brother and his wife had produced two boys and a girl, so my family name was secure for another generation at least. Laura had no male siblings, and no interest whatsoever in her family.

And now, as my sixtieth year looms obscenely in the near future, I am often left to wonder what had become of thirty-five years of my life since that day I flew away from Garrison, New Hampshire. I imagine, given enough time and careful thought, I could produce a chronicle of what my life had become in those thirty-five years; but what had taken place during those three tumultuous months of my life in 1963, I doubt I shall ever know.

About the Author

Michael Burns was born in St. Johnsbury, Vermont. His family moved to New Hampshire in 1950 where he attended high school, graduating in 1957. He deferred entrance to college to serve in the U.S. Navy for four years, seeing duty in Southeast Asia in the early days of the Vietnam War. After mustering out of the Navy, Burns returned to New Hampshire where he met and married his wife, and matriculated at the University of New Hampshire.

Encouraged by his freshman English teacher, Burns first became interested in writing fiction in 1963. He continued writing after being inspired by the late Thomas Williams, National Book Award-winning author and mentor to many young writers, among them John Irving.

In 1971, Burns joined the faculty of St. Paul's School, a college preparatory boarding school in Concord, New Hampshire. He retired from that school in 2004 after 33 years of teaching chemistry, life science, and creative writing. At present, Burns is living with his wife in rural New Hampshire where he is at work on his fourth novel. *Gemini*, his first novel, was published by Poncha Press in 2001. *Where You Are* is Burns' second novel.

ALL THINGS THAT MATTER PRESS ™

FOR MORE INFORMATION ON TITLES AVAILABLE FROM
ALL THINGS THAT MATTER PRESS, GO TO
http://allthingsthatmatterpress.com
or contact us at
allthingsthatmatterpress@gmail.com